Eleanor —

Thank you for your friendship
and care of our home.
I hope you enjoyed the book.
All the best to you and your family

Fred

PROPHECY   MYSTICISM   SUSPENSE

EZEKIEL'S VISION

A NOVEL

by

Fred Snyder

gefen גפן
publishing house בית הוצאה לאור
JERUSALEM ◆ NEW YORK

Typesetting: Jerusalem Typesetting, Jerusalem
Cover Design: S. Kim Glassman, Jerusalem

ISBN 965-229-363-6

1   3   5   7   9   8   6   4   2

Gefen Publishing House
6 Hatzvi Street, Jerusalem 94386, Israel
972-2-538-0247 • orders@gefenpublishing.com

Gefen Books
600 Broadway, Lynbrook, NY 11563, USA
1-800-477-5257 • orders@gefenpublishing.com

www.israelbooks.com

Printed in Israel

Send for our free catalogue

For my wife Gail

and for Rachel, Libbie, Aaron, and Anna

What, can these dead bones live, whose sap is dried
By twenty scorching centuries of wrong?
Is this the House of Israel whose pride
Is as a tale that's told, an ancient song?
Are these ignoble relics all that live
Of psalmist, priest, and prophet? Can the breath
Of very heaven bid these bones revive,
Open the graves, and clothe the ribs of death?
Yea, Prophesy, the Lord hath said again:
Say to the wind, Come forth and breathe afresh,
Even that they may live, upon these slain,
And bone to bone shall leap, and flesh to flesh.
The spirit is not dead, proclaim the word.
Where lay dead bones a host of armed men stand!
I ope your graves, my people, saith the Lord,
And I shall place you living in your land.

From *The New Ezekiel*
By Emma Lazarus (1849–1887)

Contents

Prologue

Approximately 597 B.C.E., in the wake of Nebuchadnezzar's successful conquests in Judah, a high-ranking temple priest named Ezekiel was deported to Babylonia, where he settled in a former labor camp called Tel-Abib. Five years after his forced move, while in a hypnotic trance, Ezekiel had a vision, which he shared with other exiles. He eventually attained prominence as a legitimate prophet.

Ezekiel, however, found himself at a crossroads. Could the Jews retain the tenets of their religion, the thread of their national identity, without the Jerusalem Temple? Indeed some of his contemporaries argued that the covenant had ended with the Babylonian conquest. But Ezekiel held fast to tradition. He called out to the Jews still permitted to live in Jerusalem, to maintain strict religious rituals, and warned that there would be terrible consequences for desecrations. Ezekiel continued to share his visions, and in doing so became a leader for the cause of continuing a national and religious identity, even in exile.

Over twenty-five hundred years ago, Ezekiel's vision, aside from predicting the destruction of the Temple, included worldwide dispersion, a catastrophic genocide, the ingathering of the survivors to Israel (where they would enjoy relatively quick economic growth), the military defeats of Israel's neighbors, and the demographic decline of Jewish communities outside of Israel.

Chapter One

Thus says the Lord God: "Jerusalem, because you have not walked in my statutes or kept my ordinances, because you have wickedly rebelled against my ordinances, even I am against you. I will execute judgments in the midst of you in the sight of the nations. Therefore fathers shall eat their sons, and sons shall eat their fathers; and any of you who survive I will scatter to all the winds, my eye will not spare, and I will have no pity. A third part of you shall die of pestilence and be consumed with famine, a third part shall fall by the sword, and a third part I will scatter to all the winds and will unsheathe the sword after you."

PALESTINE, 1936

A loud, rapid knock broke Reuven's concentration. He put down his manuscript.

His old friend, sitting across the little wobbly table, took off his wire glasses and rubbed his eyes. "Who is it? Who's calling so late?"

A sharp, high-pitched voice responded. "It's Abdul. Open quickly."

The old friend turned to Reuven, raised his eyebrows and shrugged. "Excuse me," he muttered, reaching for his cane.

Abdul knocked again, louder and faster.

"Why so impatient?" the old friend said as he slowly walked to the door just ten feet away.

The old friend, a curious look on his face, opened the door. Reuven saw a short, thin Arab, with a thick grey handlebar mustache, wearing a white robe with black stripes.

"Quick, quick, come with me," Abdul said nervously, in English, waving both hands.

"What? What is it?" the old friend returned in Yiddish.

"Must come quickly."

"I don't do anything quickly, not anymore. It's too late and dark to go anywhere. Come in. I'll make tea."

Abdul stayed by the threshold. "You don't understand. There's no time. You must come now. I'll explain as we ride."

The old friend wouldn't be moved so fast. "I've got a visitor from Safed," he pointed toward Reuven.

Abdul nodded, politely acknowledging the houseguest, but promptly resumed waving his hands anxiously. "Come, then, both of you," Abdul begged, almost desperate. "Come into my truck."

The old friend, still not very convinced, looked at Reuven and shrugged. Reuven didn't know what to make of the situation, but took his lead from his friend. He put on his black coat and hat and followed him to Abdul's truck. The two men sat alongside Abdul on the front bench and waited as Abdul tried the ignition over and over again. The truck finally started with a jolt and they chugged down the rural dirt road.

At first Abdul drove without speaking a word, offering no explanation for his urgency. When he finally drove onto the wider and flatter road which led east toward the cluster of Arab villages, he sighed deeply and began, "There's a revolt all over Galilee. The mufti has called up the same old troublemakers."

"We're old men. We're no threat to anyone," the old friend pleaded.

"They're going after every Jew. The Germans are behind it. They give money to the mufti." He rubbed his fingers and thumb together contemptuously. "The mufti and his followers are trying to ignite a revolt. And they've invited more troublemakers from Iraq and Lebanon. Petty criminals who love to fight. They don't care if they make trouble for Arabs or Jews."

Abdul fell silent again, shaking his head and sighing at intervals. At the same time the old friend offered apologies over and over to Reuven and occasionally to Abdul. After what Reuven felt was an eternity, the driver spoke again, attempting a calmer tone. "I'll take you to my house. You'll be safe there. First, we'll stop to pick up the young farmer."

"He lives around the bend," the old friend explained to Reuven. "He's a kind man. Gives me bread and eggs."

"That reminds me. Hope he has some of that cheese that I like," Abdul said, forcing a smile, apparently trying to ease the tension.

As they came around the curve, Reuven could see the farmhouse in the distance. Abdul's truck bounced and rattled as it turned onto the pot-holed dirt road.

"Something's not right," the old friend mumbled.

"What do you mean?" Abdul said.

"I don't know exactly."

Reuven pointed to the farmhouse. "Look. Smoke," he said excitedly, his pointing hand shaking.

The old friend reached for his handkerchief and wiped his face. "Something's not right," he repeated and his mouth remained open.

A few meters on, the three came to the corpse of a dark brown horse. It lay across the stony road, blocking any willing traveler. Abdul stopped the car and opened his door. "Look at that," he whispered.

The three men walked toward the skinny dead animal. The horse was on its side in mud, excrement, and blood. The flies and stench halted Reuven's approach.

"It's been shot," Abdul said quietly.

"Why?" the old friend implored, a look of exasperation contorting his face as he first looked to Reuven and then to the sky.

Reuven glanced up at the farmhouse. Heavy white smoke from many sources filled the night sky.

They returned to the truck, and after Abdul maneuvered around the corpse continued toward the farmhouse.

Now, in the distance, they could see dead cows scattered through the fields. Abdul, his complexion turning a shade of green, stopped the truck again. The three men looked at one another.

"I'm worried," the old friend said.

Abdul nodded and pleaded, "God, be merciful."

He drove again, rumbling on slowly until he parked in front of the kitchen entrance of the farmhouse.

Abdul led the two men toward the door, knocked, and called out to the farmer, "Avraham, open the door."

Realizing that the door was ajar, the Arab pushed the door in, and called again. There was no answer.

The three men walked into the kitchen and found a stove fire, burning quietly, not yet out of control.

"Should we put it out?" the old friend wondered, trailing with his cane behind Reuven and Abdul.

"Let's see what else we find," Reuven answered as he walked quietly into the living room. He was greeted by the sight of a man lying facedown in a pool of blood. The scene made him take a sudden step backward with a gasp. A sharp chest pain gripped him suddenly, but went as quickly as it came.

"That's the farmer," Abdul explained and followed with a curse in Arabic.

The old friend entered the living room. He saw the farmer's body and began to wail.

Reuven cautiously stepped closer and turned the body over; there was no doubt that the victim was dead. There was a bullet wound near his heart.

"A terrible thing," Abdul shook his head, clenched his fists, and swung out to hit the wall.

"God, tell me why?" the old friend demanded.

Reuven heard the hushed simpering of a dog from the next room. He walked into the bedroom. There, the farmer's wife lay dead, facedown on her bed. A young child was dead on the floor. The dog was nearly dead, lying alongside the child.

Now Reuven looked away and covered his face with his right arm. He walked back into the living room in a daze, stumbling over the farmer's leg.

"What should we do now?" the old friend wept.

"We can't do anything," Abdul shook his head. "We must move quickly. This didn't happen long ago. The perpetrators may still be in the area."

Reuven felt sickened and faint. He stumbled out of the farmhouse. He noticed a little of the farmer's blood smeared on his hands. The pain in his chest returned, and he found it hard to breathe. He slumped down on the ground and tried to breathe normally. Abdul and the old friend followed him out of the house and stood next to him.

I'll be okay, Reuven thought, but couldn't say anything. He tried signaling that it wasn't serious.

A few minutes passed.

"It's not safe to stay," Abdul warned the old friend. "Let's get back to the truck."

"I'm okay now," Reuven said.

Abdul helped Reuven to his feet and let Reuven walk unescorted to the truck.

Abdul turned the vehicle around and headed back along the dirt road. It seemed to Reuven that he drove too fast down the bumpy road.

"You're a good man," the old friend told Abdul while patting his forearm. "Thank you for this help."

"You've helped me many times," Abdul said. "I'm happy to do this for you."

Within ten minutes they had reached Abdul's traditional Arab villa, the largest in his isolated village, and located high and at the edge of the slope of the hill. The entire village enjoyed the panorama of the Galilee's hills and valleys.

The two men followed Abdul toward the grand house, Reuven now walking slower than his old friend.

Abdul opened the green iron gate, entered his house, and nodded to his wives and children who stood in the foyer.

Reuven tried to follow religious tradition by not looking at the women, but he noticed that they were veiled, tall, and heavy. Abdul led the two to a small room in the rear of the house. The room smelled of smoke; a water pipe, which Reuven knew was popular amongst the Arabs, stood in the corner.

"I'm sorry to ask you to stay in this dark room. You'll be safe here, but I'm afraid it may be uncomfortable."

"It's no problem at all," the old friend assured him.

The old friend stepped to the rear of the white-walled room, and Reuven followed. The room was devoid of furnishings but for a small oriental carpet in the center surrounded by chipped and worn colored tiles. Abdul left and shut the door. Reuven could hear a piece of furniture being dragged against the door. He assumed it was to camouflage the room.

Dim moonlight penetrated the room. Reuven and his friend didn't move for a while. Then Reuven suggested they recite *kiddush levana*, the prayer for a new moon.

"Why don't we wait until we get to Safed, so we can say it with a minyan?" the old friend objected.

"It doesn't have to be said with ten men. Let's say it now," Reuven urged. "We have a good clear moon, and it could be we won't have another opportunity."

They quietly chanted the prayer from memory, almost in unison, swaying back and forth. When they finished, they sat on the floor.

"Abdul's a real human being with a heart," Reuven observed.

"We've been friends a long time."

"A friend when things go well is one thing. A friend in a crisis is truly a blessing."

"Sorry this happened during your visit to my house."

"God's will," Reuven responded with a nod of deep understanding.

They were quiet a while. Reuven looked at his old friend in the near darkness and remembered him as a spirited young man of intellectual promise. They had grown up together in a village near Kiev. Almost four years ago, after Reuven had spent many years in America and finally moved to northern Palestine, he had met his old friend again.

"Are you feeling okay?" the old friend inquired.

"Better."

"Your study's a very impressive and worthy effort," the old friend said, nodding his head with approval. He scratched his chest just below his white beard and stared into space. His eyes seemed to bulge. He turned his head back, and once again his eyes met Reuven's. "You've made sense of Ezekiel's prophecy. And you've anchored it firmly in the secret traditions we've received. A significant contribution."

"We all try to understand and be guided by His will."

"You'll receive many honors as the word gets out." The old friend smiled, his eyes moist.

"Not this time," Reuven responded. "The prophecy includes a vision of horrible things to come. Still, it's God's plan. *Baruch Hashem*, bless the Holy Name."

"Terrible events. It frightens me."

"Frightens me, too. We must trust His greater wisdom. He's our shepherd."

"Are you sure the prophecy will happen soon?"

"Yes, it's been written. All three components."

"It's the first component, God's anger and punishment, that frightens me."

Reuven nodded.

"I think it happened already," the old friend said. "I think it was the Roman wars."

"No."

"The Inquisition."

Reuven shook his head.

"I still think it was the Romans."

"Can't be. The second component, the ingathering of the exiles, the establishment of a new independent Israel, comes at the end of the first component."

"Who knows what God considers a moment in time?"

Reuven shook his head with absolute confidence. "I'm afraid it's yet to come."

"God help us. I prefer to think it's only a theory."

"It'll come, the bad and the good. The timing has always been the only question. A hundred years is a blink in history, but it'll happen even sooner."

They were quiet a minute. Then the old friend asked as if to change the subject, "Have you heard from your children in America?"

"My three daughters write," Reuven said. "My son, the youngest, is another matter."

"He doesn't write?"

"Very little. He's still angry I moved to Palestine after his mother died. Strange he's so angry. I don't think he misses me. He just doesn't like what I did."

"He doesn't understand?" the old friend said.

"No."

"Does he observe any traditions?"

"Very little. He doesn't have a Jewish heart. All he ever cared about were those crazy American sports. Baseball, boxing. And he always loved automobiles."

The friend nodded.

"Sometimes I feel guilty. I must've done something wrong."

"What's his name?"

"Adam."

"Is your son kind to others?"

Reuven rubbed his beard. "Suppose so," he surmised.

"Does he live a moral life? Does he treat others as he would wish to be treated?"

"Think so." Reuven nodded.

"You didn't do so bad. Maybe he didn't make the effort to understand our rituals, but he learned something that's most important."

Reuven didn't say anything. He was recalling why he liked and respected his old friend. On the other hand, Reuven thought, the old friend was childless, and couldn't fully understand the anguish of a parent.

They chanted the prayers for retiring to rest. Then they lay on the floor. Reuven tried to relax but felt the pains return. He rubbed his chest until he seemed to get some relief. As the pains finally subsided, he was able to sleep.

*   *   *

Reuven was awakened by the sound of furniture being dragged away from the door.

"Good morning," Abdul greeted them in Yiddish as he walked into the room.

"Good morning," the old friend replied in Arabic.

"Would you like bread?" Abdul asked.

"After prayers," the old friend said.

Abdul left with a nod.

"It's kosher bread, very good bread," the old friend whispered to Reuven.

Once the men had finished chanting the morning prayers, one of Abdul's wives brought mint tea and warm pita into the room. Reuven thanked the woman and proceeded to ceremoniously wash his hands and offer the blessing over bread.

Before they could finish eating and sipping the tea, Abdul returned. "Thank you for saving our lives," the old friend said, patting Abdul's shoulder.

"God is great. God's saved you. I'm merely His servant. You know, you're welcome to stay in my home as long as you like."

"Thank you, but I'm going to Reuven's in Safed," the old friend said apologetically.

"You're sure?"

"Yes. We've much work to do for Reuven's students."

"Then I'll drive you to Safed."

"You're a generous and true friend."

"I'm happy to do this," Abdul offered.

"Thank you. One little thing, if I may ask. We left Reuven's manuscript in my cottage. Would it be too much to go to Safed by way of my home?"

Abdul stroked his moustache, seeming concerned, but then abruptly dropped his hand. He smiled. "The troublemakers attack at night. It would be safe in the morning," he said.

Abdul led the men toward the foyer and asked them to wait a few moments. He moved to another corner of the hallway and bent his knees in prayer on what appeared to be a very expensive carpet.

Reuven and the old friend walked outside where they were greeted by the morning mist. A layer of light dew covered the ground. Dawn was just breaking.

"It's warmer today," the old friend said.

"Hardly need our coats," Reuven said.

"Looks like it'll be a good day."

"Baruch Hashem."

A few minutes passed and Abdul came out to take them to their destination. He greeted them and then opened the truck door. This time, the truck started on the first try.

The drive southwest led them over roads that had a clear view of the hills of Galilee. Soon they passed the dirt road that had brought them to the farmer's house.

The three sat in silence until Reuven turned to a practicality. "I'll tell the authorities about the poor farmer when we get to Safed."

"Will that do any good?" his old friend asked skeptically.

"Not sure. I'll tell the burial society, of course, but I think we should let the authorities know, too."

"The English don't care, but you may as well tell them."

Reuven turned to Abdul. "Come visit me with your family. I'm a tailor by profession, as well as a teacher. I'll make you a beautiful robe, and I'll introduce you to my students as a man of honor."

Abdul nodded politely, but Reuven had the feeling he was made uncomfortable by the invitation.

A car pulled in front of them and stopped suddenly. Abdul braked hard, and Reuven nearly hit the windshield.

Abdul cursed. "The bandits."

The truck was surrounded by about twenty-five Arabs with rifles and handguns. They appeared to be a rough rabble, their clothes dirty and disheveled. They seemed a very different class of men than Abdul.

Abdul tried to maintain his composure. The two Jews could but stare in fear as Abdul yelled at the bandits in their own language. They answered, and Abdul yelled again.

Reuven felt his old friend grab his arm, trembling.

"Don't be afraid," Reuven whispered. "We're much too old to run or fight. It's God's will. Maybe we know too much of the prophecy and the timing's not right. Someone else will have to come at the right time. I believe it."

One of the bandits put a rifle to Abdul's head and gestured Abdul out of the truck. Abdul complied and seemed to be losing his authority. The bandit hit Abdul with the butt of his gun. He fell to the ground. Reuven saw blood. The same Arab yelled at Reuven and his friend, fiercely beckoning them with his free hand to come out of the truck.

Reuven slid across the seat and stepped out. He turned back and seeing that his old friend was frozen to his seat, he reached over to assist him out of the truck. He retrieved the cane, and handed it to his old friend.

"Thank you." The old friend patted the sweat on his face with a handkerchief, and holding onto his cane with one trembling hand and Reuven's arm with the other, he climbed out of the truck.

Reuven gazed up at the sky and knew that God had created such a bright clear day for a purpose. Perhaps God wanted him to experience once again the beauty of His creation, even in this difficult situation. He said the Shema prayer proclaiming God's unity and then, without fear in his soul, he began to chant a section from the Book of Ezekiel that he had memorized long ago. "I was among the exiles by the river Chebar, the heavens were opened, and I saw visions of God…"

As he chanted, he weaved his upper body back and forth. Turning slightly to the right, he saw that the bandit had raised and aimed his rifle.

Chapter Two

Thus shall my anger spend itself, and I will vent my fury upon them and satisfy myself; and they shall know that I, the Lord, have spoken in my jealousy. Moreover I will make you desolation and an object of reproach among the nations round about you and in the sight of all that pass by. I will send famine and will rob you of your children. I scattered you among the nations, and you were dispersed through the countries; in accordance with your conduct and your deeds I judged you. But when you came to the nations, wherever you came, you profaned my holy name, in that men said of you, "These are the people of the Lord, and yet they had to go out of his land."

BOSTON, MASSACHUSETTS, 1961

Robert Zadok tried the bathroom door again, but it was still locked. "C'mon, open up," he said. "You've been in there for hours."

There was no answer, so he knocked hard enough to hurt his knuckles.

"Get away," his sister said.

"I have to go, bad."

"I'm in here. Go away."

"Brat, open up."

Still no answer.

He went down the back stairs of the apartment building, and urinated discretely behind the trash shack. He started back, but then he noticed a

13

tennis ball on the roof of the auto body garage. He ran onto the roof, retrieved the ball, and quickly ran off.

He bounced it. Good, it wasn't dead.

He heard a noise, turned, and realized the burly garage owner was after him. Zadok ran down the alley. He heard the garage owner closing on him, a few strides behind. Zadok ran up the hill, and across an empty lot. The garage owner was still keeping up. He turned down another alley, but at the corner, the garage owner grabbed his shirt. Zadok struggled to get free.

"Little rat. I'll teach you," the big garage owner said.

Zadok saw he was about to be slapped, but another man caught the garage owner's hand in motion. It was Jacob, a wiry construction worker, and Orthodox Jew.

"What'd he do?" Jacob said. The veins on his forearm popped up as he held back the garage owner's arm.

"Tried to wreck my roof."

"Just got a ball," Zadok said.

"He's just a boy," Jacob said.

"Yeah, but he could cost me. I just paid sixteen hundred bucks for that roof. I can't let these punks ruin it."

"Sorry," Zadok said. "I didn't know. I won't go on your roof again."

The garage owner released Zadok's shirt. "Better not. Next time you'll get it good, with or without Jacob."

The garage owner left.

"Thanks a lot," Zadok said to Jacob.

Jacob smiled kindly, and patted Zadok's shoulder. "I'm glad you ran to my house," he said, sounding as if he were the one who should feel gratitude. "You learn a lesson?"

"Won't do it again."

Zadok returned home and climbed the four flights to his apartment. In his room, which he shared with his sister, he put his new tennis ball on the dresser and hopped onto his bed.

His sister finally came out of the bathroom.

"You ass," Zadok said. "You got me in trouble."

"What're you talking about?"

"Because of you, I had to piss outside. Then the owner of the garage next door came after me."

"Why'd you piss on his garage?"

"I didn't piss on his garage. He just came after me, and tried to kill me. It's your fault."

"Shut up."

"All your fault."

The knot in his stomach propelled him off his bed. He went into the kitchen where his mother was washing dishes.

"Want me to dry?" he asked.

"I'm going to defrost the fridge in a minute. Can you help?"

"Sure." He went to empty the refrigerator.

"Thank you, dear."

"Beverly's being a pain. I can't stand her."

"I wish you kids wouldn't fight so much."

"She's ugly and selfish."

"When you're older, you'll be glad you've a sister."

"Fat chance."

*　　*　　*

On his fourth lesson for his bar mitzvah readings, Zadok shyly approached his teacher's study. Yaakov Smilensky looked like a patriarch right out of the pages of Genesis. His hair was not at all receded, a blend of white and gray under his black skullcap. His beard was full, a darker gray, and reached up high on his cheeks, covering most of his face, and it ran down well below his chest. The wrinkles on his forehead and around his eyes showed the stress of a hard life, though his eyes were blue and soft. Zadok could find a vitality and trace of youth in those eyes.

Smilensky was totally immersed in the oversized, ancient leather-bound volume spread out on the dominant walnut desk. The room was small, with two windows above the desk. A small desk lamp provided the barely adequate lighting since the shades were drawn over the windows. Against two walls were volumes of books from floor to ceiling, all of them in Hebrew or Yiddish.

For a while Zadok stood on the threshold, uncomfortably clutching his book and shifting his weight from leg to leg, afraid to intrude on the old man's study. Then, suddenly, Smilensky's wife strolled into the room, passing Zadok without acknowledging him, and with the contempt of familiarity that comes after forty years of living together, lifted the shades above her husband.

"Your student's here," she said without looking at anyone. She promptly left the room.

Smilensky turned to Zadok and showed no expression, but motioned to him to sit at the chair beside him. "Begin," Smilensky said.

Zadok read two lines before he got into trouble. Normally Smilensky would offer the correct reading automatically whenever Zadok hesitated or made a mistake. Zadok looked up to find Smilensky focusing on the ring he was wearing.

"An old ring for a young man," Smilensky said, touching it. The ring was a flat gold band with an inscription that was unknown to Zadok.

"Handed down to me," said Zadok, "down through the male line. I'm the oldest son of an oldest son of an oldest son for I don't know how many generations. My father never wore it, but my grandfather did for a while. I think it's at least a hundred fifty years old."

"Your grandfather, was his name Reuven Zadok?"

"Yes, how'd you know? I'm named after him. My Hebrew name's Reuven."

"You're Reuven Zadok's grandson," Smilensky repeated quietly.

Zadok was surprised that someone thought that meant something. "You knew my grandfather?"

"No. I knew of him. I knew of some of the work he did."

"He was a tailor," Zadok said.

"No, I don't know his cutting and sewing, but some of his writings."

"He was a writer?"

"I'd say he was a scholar."

Again Zadok was surprised.

"Know what the inscription says?"

Zadok lifted his ring finger.

"Ben Hezekiah," Smilensky read.

"What?"

"A name."

"Whose name, my great grandfather's, maybe?"

"Perhaps it's to do with the champion of Ezekiel, the one who kept the book of Ezekiel in the scriptures."

"Kept it in?"

"Yes, kept it from being removed."

"Someone could take a book out of the Bible?"

Smilensky nodded. "At one time they assembled the books, and they could disassemble the books. Some thought that Ezekiel's prophecies were proven untrue, so there was an opinion to take out Ezekiel. It could never happen now."

"But I don't understand why they'd pass down a ring with that name."

"Look," said Smilensky, turning back towards his library, "I have a present for you." He pulled out a small, thin book with yellowed, missing pages and worn bindings, and handed it to Zadok.

Zadok opened the book. On the first page was a drawing in bold blue ink of a chariot without horses. Above the chariot was a small king's crown. The rest of the book was Hebrew text, totally unintelligible to him. "Thank you," he said, but he had no idea why his teacher wanted him to have this ragged valueless book.

"Your grandfather is the author of the book, and a lot of it has to do with Ezekiel," Smilensky explained, apparently sensing Zadok's confusion. "With commentary. Perhaps some day you'll be curious about commentary."

"Thank you," Zadok said, again.

"You're very fortunate."

"Fortunate?"

"And so young. Ah, to be so young…and so fortunate."

"What do you mean?"

"You'll understand when you're older."

"I don't get it."

"You'll understand how fortunate you are to be so blessed. The book I gave you is normally only given to married and intellectually talented men over the age of forty years who have studied and mastered all of the texts and commentaries. They say it's only appropriate for men who have demonstrated maturity, intellect, and character. It's complicated and not meant for the masses."

"So why give it to me?"

Smilensky smiled, revealing that he relished the question. "After all, it's written by your grandfather. I happen to have a book written by the grandfather of my student. That's some coincidence, don't you think? If anyone, one day, should read it, I think that person is you. It seems meant to be. Don't worry, God willing, one day you'll be forty. But never be in a hurry to get older. It'll come faster than you can realize."

"What's so special about the book?"

"Your grandfather was a rational thinker who didn't reject the spiritual and special connection between God and man. People today have a hard time accepting anything mystical, but your grandfather saw no conflict between mysticism and rational thought. He went back to the origins of the divine spark. He didn't dismiss the whole subject simply because it was complicated and sometimes misinterpreted by others. He took the rationalist approach of the great Maimonides and applied it to legitimate mystical thought. He didn't try to make it simple, he just tried to separate God's intent from the rest. And he made logical sense of it. He was particularly interested in Ezekiel, and wrote a good deal about the prophecies. So you see now, there is a connection between you, your ring, this book, and your grandfather."

"I don't think I'd understand this even if I were over forty and married. Besides, it makes no sense to restrict anything by age and whether or not you're married."

Smilensky now shifted in his chair. "You're so young. I'll explain. Some students of mystical materials went mad. The masters decided that they must take steps to protect their students, especially if they were unworthy of the material. A person must have his feet firmly planted on the ground if he is to reach his head so far into the heavens and not lose himself. Maturity and wisdom come with age, position in life, experience, and knowledge. As I said, you'll understand when you're older."

*   *   *

On the bus ride home, Zadok liked to stare out the window, taking in all the cars, pedestrians, and groups of people hanging out. His nose was nearly touching the glass.

He thought about Smilensky again, and liked the feeling of being special. He guessed he'd be treated a little differently and better from now on at the old man's house.

He was still confused by Smilensky's comments. It made no sense, but sometimes his maternal grandparents talked that way, and they, too, could be hard to follow. Was it a condition of old age, or did Smilensky really know more than he shared? Zadok got off the bus on Blue Hill Avenue and stepped into a puddle left from yesterday's rain. There at the bus stop, as if they were waiting for him, were Bruno and three others. Bruno was leaning back against the stone wall that bordered the perimeter of Franklin Park, a cigarette in the far corner of his mouth, a pack of cigarettes tucked under his left T-shirt sleeve. He was clicking the tap on the heel of one of his black pointed shoes. His friends, diminutive copies of Bruno, were smoking and grinning with anticipation. One of them was holding a new transistor radio up to his ear, even though the music could easily be heard from a distance.

"Get over here," Bruno said to Zadok.

Zadok looked up and down the avenue and realized he was alone with the four of them. He reluctantly stepped over to Bruno who immediately grabbed Zadok's shirt just below his throat. Zadok was still clutching his two Hebrew books.

"Been hiding from me?"

"Didn't know you were looking for me."

"Don't get wise," Bruno said.

"Punch out the little wise guy," one of the gang said.

"See this?" Bruno asked while simultaneously pulling out a closed switchblade knife. Bruno squeezed the knife's button and the five-inch blade flashed out within inches of Zadok's eye. Zadok felt a knot of fear in his stomach. He knew Bruno was showing off in front of his friends, but he didn't know how far Bruno would go.

"Not being wise. I didn't know. What do you want?"

He was ashamed of the obvious trembling in his voice. He looked into Bruno's eyes and then at Bruno's hair, which, like his own, was heavily greased with a big wave in the front and side.

"Heard you been badmouthing me."

"Me? No, not me. I wouldn't do that, who said?"

"You badmouth me, you know what'll happen?" Bruno twirled the blade slowly.

"I won't. No, sir, I won't."

Bruno smiled, probably at the flattery of being called sir. He seemed to relax for a moment, but then Zadok felt him stiffen again, as if recalling the role he had to play to command such respect.

"I hear of any more badmouthing, I'm coming after you. You. Understand? Now get out of here." He released Zadok's shirt and pushed him back.

Zadok, who barely managed to keep from tripping, regained his footing, and quickly crossed the street. He heard laughter from behind, but he didn't look back. It wasn't the first time Bruno had cornered him, but at least, unlike a few other gang encounters, he'd never been hurt by Bruno or his crowd. He never worried about any of the other gang members when Bruno wasn't with them. They'd never take the offensive without him.

*　*　*

Months later, on the street corner in front of the drug store on the avenue, Zadok was on his way home when he came upon one of Bruno's friends pushing Leo into the street sign pole. Easily fifteen years older than Zadok, Leo was an epileptic who had a deformed ear, a deformed hand, one lung, and a limp left over from a childhood case of polio. When he laughed he shook uncontrollably and sounded like a sea robin yanked out of the ocean. Leo had no friends his own age; even his immediate family had trouble accepting his handicaps. Zadok and his friends took a liking to Leo and included him whenever they hung out in the neighborhood. Leo seemed especially to enjoy their penny-ante poker games conducted in random basements.

Zadok responded instantly to the sight of a husky teenager pushing someone like Leo. A rage welled within him.

"Leave Leo alone. Get off him," Zadok called out, as he grabbed Leo's assailant from behind and pulled him away.

The husky teenager came at Zadok next, but Zadok dodged a punch and pushed the bully back up against the wall of the drugstore. Zadok noticed the confusion in the gang member's face as he apparently realized who had successfully pulled him off Leo.

"Behind you," Leo yelled.

Zadok turned around and caught another gang member about to jump him, but he managed to push the attacker to the ground. Zadok watched him roll over several times on the ground. Then Zadok's would-be attacker stopped and seemed to give up. Neither gang member made another attempt to come at him.

Zadok was surprised by his own apparent strength. "Thanks for the warning," he said to Leo.

Leo nodded.

Then Bruno marched out of the drugstore followed by another one of his friends. Bruno stopped and leaned against the mailbox. Zadok felt his heart race, he felt pure fear, and then he felt his own anger return. How dare anyone come down on helpless Leo. Zadok was scared but he didn't care.

He was dead, Zadok thought, but he wasn't planning his moves, he was reacting to his emotions. He looked squarely at Bruno and yelled out, "They were beating on Leo. I'm not going to let anyone beat on Leo."

Zadok was spitting and waving his fist as he spoke. He felt his face flush.

All eyes turned to Bruno and there was a long silence.

Zadok braced himself for the attack. He thought about Bruno's knife and how outnumbered he was, but what they had done to Leo was wrong. He couldn't walk away from it.

But Bruno just smiled and lazily turned into the drugstore and, one by one, his friends followed. Zadok stood there stunned. He and Leo were alone. There was to be no fight. He didn't understand. He opened his fists slowly. His hands were shaking.

"Thanks," Leo said.

"Want to play deuces wild?" Zadok asked, attempting to minimize the strain. Deuces wild was always Leo's choice when he dealt.

"Yes." Leo smiled anxiously.

As they walked away Zadok's words tumbled out in an adrenaline-charged rush. "I don't get it. Bruno's always threatening to beat me up, even when he has no reason. Now he had a reason."

Leo shrugged and pulled out the deck of cards he kept in his back pocket.

*   *   *

Six years later, Zadok was still fighting with his sister. Zadok thought that he was the only one who made an effort to keep their bedroom neat, and that Beverly took up eighty percent of the available space. He liked to read or listen to the radio at night, and Beverly always tried to stop him.

Zadok enrolled at Boston University's school of engineering. A year later, Beverly also began commuting to Boston University, but she couldn't decide on a major.

Sometime in his sophomore year, Zadok discovered Jewish history. It fascinated him. He began to read more and more about the fall of the First and Second Temples, the Diaspora cultures and travels, and anti-Semitism. He spent nearly as much of his time studying Jewish history as he put toward his required curriculum. The more he learned, the more his fascination and curiosity were piqued.

One evening, after a long day at the university, Zadok realized he had startled his sister when he opened the bedroom door. In a few seconds, he understood her reaction. "Don't tell me you smoked pot in our room," he said.

"Quiet," his sister said, brushing back her light brown ironed hair, which reached the small of her back. She put down the brush and began spraying pine scent. Zadok noticed she was wearing a blue granny dress with yellow flowers. On her left cheek she had painted a yellow flower similar to the print on her dress.

"You're crazy. Dad and Mom'll catch you."

"They've got no idea." She returned the aerosol to the bathroom, and came back to retrieve her bag.

"Where you going?" Zadok said.

"Your business?"

"Forget it."

"If you must know, I'm going to listen to a visiting maharajah."

"Why?"

"You're too square. You wouldn't understand." She turned to leave the room. "Later," she said.

Zadok went to the kitchen where his mother was, as usual, cleaning.

"Hear the news?" his mother said.

"What?"

"Your cousin just got accepted to Harvard medical. Isn't that wonderful?"

"So what?"

"Whaddaya mean? It's wonderful. Maybe he could help you do the same."

"Not interested. Not sure I could do it, even if I wanted. But I don't want to."

"Really, now. I know you could do it."

"Told you many times. Not interested."

Zadok went to the living room. His father was sitting in a stuffed chair. The television was on, but his father was lost in thought.

"What's the matter, tough day in the janitor business?" Zadok said.

"Be nice. Property management."

"Sorry."

"Not thinking about work. I got a call from the monsignor. Wants me to use my influence with buddies on the draft board. One of his parishioners needs a deferment." His father changed his position in the chair, apparently trying to get more comfortable.

"You going to do it?"

"I want to help the monsignor, but I don't know if I can. I served my time, almost four years overseas. I'm in the Veterans of Foreign Wars, and the American Legion. I was a commander of the V.F.W. lodge. This goes against everything."

Zadok observed his father agonize over his decision for the next three days. On the fourth day, his father seemed to relax. He told Zadok that a doctor, whom the monsignor had also approached, had agreed to provide a medical excuse to help the parishioner obtain a deferment.

"Relieved now?" Zadok said.

"Very." His father turned on the television, and sat in his favorite stuffed chair.

"I'm glad. But I think you'd have been outraged had a rabbi asked you to do the same," Zadok said.

"Not true." His father continued to watch television, and waved off Zadok's suggestion.

"It is true. You're still trying to be accepted by your Irish and Italian friends."

"That's enough." His face flushed, he stood up and pointed toward Zadok's bedroom. "Out of here," he said.

* * *

A week later Zadok woke suddenly when his sister turned on their bedroom light.

"You brat. Turn off the damn light. Having a great dream," he said.

"Just need to see for a second. Go back to sleep."

"Hippie weirdo, now I can't sleep. What time is it?"

"About two."

"Two in the morning? Where've you been?"

"With friends."

"You're high, aren't you?"

"You're so square, such a boy scout. Go to sleep." She turned off the light.

"Did you see that maharajah guy again?"

"That was last week. It was great. Very, you know, very spiritual. Liked it. You know, a lot more fun than synagogue."

"You really think Judaism isn't spiritual?" Zadok said.

"Just a bunch of old men reading out loud, very fast, mumbling in a language they don't understand."

"Really? That's all you think there is to Judaism?"

"And the maharajah spoke about a higher spirituality, of communing with God and nature, ethics, yoga, great stuff."

"All you've proven tonight is your ignorance."

"I'm ignorant?"

"You reject Judaism and use your lack of knowledge as some kind of justification."

"You're the one who's afraid to experiment, learn new things, new cultures, new experiences. You're provincial."

"At least I know more than you about my heritage."

"Just talk. You're not even religious. How often do you go to synagogue?"

He waved his arm. "Shut up. No point talking to you."

Beverly was quiet for a while, and Zadok rolled over to try to go back to sleep. Then Beverly said, "Why don't you date non-Jews? You know, you're really limiting your possibilities."

"There's no way the Jewish line, after thousands of years, will end with me. So many hardships and triumphs. Such a rich culture and history. I can't see throwing it away. Now, good night."

"Oh, Bob. Does it really matter? Life's short. Who cares what happened fifty years ago? A thousand years ago? Two thousand years ago?"

"I care. But you're right, most of my friends don't care whether we continue as a people. And it breaks my heart."

Zadok turned the light out and rolled over. He smiled as he recalled that he'd be seeing a Red Sox and Yankees doubleheader in a few days.

Chapter Three

I will lay the dead bodies of the people of Israel before their idols; and I will scatter your bones round about your altars. Wherever you dwell your cities shall be waste and your high places ruined. And if any survivors escape, they will be on the mountains, like doves of the valleys, all of them moaning, every one over his iniquity. All hands are feeble, and all knees weak as water. They gird themselves with sackcloth, and horror covers them; shame is upon all faces, and baldness on all their heads. They cast their silver into the streets, and their gold is like an unclean thing; their silver and gold are not able to deliver them in the day of the wrath of the Lord, they cannot satisfy their hunger or fill their stomachs with it.

The Six-Day War, and Zadok's subsequent discovery of Zionism, helped him to understand his individualistic feelings. For one thing, he realized that his perspective wasn't so unique or original.

He realized that the early Zionists had argued that remaining separate in many countries would invariably lead to resentment, prejudice, and persecution, while full participation would often lead to assimilation. If the end results of both options were undesirable, then the conclusion was that Jews should live in their own land, as they once did in the land of Israel.

Zadok wasn't alone in his awakening. He learned that after the Six-Day War, new groups formed in every major city for the purpose of sharing information on immigration to Israel.

These parlor meetings in alternating member homes usually consisted of a talk by a visiting prominent Israeli or a successfully settled American emigrant. The conversation usually focused on practical considerations: what kind of appliances to buy in Israel, or to take from America, where to settle, how to learn Hebrew, how to find long-term housing, how to conduct a job search. The information was useful and the group meetings were supportive, but the lack of ideological discussions limited the momentum.

It seemed to Zadok that there were almost as many different motivations to immigrate as there were potential candidates, and there was no charismatic leader.

Zadok contrasted this to the leftist ideologies that were dominant in the campuses at the time. He knew that people like his sister could only be responsive to the more mainstream politics of their peer group.

Yet, the parlor meetings did constitute a genuine grassroots movement. It was the purest form of Zionism in the West since the creation of the Israeli State, and the largest ever emigration from the affluent and free Western societies. When in the history of the world, Zadok wondered, did tens of thousands emigrate from rich, free societies in preference to a lower standard of living in a war zone? Perhaps ironically, the new and increased interest in emigration from North America was totally independent of the established American Zionist organizations who continued in their role as charitable benefactors, or as sterile representatives of the various Israeli political parties.

Long after he'd graduated, when the time came for Zadok to inform his family of his plans to try living in Israel, the response was even worse than he had anticipated.

His mother said, "Are you crazy, are you stupid, what a son, what an ungrateful son, how can you leave us? You're leaving your old parents, taking away our chance to see our grandchildren, to live like a refugee. They all want to come here and you want to go there – how stupid and selfish can you be?!"

She worked herself up until she appeared to faint. She just fell flat on the kitchen floor. Then everyone's attention focused on reviving her. Beverly ran for a washcloth and came back and wiped her face. She was conscious, but it was a shock to everyone to see her lying on the floor.

"Look what you've done to your mother," his father said. "What's the matter with you?"

"I can't breathe." Zadok's mother put her hand over her heart.

Zadok brought her a glass of water.

She turned away, and the outpouring of guilt started again. "Work all your life and this is what children do to you. You want to live with war. I know what it's like to struggle. I worked all my life so you wouldn't have to struggle. You want to be stupid. You want to be selfish."

She continued shrieking and crying and admonishing her son, and when it seemed she was slowing down, his father started.

"When I was in the war I never ever imagined – it never entered my mind – that a son of mine would want to leave the United States. How can I show my face at the lodge – a post commander's son doesn't want to stay in this country? Many of their sons are in the service, some fighting in Vietnam, and my son runs away. I wouldn't even be able to enter the building. I don't believe it. I never imagined it. I can't accept it. I'm sorry, I'll never accept it. Never."

"There's no future for Jews here," Zadok said. "All my friends want to assimilate. The Jewish future is in Israel."

"I can't breathe," his mother said with pathos.

"What kind of a son are you? What kind of a person, what kind of a young man are you?" His father shook his head and bent down to assist his wife. "If you dare to continue with this nonsense, if you do this terrible thing to your mother, then I don't want anything to do with you. I don't accept you. I'll never accept it."

Zadok went to the bathroom to throw up in the toilet.

Later in his room, his sister said, "That was terrible, wasn't it. Still moving?"

He nodded. "But I'm feeling guilty."

"Maybe you should. You're going to help people you don't know, while you hurt your own family who needs you here."

"Don't know about helping anyone else. This is something I want to do. I need to do. Why can't you or Mom or Dad support me? It's my life."

"It's hard to support someone when you don't see them. They'll miss you."

"And I'll miss them."

"Even I, you know, will miss you."

"Really?"

"Well, I hope you find what you're looking for."

"I will."

"If you don't, you can come back, you know. I think you'll be home pretty soon."

Such was his family's send-off, as Zadok, a Zionist, prepared himself to contribute and participate in the building of the first Jewish State in two thousand years.

*   *   *

Zadok went to say good-bye to Jacob, with whom he had developed a casual friendship ever since Jacob rescued him years ago from the agitated garage owner.

Jacob was not well now, and was confined to bed rest most days. Zadok climbed the four flights to find Jacob's daughter waiting for him at the top landing. She was a frail-looking woman with short brown streaked hair. She welcomed him and offered coffee.

"Do you have tonic?" Zadok asked.

"Coke?"

"Fine."

"I'll get some."

She led Zadok to her father's bedroom. He was lying on a twin bed against the far wall, his head propped up by a few pillows. He was unshaven, his hair disheveled and whiter than ever. Zadok walked towards the bed and as Jacob recognized him, Zadok could see the sick man's expression come alive. Jacob motioned for Zadok to pull the chair over and sit down.

"How are you today?"

"Okay," said Jacob, but his voice telegraphed otherwise.

"Well, I'm finally doing it," said Zadok, "moving up to Israel."

Jacob nodded. "How're your parents taking it?"

"As bad as expected."

"Too bad. They should've been proud."

"Not my family. They're all assimilated."

"Your grandfather would've been proud."

"You mean my father's father, Reuven?"

Jacob nodded.

"I've heard about him. But no one in my family talks about him. So I don't know too much about him except that he wrote a book in Hebrew."

Jacob tried to sit up. "When I was young I went to the same synagogue as your grandfather. He was a lot older so we didn't talk much, other than to wish each other *gut Shabbos*, 'good Sabbath.' I knew he was liked and respected. Someone once described him to me as a genuine scholar, a real smart head, as they used to say. But more than that, he was seen as a good and righteous man, someone who was kind and who'd share everything he has with anyone who has a need. But after his wife died, they said he changed. They said he became so absorbed in his studies that he was a different person, like he had something to prove. A few years later he went to Palestine and began to write."

"I have one of his books, but I can't read it. What did he write about?"

Jacob coughed and shrugged. Then he cleared his throat and shook his head. "I don't know. I never read his material."

*   *   *

After the meeting with Jacob, Zadok decided to call his Aunt Bella, his father's oldest sister, to ask if she might know anything about her father's writings. She said he had written about religious matters, from which Zadok gathered she had little insight or interest in the subject. But then Bella said, "I might have some of his old letters in the basement. Want me to look?"

"Yes, thank you. I would appreciate it very much."

*   *   *

Zadok elected to go to Israel by ship. Plane hijackings were common, and he had the time, freedom, and inclination to enjoy a two-week cruise to Israel aboard a Greek luxury liner.

Zadok went alone to New York to begin his cruise. He regretted that there was no one to see him off, but he dismissed it as another test of his resolve.

He was finally doing it. It was really happening. He believed he'd just made the most difficult and most significant decision he would ever have to make for the rest of his life.

He unpacked in his tiny cabin in the lowest level of the ship. He lay for a while on the lower bunk. Then, when it was time, he went down for dinner, but after one bite he couldn't eat any more. He got up, said nothing to the others at the table, and walked out of the dining room and up the stairs to the promenade deck.

Outside, the new air greeted him gently in gusts. It was soothing and the tightness in his throat and stomach was going away. He leaned over the leeward rail. He wasn't sure if it was seasickness or the recent emotional turmoil that had affected him.

It was not very cold. He was only aware of the wind's strength as he leaned over, and then he became more aware of the sea. He was all right now, he thought. But the feelings of guilt were still very strong.

He was alone and relished it. He would be alone and just eat, sleep, do nothing and worry about nothing. He wouldn't need anything or anyone.

Then the ship passed the Statue of Liberty. The deck seemed too quiet as the emigrants on board studied the statue, and reflected. Zadok knew what it had meant for his mother when she had immigrated to America, and he imagined her as an anxious and hungry little girl, leaning over the railing of an old freighter, filled with excitement and joy. He knew he'd miss his family. Why couldn't they have understood? Would he ever get over the guilt?

Later he found himself against the rail on the other side. There was a floodlight above that exposed the mild dipping and churning of the ocean. Beyond the light he could see nothing and there were no stars. It was more beautiful before, he thought, the gulls and slipshod tide, when the tug had pushed them out and turned them around.

There was an old man leaning against the rail beside him. Zadok looked into the sea exposed by the light and thought that he, too, was like an old man. He was thinking too much of the past.

Inside there was Greek music, and several Greeks were sipping thick black coffee and chasing it with cold water. He passed them and went upstairs to the bar.

There the mood was dark and depressed, and unexpectedly he recognized the solitary figure at the bar.

"Hey, where you been?"

"Just outside," Zadok said. The man at the bar was to be his roommate.

He was short, very Brooklyn, and thought he looked good with a foolish bushy mustache. He had big dark eyes that were afraid to look at anyone. Zadok was trying to remember his name.

The roommate complained that if he had known the ship would pull out so late he'd have had some people come down to give a big proper send-off. He lit up a fresh cigar, and then offered one to Zadok.

"Don't smoke, but thanks anyway."

After a few more drinks the roommate turned as if to tell a secret and said, "I'm not ashamed to admit it. I'm running away. It's true. I know it."

Zadok didn't understand but nodded as if he had.

"Why are you moving to Israel?" the roommate said to Zadok.

"I want my grandchildren to be Jews, and in America there's a high likelihood that my grandchildren or their children won't be. I want to be a part of what's happening in Israel."

The roommate nodded.

Then the conversation shifted to their impressions of the women on board.

Nate – that was the roommate's name – suggested that there was a girl at his dining table who was about Zadok's age. Nate added he had met another woman at his dining table, "a sexy dish, you know what I mean. She has a body you wouldn't believe. But she knows she's got it. I don't go for that type. Know what I mean? It's what's here that counts," pointing towards his heart, "believe me, I know."

They sat and drank and laughed another two hours. Then they left the bar and went to the Zebra Room for a scheduled ceremony to meet the captain and to take a picture with him.

They were seated in a table in the back near a small bar. The chairs and tabletops were a mock zebra pattern. After they were comfortable, the waiter brought complimentary whiskey sours.

"Nice of the ship to buy the first round," Nate said.

"*L'chaim.*"

"*L'chaim*, to life," Nate repeated, motioning with his glass. "What'll we drink to?"

"To us. To us in Israel," Zadok said.

"Yes, yes," Nate chuckled. "To our second life."

He began to laugh and Zadok had to smile with him. Nate bought the next round.

"I'm told imported scotch is very expensive in Israel," Zadok said regretfully, holding the wet glass of scotch up high.

That was when he saw the woman whose turn it was to meet the captain. She was evenly tanned and smiling wide. The captain shook her hand and managed to keep his sober expression. No other officer in the reception line did.

Sometimes, Zadok thought – perhaps very rarely, but sometimes – you meet people who are naturally beautiful, so full of life that they instantly be-come the focus of attention and activity. If you don't meet them and come to know them, then you feel you're missing something.

This woman was such a person. Zadok didn't take his eyes from her until he realized he was staring.

She was wearing a two-piece, leopard-skin outfit with a bikini top that lifted and slightly squeezed her breasts. Her tight bell bottom pants were contoured from her waist to her thighs. Even at a distance Zadok could see her taut shape and the curve of her muscles.

"That's Vicki Amour," said Nate. "You meet her?"

"No." Zadok took a sip.

"I told you about her. You know, the sexy dish."

"I remember now," Zadok said.

She moved so elegantly. She smiled, almost laughed while they took her picture. She went to a table. Nate was laughing with appetite about something he had said.

"What?" Zadok couldn't understand Nate's giggle, something about New York. To be polite Zadok laughed along and took another sip.

She was the most beautiful woman he had ever seen. She was wearing about ten gold bangles on her right forearm and had a little gold pocket book that matched her shoes.

Two rounds later, after the ceremony was over and most of the people had left, Nate said, "Hey, want me to tell you something? Want me to tell you how to be happy, really happy?"

"Yes."

"You want to be happy, find a good woman. You think I'm joking? It's not simple. It may be very hard. But find a good, considerate woman, one who'll respect you, that's the only way to be happy. Believe me, that's the way."

"That's the way, huh?"

"Ever meet a playboy who's really happy? I mean really happy? Deep down inside, satisfied with himself?"

"Don't know."

"Don't believe it. You've got to have companionship. That's what it's all about. I know, believe me. I hope to God you never experience what I did."

"What's the matter?" Zadok said.

"The ex, the Goddamn ex." Nate's voice was heavy and slow. "There's nothing worse in the whole wide world than to be married to an inconsiderate, evil person." He waved his arms wildly for emphasis. Ashes dropped on his shirt. "You know what she's doing now? Started up with a nineteen-year-old kid. Can you imagine? Lives with him. He's just a kid, younger than ours."

Zadok didn't say anything.

"The whole Goddamn thing's just a joke."

*   *   *

Zadok attended the movie alone the next day. He found the ship's daily movie to be a welcome escape from thinking of his family or anything else. It was like being in a time capsule. When the movie ended Zadok found himself thinking about Nate, and the likelihood of Nate's success in Israel.

Zadok followed the crowd out of the theater and, in the passageway, passed Vicki Amour. She was trying to open her door, but the lock was giving her trouble.

"Can I help?"

"It's these keys. I don't know how to work them."

"Let me try." At first he pushed the key in too far, but he tried again. He pushed on the handle and it opened.

"You did it," Vicki said, clapping her hands together.

"Of course."

They smiled at each other.

Her beauty made it so pleasant and exciting just to be near her.

She looked up at him, her hazel eyes bright and appreciative. Zadok realized it was easy for her to flatter a man.

"Want some fruit, an apple maybe?"

"Okay," he said.

"Come in."

Her room was tourist, a better status than his, but the only difference – aside from the price – seemed to be its location on a higher level of the ship.

"Who's your roommate?" Zadok said.

"A Greek lady. I don't know where she is. She's never here. Comes in late at night and admires my clothes. Here, have an apple." She took an apple from a braided straw basket on the floor, three feet high, laced with pink and yellow ribbons.

"Thank you."

"It was full of fruit and very pretty. I gave most of the fruit away. A friend telegrammed it to the ship."

"Boyfriend?"

"One of my boyfriends."

He sat on the couch and she on the chair by the dressing table.

"You're Nate's roommate, aren't you?"

"You know?"

"He pointed you out to me."

"That's right, you're at the same table, aren't you?"

"Yes we are. My name's – "

"Vicki Amour."

"Oh, so you know me."

"Nate pointed you out, too."

She laughed. "Where's Nate? Haven't seen him today."

"Poor Nate," he said.

"What's the matter?"

"He hurt himself last night. He fell out of bed and cut his forehead and they stitched it up. He insists he looks like Frankenstein and won't come out of the room."

"That's terrible. Tell him I hope he feels better and that he doesn't look at all like Frankenstein. Dracula, maybe."

They both laughed. "We should go down and see him. Would that make him feel better?"

"Don't know. I'm afraid it'll just embarrass him," Zadok said.

"Well, I hope he feels better. Doesn't he eat?"

"The steward brings his food."

"We wondered at the table. What's your name, again?"

"Bob Zadok."

"Where were you going when you saw me?"

"I just came out of the movie."

"Any good?"

"I liked it. About long-distance runners."

"There's not much to do here, is there?"

"What's the matter, you don't like bingo?"

"No."

"What about the night club?"

"I was there. I didn't care for the people I met. First I was with this Canadian divorcé. He told me he was looking for a Jewish girl this time. Then I was with an Israeli. He was all hands, an immature kid."

"Maybe you'd like to go for a walk. Maybe down to the bar? Can I buy you a drink?"

"I'm not dressed for the lounge."

"You look fine to me."

She looked up at him and smiled. "Okay."

He noticed that she pronounced certain syllables as a non-English speaker. He didn't know her accent.

They sat at a dark, candlelit table. She wanted sherry. A visible reel tape recorder provided the Greek music.

"And where are you from?" Vicki asked.

"Boston."

"Oh, yes. Nate told us. I'm from L.A. I really love it there. This was my first time in New York. I was there two days before the ship left. Is Boston like New York?"

"It's smaller."

"My agent said I may have to do some work in New York. I hope not. I want to stay in California."

"You're an actress?"

"A dancer. I've modeled some, too. I'd like to do some acting."

"Sounds interesting."

"I've been very lucky. Got my breaks easily. Ever seen the Dean Lewis show?"

"Of course."

"I was a regular there for a while. Now I don't have anything scheduled. My next job might be in Vegas. It's not so convenient for me to work in Vegas but there's always work and good money there. I told my agent that I prefer California to Vegas. He's really a nice person, very good to me. I've really had it very easy. Some girls have to really struggle. I might even get a job in a film next year."

"Good," Zadok said.

"Going to Israel?" she said.

"Yes."

"Oh, I am, too. Going to Kiryat Shmone. Relatives there. I have relatives all over Israel."

"Hope you're not expecting much in Kiryat Shmone. I mean, it's not Vegas."

"It doesn't matter. I won't be in Israel all that long, anyway. I have to go back to L.A. in December and I want to tour Europe. I'll stay in Israel only three weeks or so."

"Sounds like an exciting trip."

"Look at that poor man over there," said Vicki. She pointed to an old Greek leaning against the bar. He was alone and drunk. "He's so lonely, poor man. I have everything so good. I'm so lucky and I hate to see other people sad. I wish I could do something sometimes. It bothers me when I have so much and others don't have anything."

Zadok nodded. "I'm moving to Israel," he said.

"Really? Why?"

"It's where I belong. It's who I am. I never ask myself whether being Jewish is important. It's an emotional thing, really. I want to be part of building a country. I want to…" He stopped talking when he realized she was more interested in the image of her lipstick in a pocket mirror.

They went out onto the promenade deck and then to the upper deck. It was colder and windier that night as they went higher. They stopped for a moment and sat on a bench. A few people went by. Then they were alone. They could see the white-tipped waves in the distance.

They stood up and walked toward the bow. It was as if they were alone, sailing a little sloop. The stars thickly spiked the black sky.

They were at the bow where the wind was the strongest, leaning forward against the rail. Her hair was lifting and waving in the wind. She was wearing a white shawl. He put his arm around her and the shawl felt very soft and luxurious. She didn't seem to notice. She continued to look into the sea and up at the stars.

"Ever see so many stars?" he asked.

"All the time," she said, "when I was just a little Jewish Sephardic girl in Morocco." She sighed and rolled her eyes as if she were going away. Then, talking to herself, she mumbled, "So long ago, and yet like yesterday."

Later he walked her back to her room. They said good night and he watched her go inside. Then he decided to go down to the bar.

He mounted the high bar stool and called for scotch and thought about

Vicki. She was an exceptional woman. He should have known she was Moroccan when she said she had relatives in Kiryat Shmone. Vicki was truly beautiful. He wouldn't mind being with her. Not at all.

* * *

When the ship docked in Lisbon, Zadok and Vicki took a taxi and toured together. After taking a series of pictures, Vicki gave her camera to the driver and invited Zadok to put his arm around her for an affectionate pose. Vicki spoke to the driver in Portuguese.

"Languages are easy for me," she explained to Zadok.

Several hours later the taxi returned to the port. Zadok paid the driver and thanked him and they got out.

"Where's the ship?" Vicki said.

"I don't know," Zadok said. "There it is, I think. At the end of the wharf."

It was not their ship.

"How late are we?" Vicki said.

"About twenty minutes."

"We can't be the only ones late. You don't think they left without us? Could they?"

"Must be around here someplace."

"What'll we do if they left?"

"Rent a row boat."

"I'm serious."

She stopped to talk to the longshoremen and Zadok went ahead a short way. Then she caught up with Zadok.

"They don't know it," she said. She was worried. "None of them know."

"Never mind. I think I see it."

"Where?"

"Around the bend, on the other side of the fence. Do you see it?"

"They're pulling up the stairs."

"We better hurry." He took her hand and they ran until they came to the fence.

"Hold my camera," Zadok said.

It was a wire fence with horizontal iron bars that held it together. He would have pulled himself over in one hop, but instead stepped on one of the bars and carefully went over the way he thought she would want to do it.

"Now you," he said.

He took the cameras and her pocketbook. She held the top bar and kicked her right leg straight up and then the left and went over in one hop. He took her hand and they ran again.

"Stop that ship," she shouted. She smiled but still looked worried. "Wait for us. Put down the steps."

"Keep running," he said.

They reached the bow and ran on the dock alongside the ship and everyone on the sundeck cheered.

"Wait for us. Don't leave. Don't start without us," Vicki yelled.

"They're letting down the ramp."

"They see us now," she said.

They reached the ramp and went slowly up the stairs. They were breathing hard and laughing.

The steward admonished them. "Can you tell time? Don't you know what time it is? We should have left you. That would teach you. You're late. Look how late. You can't read time."

They ignored the steward and went up the companionway to the sundeck. They were still laughing and breathing hard, like children reliving a good time. They leaned against the rail and watched the ship pull away.

"I can't believe it. We just made it," Vicki said. She was trying to comb her hair back in place. "I've got to catch my breath."

"Like a drink or something?"

"No," she said, then changed her mind.

Zadok went to get her a ginger ale. He came back and gave it to her and she thanked him. She wanted to give him five dollars.

"What for?"

"Cab fare."

"Don't be silly," he said.

"No. I want you to take it."

He laughed. "Easy come, easy go."

"It won't be coming easy where you're going."

He leaned against the rail and looked back to Lisbon. All that was visible now were the hills and a faint statue on the top of the largest hill.

Soft classical music began from the public address system, and there were no longer many people on the sundeck. Vicki was looking toward the horizon, thinking, perhaps dreaming. She seemed far away. Zadok took a picture of her.

"That was sneaky," she said. "I wasn't ready." She smiled and tried to push her hair back with her hand.

"Impossible to take a bad picture of you."

"Oh, I'm not so sure."

"Well, I think so."

"That's good. I'm glad you think so." She paused and looked back to the sea. "It was fun today in Lisbon. Did you see the way the people on the streets looked at us?"

"Yes."

"Like we were millionaires."

"I know what you mean."

"Very lucky, aren't we?"

Chapter Four

Their beautiful ornament they used for vainglory, and they made their abominable images and their detestable things of it; therefore I will make it an unclean thing to them. And I will give it into the hands of foreigners for a prey, and to the wicked of the earth for a spoil; and they shall profane it. I will turn my face from them, that they may profane my precious place; robbers shall enter and profane it, and make a desolation. I will bring the worst of the nations to take possession of their houses; I will put an end to their proud might, and their holy places shall be profaned.

Zadok and Vicki spent the next few days together. In the evening they went to the Zebra Room and after two nights knew the band's entire repertoire. Vicki made friends with several French- and Spanish-speaking passengers. Zadok felt he had become known as the one she was always with. Anyway, being her escort gave him a feeling of celebrity by association.

"Shall we dance?" Zadok offered, as he often did when he felt he was losing her attention.

He followed her to the crowded little dance floor and took her and held her tightly. She came up to his chin and he gently rested his cheek against her head. Her hair was black and soft and comforting, and he loved the feeling of it in his face. They danced slowly and he could feel the motion of her legs as she stepped. He drew her even closer. He thought about how she might be responding and what to do.

He began to daydream about what might possibly develop between them, but he didn't take those thoughts seriously.

When the music stopped, he relaxed and took hold of her hands. The next dance was also a slow Mediterranean ballad. She smiled, her eyes wide and eager. He put his arms around her and felt her hands on his back. He wanted to stay there and never be found.

Her French-speaking friends called and waved good-bye.

"What did they say?" Zadok said.

"They said it's too hot and stale in here for them. They're going out for a walk and for air."

He held her close again and tucked her head back under his cheek.

They went back to the table and ordered drinks.

"How's your roommate? I saw him today. He came to eat." She leaned forward and took his hand. "What does he expect to find in Israel? It won't be easy for him."

"Wants to start fresh. He had a tough time of it."

"Poor man," she said. "I feel sorry for him."

"I like him. In his own way he tries to do what's right."

"He's funny. I think it's very hard for him to do what he's doing."

"I'm doing the same thing."

"But for different reasons. And you're much younger."

"Does that matter?"

"Yes. Don't you think so? I was very young when I came to America. I think only the very young can be good immigrants. My older sisters will never speak English well."

"Well, when you come back to Israel in a few years, come and see me. I'll let you know how I'm doing."

"Okay, I will."

"And you can see how Nate's doing, too."

"If he's still there."

Vicki wasn't finishing her drink. She released his hand and leaned back. "It is warm in here, isn't it," she said.

It was better outside. They walked the sundeck, holding hands, until they came to the railing by the floodlight where they had stood when they had sailed from Portugal. He looked as far as the floodlight would allow, put his arm around her and rested his hand on her shoulder. America already seemed far away. It was like Nate had said, a second life, and he must not look back.

"What're you thinking about?"

"Nothing much," he said.

"Yes, you are. But it's all right, you don't have to tell me."

"I was just thinking about what we had talked about. About how it is to be an immigrant."

"You don't have to be."

"I know, but in a way I do," he said.

He turned to her and kissed her. He went to her slowly, slightly squeezing her shoulders and tilting her neck back, finding her lips fresh and sweet and wonderful. He relaxed and moved back to look at her, to look in her eyes.

"That was sudden," she whispered.

"I was thinking about it for a while," he said. He touched her cheek. "You have so many tiny freckles."

"Like them?"

"They're beautiful. You have many."

"But not too many."

"No, just enough. Has anyone ever told you that you're beautiful?"

"Yes." She smiled.

"It's true," he said. "That's what I thought the first time I saw you."

"When was that?"

"At the captain's cocktail hour."

"Really?"

"Yes, I was with Nate."

"Poor Nate."

"It seems some time ago. I didn't know you then."

"Now you know me and I know you. And I like you. You're very different from the Hollywood crowd back home."

"How so?"

"You're interested in something besides your own ego, or your own career. You aren't out just for yourself and the hell with everyone else. And you aren't affected by what other people think. You think for yourself. So refreshing. You're not driven just by material things. You're not plastic, you're real."

Zadok nodded. "I'm glad you approve."

"And you're just different. Something about you…" She was think-ing and looked away. "But it's a good difference," she assured him as she turned back.

They went below to her room. "Wait a minute. Don't come in now," she said. "I want to see if the Greek lady's here."

"All right."

She went in and called back. "Okay, come on. She's not here."

He went in and shut the door.

"I still have some fruit left," she said. "Want some?"

"No, thanks." He sat on the sofa. "This reminds me of when we met," he said.

"Not so long ago." Vicki joined him on the sofa. She put her arms over his shoulders. "You have very broad shoulders."

"Thank you."

They kissed. He put his arms around her and pulled her as close as he could and pressed his weight against her until she was on her back on the sofa. He was very hungry for her but tried to be gentle. His fingers were in her hair, then lightly caressing her face.

"No, we can't," she said.

"What?"

"We can't." She put the bra loops back over her shoulders.

"Oh, come on," he said, and tried to embrace her.

"No."

"What's the matter?"

"My roommate. She'll be here any minute."

"We can lock the door."

"No, it's no good. We can't."

"We'll go to my room."

"Nate's there," she said. "He never goes out."

"No," he said. "I think he's out tonight."

"Where?"

"I'll go check if you want. But I'm pretty sure he's out."

She didn't say anything.

"I'll be just a minute," he said. "I'll be right back. Don't go away."

"I'm not going anywhere."

He left and went to his room. Nate was asleep on his bunk.

"Wake up, wake up. It's me." He shook him until he got a response. "Hell, get up. Come on."

"Huh, what is it? Something wrong?"

"It's me. I need your help."

"What?"

"Do me a favor?"

"What is it?" He was sitting up now.

"I need the room for a while."

"You need the room?"

"Yes."

"When?"

"Tonight. Now."

Nate turned away and smiled. "Okay, okay. I'll get dressed. I'll get dressed."

"Thanks."

"It's okay. Anything for a friend. You know me. I don't give a – "

"Come on," Zadok said, "please hurry."

"All right, I'm going, I'm going. What the hell do I care."

Zadok found Nate's shoes and socks. "Come on."

"What you do's your business. I congratulate you." He got dressed. "I mean, I don't care, you know, what the hell. You know me."

"I really appreciate this."

"I know it. Where's my shoes?"

Zadok gave them to him.

"Come and get me at the bar when I can come back," he said.

Zadok nearly ran back to Vicki's room. "It's all right. Nate's gone. Let's go to my room."

"You sure?"

"Yes. Come on now."

He took her hand and they went to his room. Once inside he locked the door and fastened the chain and bolt.

*   *   *

The last evening before docking in Piraeus, Vicki and Zadok went to the Zebra Room. She wore a black dress, slit on both sides, with gold, high heel shoes. She had on big gold earrings, shaped like her wrist bangles, and used heavy eyeliner to create a showgirl effect with her eyelids.

They went to the dance floor. Zadok put his arms against her bare back and hugged her. They danced slowly, hardly moving at all.

After that dance, Vicki and Zadok returned to their candlelit table. They decided to order drinks so Zadok called over the waiter and they placed their orders.

A few drinks later, Nate came over to their table, holding his drink in one hand and a cigar in the other. After putting the cigar in his mouth, he put his hand out and shook hands.

"Sit down," Zadok said.

"Just came for a minute, you know, just to say hello."

"Hello," Zadok said.

"Thanks for buying the last round," Vicki said.

"My pleasure," he said, grinning. "My pleasure."

"You were at the bar on the deck over us?" Zadok said.

"A little while, you know."

"Excuse me," Vicki said. She got up. "I'll be right back. I'm going to the ladies room."

"She's all right," Nate said. "I was wrong about her. She does have a good heart."

"She's okay. You're okay, too," Zadok said.

"You like her, huh?"

"I guess so. But it's just for the cruise. When the cruise is over, she goes her way, and I go mine."

"You think so," Nate said looking away. "I'll tell you something. I been round a long time. I met lots of people. One thing I know and that's people."

Zadok didn't know what he was talking about. Nate put his hand on Zadok's shoulder, flaking ashes from his sweaty, little fingers. He sprayed in Zadok's face when he said, "People can only be what they are. That's a fact, you know. I know people. Been around a long time and I've seen that people can only go the way they can go. Am I right?"

Vicki returned and her presence seemed to have a sobering effect on Nate.

"You like to sing?" he said to Vicki.

"Yes."

"She's a professional dancer," Zadok said.

"I know, but have you done professional singing?"

"Sometimes we sing while we're dancing."

"Would you sing for me?"

"Well, I don't – "

"She can't sing here," Zadok said.

"Why not? I'll have the band play for you. Okay? I'd like to hear you. Go ahead."

"Can you get the band to go along?" Vicki said.

"I'll speak to them. Will you do it?"

Vicki didn't need much encouragement. Nate spoke to the lead singer and then came back to the table.

"All set," Nate said. "Now it's up to you."

"Okay," she said, happily.

The band leader introduced her in Greek and English and handed her the microphone. She had all the professional hand motions and facial expressions. There was no accent in her singing, and the amplifier seemed to give her voice more depth. She sang a chorus and danced a few steps with an imaginary partner. The audience applauded crazily and whistled and yelled for more. She returned the microphone to the band's singer. She thanked him and came back to the table.

Bursting with enthusiasm she thanked Nate, and came to Zadok who had stood up. She kissed Zadok on the lips and took his hand. It was then that the real feeling of pride came to him. They both sat down as the cheering quieted away.

"You were wonderful," Zadok said.

"Thank you, sweetie," she said, smiling brightly.

"You were fantastic," said Nate.

"Thank you."

"Fantastic," Nate said.

"She was," Zadok said, squeezing her hand.

The band began to play again and Vicki turned to Zadok. "Now I'm in the mood to dance. Still want to?"

"Sure," Zadok said, following her to the crowded dance floor. "You're just great."

"Why do you say that?"

"Because you are."

"You sang very well," said a nearby dancer.

Vicki thanked the woman.

"It's so easy for you to make friends," Zadok said.

"I have a lot of friends," she said. After the dance she invited Zadok back to her room.

*　*　*

The days passed quickly. The air was colder and the sea higher. All of the Greek passengers disembarked at Piraeus and now the half-empty ship was sailing through the Aegean sea, which was quite rough. The waiters had put up the edge lips on the dining tables but still there was breakage. The dining hall seemed empty now.

Zadok and Vicki sat together at dinner, though the sea had taken away their appetites. Afterwards they went to the Zebra Room but it was their last night and they wanted to be alone. They decided on a last tour of the promenade and sundecks. It was cool outside but refreshing. Zadok held her shoulder.

"It was a good idea, this walk," she said, "but I wish it weren't the last night."

"You've made this a very enjoyable trip for me. I've had the best time I can remember."

"You've made it just as wonderful for me."

He kissed her and they continued their last slow walk on the ship in the night.

"There's no pollution here," Zadok said looking up.

"It's beautiful," she said.

They stood a moment in thought.

"Shall we go in now?" he whispered. He was getting excited.

"I don't know."

"I'll remember you and the ship a long time," he said.

"I don't want to leave this."

"It's really beautiful."

"It'll be sad to leave," she said.

"But it's getting cold."

"It's so lovely."

Her little room was not nearly so inspiring, but it was warm. She wanted to put the mattresses on the floor.

*　*　*

They held one another close, both drifting in and out of sleep.

"How you feeling, darling?" Vicki asked.

"Finer than ever," he said.

"I want you to tell me everything that comes to your mind," Vicki said. "Tell me what you're thinking."

"I'm thinking about us. About our trip. The ship, the people we met. Everything that happened the last two weeks. I'll remember you a very long time."

"And I'll remember you," she said.

"Even after you leave Israel, go to Europe, and return to Los Angeles?"

"I'll always remember you," she said.

"How are you feeling?"

"Fine."

He rolled back and looked at the ceiling. It was over now, he thought. It had been good. Tomorrow he would be in Israel, and there were things to do.

*   *   *

The ship arrived in Haifa bay in the night, but to avoid dock fees, waited until morning, then slowly floated in like driftwood. The tug came out and Zadok took pictures of the blue Carmel and the sea mines that Nate had excitedly pointed out to him. Nate was very sober and looking more hopeful and confident than he had during the entire voyage.

A family of returning Israelis pointed out spots they could remember. There was an old European expressing regret over his lost youth. There was a small group of young Americans, on their way to begin their communal farm, who began to sing. A young religious family prayed that, with God's help, they would succeed in their new life.

It didn't take long for the ship to dock and for them to enter the customs building. Zadok noticed a poster of Herzl, the famous Zionist, high on the wall. It read in Hebrew, "if you will it, it is no fable."

It was a familiar and reassuring symbol that he was in the right place. He felt a stronger identification with early Zionists from Western Europe than with natives or immigrants from distressed situations.

After going through the customs building, he waited for a taxi to take him to Kibbutz Netzer Sereni, the communal settlement where he'd spend his first six months learning Hebrew. He'd been advised by the Jewish Agency to immigrate on a tourist visa because he wouldn't need his immigrant benefits in the settlement.

While Zadok was waiting, he saw a tourist who'd elected immigrant status apparently because he had no concern about losing long-term benefits. This tourist was being picked up and taken to a communal farm free of charge, while Zadok, the real, intended immigrant, had to wait. Then he noticed an American philanthropist being greeted by a bevy of government officials and politely ushered into a posh limousine.

Zadok continued to wait. "Taxi," he called.

He was the one who had brought all his money to Israel, who had said good-bye to his family and friends, who had sold everything he owned, who could not afford to waste a single day of government benefits. For him there was no one to say hello, welcome, or we understand. "Always keep your sense of humor," they'd told him at the parlor meetings. So he shrugged and tried to laugh about it.

He was the real new immigrant, after all, in mind and deed, and despite the unworthy welcome, he managed to embrace his own personal reception. It was a reception of visceral excitement, of sudden discovered pleasure, of larger-than-life experience. He felt his heart pound. He was doing what he had wanted to do for a long time.

He couldn't be bothered by routine annoyances like arranged rides, traffic, long queues, or value-added taxes. He was coming from a higher place. The euphoria continued to escalate, as he looked out from the customs building grounds, past his fellow travelers and their Israeli friends and family, past the taxis and limousines, past the village and highway, to the Carmel, the hills of Haifa.

He felt his first steps in the land weren't taken alone. He was accompanied by other invisible steps. He felt fortunate that in his lifetime most Jews were free to leave the Diaspora. He was an immigrant of the noblest idealistic purpose. He was completing the circle, the final journey. He was fulfilling the hopes of those who didn't have this opportunity.

He loved the healthy, strong vitality of the young Israeli men and women, his peers, in their uniforms. He loved the close, warm sun, centered directly above in the sky.

He loved the merging scents from the fish, fresh from the nets, from the active harbor area, from the open-air cooking at the nearby bazaar, from the diverse humanity everywhere.

He loved the light touch in the air from the yellow sand stirred by a subtle breeze.

He knew he would soon join everyone else with mundane concerns like earning a living, building a new social life, speaking and writing the language, learning the system.

That would come later.

Chapter Five

When anguish comes, they will seek peace, but there shall be none. Disaster comes upon disaster, rumor follows rumor; they seek a vision from the prophet, but the law perishes from the priest, and counsel from the elders. The hands of the people of the Land are palsied by terror. And the food which you eat shall be by weight, twenty shekels a day; once a day you shall eat it. And water you shall drink by measure, the sixth part of a hin; once a day you shall drink. And you shall eat it as a barley cake, baking it in their sight on human dung.

The road from Beer Yaakov went directly into Kibbutz Netzer Sereni. As Zadok passed the factory there was a dirt road that went past the high school and led to the old mission. The mission was now used as an ulpan, a place where conversational Hebrew was taught to adults at all levels of proficiency.

The ulpan was a lofty stucco, looking over the valley. It had been a mission until World War I when the British came and took it over for their headquarters. The settlers also mentioned that when the kibbutz founders had come after World War II, they'd all lived in that building. They had one room to a family.

The fields were a full, straight green, making a grand view from Zadok's room on the third floor. The shutters, which opened from the inside, could not be completely closed. He hung his work clothes on the nails in the walls, and on the window shutters. He could see Ramle and to the west, a young development town that appeared cubical and colorful like a plastic model. Far beyond the fields, the long stretch of Judean hills appeared grey at dawn, and by noon seemed to change to a purple, almost pinkish hue.

The palms had no motion until the night when the breeze came across the fields with a distinct but not unpleasant odor. Irrigation was intensive.

In the ulpan there was a missionary from Oregon. Every night the missionary would go from room to room to proselytize the ulpan students, of whom all but three were Jewish. No one took him seriously. Zadok thought it was ironic that he had come to Israel to preserve his Jewish identity, and this missionary had come to the exact same place for the purpose of converting the Jews.

Yet Zadok might have been the only one in the ulpan who respected him. He respected people who acted on their beliefs. He just wished the missionary would take his beliefs back to Oregon. Eventually when the kibbutz became aware of the missionary's activities, they asked him to leave.

Zadok was one of the last to arrive and on his second day, just before the commencement of work and Hebrew lessons, they planned an evening get-together, a bonfire.

The man in charge of the ulpan group was a young Turk who had married into the kibbutz. He rose and said his name was Mordy and spoke in perfect English with scarcely an accent after having first apologized for his "terrible" English.

Then he followed in his native Spanish and then French.

Kibbutz Netzer Sereni was founded after World War II by concentration camp survivors mainly from Germany and Poland. They had originally chosen the name "Kibbutz Buchenwald" but the government insisted they change it.

Mordy spoke about the kibbutz and about the ulpan program, how they would work a half day and go to Hebrew class the other half, how he would give out work assignments. Most of the people in this ulpan weren't immigrants. He didn't want to dwell on those things and tried to start group singing.

Zadok tried to join and clap with them, but something was wrong, something was missing. He didn't feel like singing. He got up and walked back into the orange groves. He stayed on the main path, figuring it would take him to the dining room. It was a black, cloudless, lovely night like the nights on the ship with Vicki. He could not help thinking how it had been with her. He looked back toward the campfire. He saw the yellow glow and smoke but could only faintly hear the singing and clapping. He continued walking now, unsure of where the road would take him.

He stopped and sat on the ground by an orange tree. It was a warm, delicate night, a rare night that shouldn't be wasted. He couldn't enjoy it without Vicki. He picked up a stick and drew a six-pointed star in the dirt. He leaned back and rested his head on his arm. He could smell the soil, fertilized and turned, seeming now at rest.

He'd been busy and, until now, hadn't had the time to think about Vicki. Now he thought about the ship. He took a deep breath. He missed her. All he could do was write to her in Kiryat Shmone and tell her.

*   *   *

Zadok was assigned work in the factory where they made tank transports and mobile kitchens for the army. While he worked, he pretended Vicki was with him.

"See how I fasten the tubing," he said to her.

How proud she must be making her cousins, he thought. To them she'd be a celebrity, a rich American television star.

He was determined never to leave Israel, but he had just started realizing how much Vicki meant to him. That was the beginning of another fight within himself, and he fantasized, while working, what it could be like moving with her to California. Moving back to the States, even California, would please his family. She was someone special, and everything would come so easily in California. In America, they'd have two days free each week and they'd be able to travel and buy anything.

After work he lay back on his bunk and read his first letter from home, from his sister. "How's things in milk and honeyville?" she wrote.

She thanked him for his recent letter, explaining that she used the term "recent" like geologists speaking of the Pleistocene age. Then after an update on weather, her boyfriend, local friends, and their parents she wrote, "You know we miss you very much (and would even let you come back). You can't expect us to feel the same way as you do, not everybody's inclined that way. You have to respect how we feel, too."

He also received a letter from Aunt Bella. She didn't write about events in the family. She just wrote that she had finally found a portion of a letter or a diary her father had kept before he had moved to Palestine. It was writ-ten in Yiddish, and she couldn't help him because she didn't read Yiddish handwriting well. But Zadok had no trouble finding a translator amongst the kibbutz membership. She was an older woman from Germany. She was anxious to help, and she translated the portion slowly into English.

"After prayer I went for a walk beside the river. It was cloudy and cold, but I needed rest, so I found a park bench. I watched the wind pick up and send the loose trash and papers in all directions. The river, too, was begin-ning to rise and hit the rocks hard. I figured a storm was coming in, so I got up to go home. But then I realized the wind and storm were limited to me. Only a hundred yards or so from where I stood, there was no wind, no trash blowing, no gray sky. I stopped walking and sat on another bench. I rubbed my hands together to try to get warm, and tried to understand what was happening. It made no sense. I feared I was losing my sense of reality. My whole consciousness was out of balance.

"I looked up to the sky and felt more fear that I have ever known. I felt fear, doubt about my vision, my sanity, and at the same time I felt excite-ment and awe. I will attempt to describe what I saw, ever aware of my per-sonal limitations and the fear that I still experience at the recollection of those events. *Hakadosh Baruch Hu*, the Holy One blessed is He, He is my witness, and this is my best and honest memory.

"The wind turned dark gray with a form in the center, a form that seemed to emerge from streams of varying gray winds. At the top of the form was a dome. It was nearly transparent. Through the transparency I was able to make out what appeared to be a king's throne. It was brilliant, bright, and blue, glistening like a precious jewel. There was a large, gray figure whose detail features were hard to see, but the figure was unmistak-ably sitting on the throne.

"Beneath the dome was a vehicle, like an old chariot, but different. It seemed to be able to propel itself in any direction in a flash. Then the form would flash up or down, or left or right, back or forward. The cold wind blew in front of this whole vision, up, down, sideways, sometimes like pillars of spinning wind. And strangely, one hundred yards away, ev-erything was calm. I was very frightened and anxious as I stood before the form, unsure of what it meant, and unsure of my own stability. I thought I could have died, that I may have entered a new stage of existence. I began to shake, more from nerves and fear than from the cold. Then I received a message from the form. I didn't hear the message; I just felt it come to me. But it didn't feel strange to receive a message in such a way. It felt natural. And I was trying very hard to understand what was happening and I didn't think much of the message at the time. My only thoughts were about what was real. And why was it happening? Then suddenly the form was gone. I looked around and everything was quiet, calm. The sky was pale blue and cloudless. How could this be? I now saw other people walking or sitting on the benches and the grass. A woman passed by pushing a pram. Children played and laughed. Where had they been before? Did they not see what I had seen?

"I went back to the bench and continued to shake, even though it was warmer now. My face felt flushed, and I had difficulty breathing.

"Yes, I had received a message or thought that I had. But I had heard no voice, so how could I have experienced the message? *Hakadosh Baruch Hu*, please help me, for I don't understand what the experience means. Nor do I understand what to do with the message. But I will try to understand. I believe it is my destiny, my purpose and responsibility to understand. I think I know how to approach this mystery. I need to discover the point of it all."

The old German woman put down the paper and looked sympathetically at Zadok. "He signed his name, Reuven Zadok," she said. "And he wrote the date, March 1932. That was the same month Hitler ran for president." She looked away for a moment and seemed to go back to an unpleasant memory. She continued, "In the margin down below he wrote four letters: *resh, mem, chet, lamed,* 'RMCL.' Does that mean anything to you?"

"No."

"Look here," she said. She showed him the four Hebrew letters at the bottom of the last page. The letters were written in pencil, not ink like the rest of the text.

Zadok shrugged.

"I'm sorry." She shook her head. "The writer appears to have been very troubled and confused. Must be difficult to hear. He was your grandfather, you said?"

"He never explained the message he had received," Zadok asked.

"No," she replied, returning the papers to Zadok.

* * *

After dinner Zadok went to his room to study. He wanted to learn how to say "get drunk." He tried to look it up in the dictionary. He found that it was impossible to recall words if you just looked them up in the dictionary. He had to say them over and over as they did in class or there had to be a strong association. When he was laughed at for using the wrong pronunciation or the wrong word, then he remembered the correction. He remembered phrases best if they involved money. Looking words up in the dictionary was useless.

He was curiously looking through the dictionary when he heard someone call his name. It was the big South African, who called again. Zadok got up and went to the stairwell.

At the first landing, there was Vicki, tilting her head, smiling up at him. "Hi," she said.

There was never anyone so beautiful, he thought. He knew he was in love with her.

"Hello." He wanted her and couldn't wait.

"Glad to see me, darling?"

"You have no idea. Hey, like my new outfit?" he asked. He felt hot and dirty in the kibbutz-provided work clothes.

"Oh, that's all right." She laughed.

He took her hand and they walked out of the ulpan, a little way up the road.

"How you feeling?" she asked happily.

"Okay. Now that you're here. My God, you've no idea how I've missed you. You're all I've been thinking about."

"I missed you, so I came to see you."

"I was hoping you'd come, all the time. I think about you in class, at work, and at night. And then I dream about you."

"I'm here."

"Really?"

"Yes, I'm here."

"Not imagining it?"

"No."

He released her hand and took her and kissed her. "I'm happy now."

"I've missed you, too," she said. "Really. And I've thought about you. Kiryat Shmone's too far."

"Too damn far." He took her hand again. "We can leave tonight for Tel

Aviv. I'll take tomorrow off and Friday begins the Sukkot holiday. We can be together again."

She began to sing softly and slowly.

They walked to Beer Yaakov, and from there took two buses to reach the Tel Aviv waterfront. The desk manager at the Gruner Hotel agreed to negotiate a discount for them.

The first thing they did after unpacking was to run a bath.

"Too hot?"

"No. It's okay. I'll just have to get used to it." Vicki lowered herself slowly into the tepid water. "Feels so good," she said. "What happened to you?"

"You mean these? Mosquito bites."

"So many."

He watched her wash her arms and breasts. He was beginning to relax and the soreness was going out from his back and neck.

"They should do something about those mosquitoes," she said. "Do they have ants, too?"

"Could be worse," he said.

"They have horrible ants and roaches in Kiryat Shmone. They even have scorpions."

He helped her wash. He kissed her and washed her breasts and shoulders. He kissed her again and washed her back. Then she washed his back and legs. Then they dried each other off with the towels and went to bed.

It was wonderful to lie on a soft mattress with clean sheets. It was wonderful to be with Vicki. And to be relaxed without the stiffness and aching and itching. Vicki massaged him and he couldn't think of anything except the cream she used on him and her hands on his back. She knew how to make him warm and loose and happy. He didn't want her to stop, so she gave him a good, long rubdown.

Then it was her turn and she lay down where he had been and he massaged her back until he was so excited that he couldn't do it anymore. He bent down and kissed her, pulling her to him.

*　*　*

Two hours later she asked, "How you feeling, darling?"

"You're all I've been thinking about at the kibbutz," Zadok said. They were lying together in the darkness.

"I've thought about you a lot, too," she said, softly.

"It was never the way it is with you. When you really feel for a person, it's so much better."

"Something completely different."

"That's what I'm trying to say. Something different and better."

"I know, my darling, my lover." She was quiet a moment and looked away. "I'm only going to be in Israel a short while. I keep thinking maybe it's too sudden. Why should we make it hard for ourselves when I leave?"

"All I know is how I feel right now. That's all that's important."

"It seems almost make-believe. Like a dream."

"Like a beautiful dream. You're the best thing that's happened to me in a long while," Zadok said.

"I feel the same way."

"You'll see. Everything's going to be great. As long as we feel this way. As long as we have each other."

"All right, darling. All right." She closed her eyes.

He'd been exhausted all day, but now, suddenly, he wasn't at all tired. He had to roll back and try to go to sleep.

He loved her but it wasn't enough, he thought. She had millionaires and actors and was happy in California. He was a new immigrant with little money. Soon she'd go back to Kiryat Shmone while he returned to the kibbutz. He'd miss her terribly, he knew that. There was always the chance she'd change her mind. That would be wonderful. He would get an apartment and a job and they'd get married and never have to separate again.

The reality was he couldn't bear the thought of losing her. He began to actually consider going back with her to California.

When the brief holiday was over, Zadok did go back to Kibbutz Netzer Sereni, and Vicki continued visiting her relatives in different towns. When she was able, she came to visit him on the kibbutz for the Sabbath. When he could take more than one night off, he would meet her in Tel Aviv, Jerusalem, or at one of her relatives' homes. They began to spend more of their time convincing one another of the advantages of permanently moving either to California or to Israel. Vicki cancelled her plans to tour Europe. Zadok knew that she did it partly because he'd suggested to her that he might consider California.

He really was considering the move back to the States. He wondered what Vicki saw in him when she could have her choice of wealthy men who were already living in California and were happy to live there. But they were her Hollywood crowd, and he was flattered that she could appreciate that he was different, that he had something the others lacked. And he knew that Vicki, a beautiful dancer with a seasoned diplomat's understanding of the world and its people, truly believed that he'd soon tire of Israel and agree to fly back with her. Maybe she was right.

The time went quickly and the seasons changed. The rains had come.

On Friday there was little work. The rain hammered against the corrugated tin roof. Nobody wanted to work and the supervisor wasn't there, so Zadok left early.

As he came out of the factory he saw a young soldier walking up the road. He was carrying a full duffle bag over one shoulder and his rifle over the other.

"Just get back?" Zadok said.

"Yes," the soldier said. He dropped the duffle bag to the ground and wiped the rain from his face. "Bag's heavy. I hitched a long ride, but had to walk all the way from Beer Yaakov."

"Good walk."

"You should join the army," he said. "Be good for you. You run a lot and they keep you busy and you don't have time to think about your problems."

"What problems?"

"I mean about your girlfriend."

That surprised Zadok. What kind of grapevine did this farm have?

The soldier picked up his duffle bag with a grunt and waved. Zadok returned his wave and started toward the ulpan.

His work boots were too big and he could feel mud in them. The parka they'd given was good. It kept the rain out of his face and had a pouch, like a kangaroo's, for his hands. He stayed on the path, keeping to the grooves made by the tractors and horse carts, because they were less muddy and slippery. It rained heavily.

He reached the ulpan and climbed the three flights. The roof wasn't holding the water well. He knew the ceiling in his room would be stained wet and dripping.

Vicki was inside, sitting on his bed.

He was surprised and happy to see her, but immediately the decision facing him came to mind, making him uneasy and worried. He reached over and kissed her.

They decided to go to Tel Aviv where they checked into the Gruner Hotel. Zadok went to bed first and watched Vicki meticulously fold her clothes. Then she went from the closet to the bathroom and he waited. She came out of the bathroom and danced her way to the bed. She pulled back the sheet and blanket, quickly hopped in and pulled the blanket over her head.

They were both tired but the hotel was like a sanctuary. The kibbutz, Kiryat Shmone, and crowded buses were forgotten. They listened, with the light off, to the rain and wind against the window.

He rubbed her cheek with his finger. He put his finger over her lips and drew it around them. Then he slid his finger between her lips and she bit at his finger. They both smiled but didn't say anything. He was looking into her special hazel eyes.

They slept through the Sabbath morning. They'd missed the complimentary breakfast, so they were hungry after they had dressed. They decided to go out for shishkabob, out into the rain, a steady, monotonous, depressing rain. They went across a few blocks to Dizengoff Street. The restaurant they had in mind was closed for the Sabbath, so they found another nearby.

After eating, they strolled into several tourist shops, and Vicki carefully selected gifts for her family in California.

After they finished and were on their way back to the hotel, Vicki started talking about California again. He didn't want to talk about it, so he didn't listen. When they got back to the hotel she went on about being in California and going places together. It was true she'd given up her plans to tour Europe because of him. She did love him. Maybe she wouldn't leave, he thought. He wouldn't let her leave.

"And everybody enjoys Disneyland. Wouldn't you like to see Disneyland?"

"Yes, of course." He sat on the bed.

"Maybe we'll live in Beverly Hills. You'd like it there."

"Probably would," he said.

"I can't wait. I don't think I can stay here much longer."

"Course you can."

"I'll stay. I'll be with you. I didn't go to Europe, did I? I'll stay with you until you finish the ulpan."

"That's good," he said.

"I can't wait, that's all."

"Stay with me in Israel. I'm not going to leave Israel."

"Oh, darling, really."

"I'm staying in Israel."

"What?"

"I said I'm staying in Israel."

"You can't be serious."

"I'm serious. I'm a new immigrant. You know that. I'm staying."

"What're you saying?"

"I want you to stay here with me in Israel."

"You said you'd come to California."

"Did not."

"You did so."

"I said I'd think about it."

"You don't know what life here is like. You have no idea. All you know is the propaganda the government gives the tourists."

"I'm not blind," he said. "Stay with me and try it. It'll work out."

"You have no money. Do you know how long you'll last here with no money? How will you live?"

"Listen, I'll get a job. Look, please, stay here with me. I know it'll work out. I know."

"It'll work out? Like my cousins. Six of them living in one rotting room. That's how it'll work out."

"No, it won't. Of course, it won't. But so what? I love you. If we have each other, that's all that matters."

"Is that everything?"

"I love you and I need you. That's all I know."

"Why do you need me?"

"I need you to be happy," he said.

"And I need you, too, darling, to be happy. Oh, darling, I do need you. You must come with me."

He tried to study her without saying anything.

"You don't understand," she continued. "You'll never last here without money. They don't want Americans like you. They want the ones with businesses. They want the ones who can bring money. You don't stand a chance."

"We'll have enough. Trust me. That's all I ask."

"I've known this life already and I don't want any part of it. I want to get away from here. I'd have been gone a long time ago if I hadn't met you."

He didn't say anything.

She shook her head. "New immigrant. You call yourself a Zionist. I wonder how long that feeling will last."

"I love this country," he said.

"You love Israel? You said you love Israel? Okay, make love to Israel. Let me see you sleep with Israel." She lay back and turned on her side away from him. "I don't believe it. You're an American. Born in America. And you prefer this? You must be crazy."

"Not crazy."

"Must be wanted by the police or by the army or something. I can't believe it. There must be something wrong with you." She paused. "It's not worth it to you. Believe me, leave your family and friends – whoever heard of such a thing?"

She doesn't understand, he thought. There was just no point. Could she understand the concern for Jewish continuity and the Jewish future? Not a chance.

"Okay," she said, "so you wanted to come to Israel. Okay. But now you've met me. And you say you love me. Isn't that enough to make you go back?"

"I do love you."

"But you won't leave. You're crazy. How many men do you think wouldn't want to live with me in America? How many Israelis wouldn't come to America with me?"

"You're not telling me something I don't already know."

"You're not even a real Israeli yet. Do you even speak the language?"

"I speak with them in the factory."

"Listen to me. I'm trying to help you. So you won't have to learn the hard way. You don't know what kind of people are here. They aren't your people. You want to live with crap? You don't know what you'll have to contend with. The poorest, most wretched, most ignorant ones came to Israel. My cousins are high-class compared to some of the ones that are here. Some of them crawled out of caves. Anybody with any money or education went to France. I was there in Morocco. I know. I know what kind of people went to Europe and what kind of people went to Israel."

He was ready to answer her but then realized it wouldn't solve anything. It wouldn't make any difference. They'd only begin to fight.

"In America you have everything," she said. "You can study anything, be anything. A worker can have his own home, what they call a villa in Israel, his own car. Two cars. I know what you're thinking. I like nice things. Why not? Things make life easier. Haven't you seen the faces of the older people, how tired they look? You're young and strong now, but think how it'll be when you're sixty, how tired you'll be. Think about your future."

"I'm staying in Israel. I belong here."

"Nobody gets out of this world alive. You have to make the most for yourself. You have to enjoy life. Make it easy for yourself. You're not helping anyone by staying here. You're not changing history. I don't know what you could be thinking. You'll just be suffering and struggling along with them. Sure, they'll tell you to stay. They'll tell you anything. They want you to suffer, too."

"That's enough," Zadok said.

"I'm trying to make you understand."

"I don't want to talk about it anymore. I want you to stay. You want to go? Go. Go back to America."

Then she began to cry. "You made me love you. You had to make me love you. You couldn't let me go to Europe. I stayed for you. You said you'd come to California. You had to make me love you. I could've had any man I wanted. You jerk. Why didn't you let me go? Crazy."

He got off the bed and walked toward the window. Hell, he thought. He never dreamed it would be like this. He finally had the two things in life he loved and had dreamed of for years. But they were incompatible.

He had wanted to make her happy, but he was making her miserable. He couldn't stand her whimpering, soft, choking tears. It made him ache. He wanted to go back and tell her anything. Just so she would smile. She was so beautiful when she smiled.

The rain hit hard against the window. He watched the drops on the glass join and run together to make bigger drops and fall.

There was nothing more he could do. He realized it would be better to go back to the kibbutz as soon as the buses started running again.

* * *

Three days after he returned to the kibbutz, Vicki telephoned.

"Darling, I'm sorry we got angry."

"So am I."

"I'm really sorry. It should never happen between us."

"Where are you?"

"In Tel Aviv. I'm at the Gruner Hotel."

"What are – "

"I have to tell you something."

"What are you doing at the hotel?"

"I got a telegram from my agent."

"A telegram?"

"Yes, darling. He has a job for me. You understand?"

"Yes."

"I've got to go. I've decided to go back."

"I see," Zadok said.

"It's a very good job. I couldn't turn it down."

"No, you couldn't do that, could you? Is it in Vegas?"

"No, Hollywood."

"That's better for you. That's what you wanted, isn't it?"

"Yes. I'm very happy."

"When you leaving?"

"Tomorrow."

He could not believe it.

"You understand, don't you, darling?"

"Yes."

"I knew you would. It's a very good job with good chances. I'll meet some important people."

Just then the phone went dead. He pushed the buttons and hit the phone. He hung up. He knew what had happened. She'd called from a pay phone and didn't watch the number of telephone tokens.

The phone rang.

"Sorry. The tokens I'd put in were used up and I forgot to put in more."

"It's okay," he said.

"It's a crazy system. You can go crazy with these tokens."

"I know."

"Anyway, listen. I'm leaving tomorrow but I'd like to see you again and I'd like you to come with me to the airport. Will you? I'm leaving very early. Why don't you come to the hotel and tomorrow we'll leave together for the airport."

"All right."

"You'll come?"

"Yes. I'll be there tonight."

After supper he took the bus to Tel Aviv. He sat alone in the back of the bus staring out the window. It was cold and drizzling with the wind hitting. The bus started with a jolt and the wheels pushed hard through the puddles.

When he got to the hotel, he asked the clerk for Vicki's room number. He went straight up a nearby set of stairs. As he did, he noticed an interesting propaganda poster. It showed a picture in the Golan of a handsome young farmer and his white work horse. One part was in English for the tourists. The Hebrew said, "He is settling Ramat Golan. Are you doing your share?"

He knocked on the door.

"Hello, darling," she said. She was suddenly there, lovely and vivacious, and he wanted her. He forgot about everything else except that she was beautiful and that he must be with her.

He went in and closed the door and kissed her hungrily, bending her over backwards. He was thinking how much he needed her, how good it was to be with her. She was indeed very beautiful. He'd never find another like her.

"I'm glad you're here," she said, pulling away and looking up.

"You knew I'd come."

"How you feeling?"

"I'll miss your asking me that."

"How you feeling?"

"Tired. But all right now that I'm with you." He led her toward the bed.

"What is that on your arms?" she said.

"Impetigo."

"It's all over your arms."

"Legs, too," he said.

"What is it?"

"Nothing. I'll see the doctor next week when he comes. It bothers you?"

"Nothing bothers you, does it?" She looked up at him, giving him that stare, shaking her head. "You'll put up with anything as long as it's in Israel, won't you?"

He was glad that was all she said.

She sat down on the bed and he sat beside her and helped her get undressed. He was already quite excited. She was good to him and endearingly sweet. They made love slowly.

They let the portable electric heater run all evening. They pretended they'd always be together. Other times they'd spoken of the future, maybe they never meant it. Maybe it was always just for the moment, even the things they had needed to tell one another.

In the morning she was already packed. They had a quick breakfast and went out to negotiate with a taxi driver.

"Your Hebrew's coming along. I don't know what you said, but it sounded quite impressive," she said to him, after she finished looking in her pocket mirror.

"The Hebrew's beginning to fit together," Zadok said as they got into the cab.

"What'll you be doing when you finish the ulpan? Found a job yet?"

"I'm going to join the army," he said.

"Join the army?" She paused. "Are you kidding?"

"No. I'm going in two, three months."

"Why?"

"Let's not get into that again."

"Are you sure you really want to?"

"I want to."

"I will always remember you. You're definitely different."

"You used to like my being different."

She nodded.

"You once said you were attracted to me because I'm different," Zadok continued.

"Yes, you are a refreshing change from the scene back home."

"And you know I want to live here because of those very qualities that you find attractive?"

Vicki tilted her head and looked up at him, opening her eyes wide and dropping her chin. It seemed as if she needed a moment to digest his comment. The she smiled, giggled, and gently patted his arm.

At that moment Zadok was reminded how sweet and beautiful she was. The realization hit him suddenly like a bolt to his gut, and he felt remorse and hurt. He didn't want to lose her.

She touched his shoulder and said, "I guess I'll have a lot to think about on the long flight home, won't I?"

It was overcast but not raining. He was wondering if the weather would hold. The driver was making good time, pulling up to every car, within a foot, and passing all of them. They turned by the big airplane factory and into the airport grounds.

"Take us to the front," Zadok told the driver.

Inside the terminal, he gave Vicki ten and a half lirot for the airport tax. They got rid of her bags and bought some coffee. She purchased a French magazine and they sat down and waited.

He said, "Give my regards to the affluent society."

Vicki didn't say anything.

They got up and he walked her as far as the escalator. An airport guard checked her ticket. She was ready to go. He took her hand to pull her against him and kissed her. He still felt it wasn't really happening.

"What can I say," he said.

"Don't say anything." She tried to smile.

She turned and went to the escalator. He watched her as she went up. She never looked back.

*   *   *

The ulpan ended and Zadok was asked to leave the building. He wasn't given a new residence and each day he would scour the settlement to find an available bed.

During this period he had to travel into Tel Aviv to the Office of the Interior because his tourist visa had expired, and he had to change his status to join the army. That was his first real exposure to an Israeli bureaucrat, for which the parlor meetings had not prepared him. This government employee was an overweight woman who carried her arrogance and authority in her bearing. She yelled at him so fast he couldn't understand her. Then, before he could explain to her why he had traveled so far, she began to interrogate him. Zadok traveled the whole day and had accomplished nothing.

On the way back, he had to transfer buses. As he walked toward the bus stop, he realized that the bus at the traffic light next to him was the bus he needed. If he missed it, it could be another two hours before it would come again. He banged on the door and pleaded. The driver pointed to the scheduled bus stop across the street. So Zadok ran, dodged traffic at the intersection and reached the other side just in time to see the bus pass him and stop briefly at the appointed stop. But the driver wouldn't wait for him.

It was a windy day. Zadok shielded his eyes from the blowing dirt and sand as he sat on the bench in the bus stall. It seemed like over two hours had passed. Then he saw a blue bereted female soldier cross the street and he got up to ask her if she had the time.

"Excuse me," he said.

As he approached, she ignored him, turned and walked in the opposite direction. He realized she had taken him for a lowlife who was making a move on her. Well, at least he wasn't being taken for a tourist anymore.

That night, the only bed he could find was a caved-in mattress on the floor of a supply closet. It was too much. He felt as if his spirit had finally been broken. He'd hurt his parents, lowered his standard of living, left his friends and family, and let go the woman he loved, all for the privilege of sleeping on the floor of a damp, dirty, supply closet. He stared up at the cobwebs above him.

He thought about the useless bureaucrats, the bus driver, and the soldier. What did they want from him? God knew, he'd tried. He had really tried.

The next day he was given a private room in an older, but attractive section of the settlement. Things began to look a little better.

The bureaucracy in the army, though, was hard for him to adjust to. It was not much different from the Israeli bureaucracy he'd experienced in civilian life. The primary difference was that younger people were able to abuse their authority. And the army didn't help him to forget about Vicki.

Once on leave, he went to Tel Aviv and checked into the Gruner Hotel. The desk clerk, on renting a room to a soldier in uniform, scratched his bald head and shrugged. Zadok asked for a discount, but the clerk said he couldn't. Soon Zadok realized how different it felt to be alone there. Vicki had a charm that attracted everyone, and he remembered how strangers made an effort to be pleasant when he was with her. She was so beautiful that everyone in the hotel would wish them a good day, smile at them, or at least turn their heads. It was a very different feeling without her.

After checking in he went outside for a walk along the waterfront. As he passed the various shops he'd visited with Vicki, it all started coming back to him, from the ship to the day he took her to the airport.

He crossed the street and went to the wall and watched the waves crashing into the breakers. He realized that if Vicki had told him she didn't love him he could've forgotten her.

He had not resolved his guilt over leaving his family. It stayed deep within and would always bring pain whenever it came to mind. He now wondered about his decision to let Vicki go. Would she always be the love of his life? Would the thought of her and the loss of her love bring pain and regret forever?

He went into a restaurant overlooking the sea and ordered a glass of Israeli cognac. It was much cheaper than imported whiskey. He sipped the drink slowly and watched the sunset.

When the stars came out, Zadok was astonished to recognize a celestial formation of the chariot, depicted exactly as he remembered the first page of his grandfather's book. "Couldn't be," he said to himself, and yet it did somehow make him feel spiritually connected. Then he laughed. Now he understood how zealous students of the mystical could drive themselves mad.

Chapter Six

And you, O son of man, take a sharp sword; use it as a barber's razor and pass it over your head and your beard. As men gather silver and bronze and iron and lead and tin into a furnace, to blow the fire upon it in order to melt it; so I will gather you in my anger and in my wrath, and I will put you in and melt you. I will gather you and blow upon you with the fire of my wrath, and you shall be melted in the midst of it. As silver is melted in a furnace, so you shall be melted in the midst of it; Son of man, these bones are the whole house of Israel. Behold, they say, "Our bones are dried up, and our hope is lost; we are clean cut off."

The Sinai sands shifted all night, the mist of the top sand blew aimlessly, seeming more sinister than simple surf spray reflecting innocently from rocks.

In the morning, the desert was like a different planet. The morning brought an unrelenting, stale heat and stillness. It was an oppressive, long day until the sun came back down to the horizon, then the wind and cold came and blew the sand again. The sand blew with the cold, so Zadok felt and smelled it inside and outside, everywhere cleansing and soiling, soothing and burning. This was a lonely and unsympathetic place.

Damn this duty, the ominous night watch by the bunkers along the canal. Zadok shivered.

He stretched, yawned, and paced. He put down his binoculars. He

desperately wanted to end the boredom and shake the sleep that beck-
oned him.

Three hundred kilometers away was another world, he thought. There,
people didn't fear to sleep. Infants might be crying and their parents would
get up to feed and care for them. The prominent beat of traffic must've
slowed to nothing. Even the prostitutes surely had retired for the night.

There, in only a few hours, the farmers would rise early to avoid working under the harsh afternoon sun. With the first light, the irrigation sprinklers would sluggishly begin their rhythm. In the cities people would jam
the streets and buses, shoving and pushing. The vendors would shout their
prices. The strikers would parade. The black market would flourish. Politicians would bicker. The bureaucracy would strangle. All to the driving
crescendo of our music.

But Zadok was here in the bunker, along the canal, in his newfound
role as protector, looking at Egypt through his binoculars. It seemed a
hundred years ago he was a student at Boston University, but it was only
three.

Zadok looked back toward the desert cliffs, which were magnificent
and beautiful, but they seemed to rise over the plain with a menacing,
haunting presence. It seemed like an arched cobra waited above him.

Hell, he was spooking himself. It was a damn long, eerie watch until
dawn. But he had to admit that the power of the desert mountains could
lure him and frighten him at the same time.

With the first suggestion of light, the dust and sand seemed to settle. A
strange, lurid quiet descended. The canal became distinguishable and the
tide was higher. Zadok stopped thinking of other places.

He focused and panned his binoculars a few times, until he was sure
there was a vehicle, probably a jeep, which was rapidly approaching. It had
been hard to tell because of the sand the vehicle had kicked up, but now at
about two hundred meters away it was becoming more definable. Zadok
put his left hand over the field glasses to keep sand from building up on the
lenses. He noticed the jeep was bouncing and twisting over the serpentine
road, which wasn't really a road, but packed sand that had been crossed for
years by tanks and transports.

The jeep arrived and Zadok walked out from his post behind the sandbags to greet the driver.

"You're fast. I watched you," Zadok said, cheerfully.

The driver didn't answer him. He lifted his goggles to his forehead and rubbed his eyes. The circles around his eyes were free of sand, highlighting just how much sand and dirt was caked onto the rest of his face and beard. Zadok offered him a canteen, but the driver didn't acknowledge the courtesy.

"Where's Captain Shani?" the driver said, showing his identification. "He's in command?"

Zadok nodded and pointed. In response to the driver's apparent hostility, Zadok made no further effort to talk to or assist him.

The driver reached behind his seat to pick up a radio phone. By this time Captain Shani had come out to investigate.

"Okay, finally someone brings us the radio," the captain said, easily.

"You're Captain Shani?" the driver asked. He stepped out of the jeep, instantly revealing how tall and agile he was. He carefully placed the radio phone next to Captain Shani.

"Thanks," the captain said. "Ours has been dead for a few days. We've got a good radio man, but he either complains about the lack of equipment to do a proper repair job, or he gives us overly optimistic assessments of when the radio will be working."

"Call Southern Command, they want to hear from you," the driver said, maintaining his level of impatience.

Zadok dismissed him as a classic, rude, native-born Israeli.

"Sure," the captain said. He offered him a canteen of water.

This time the driver took it. He seemed to empty it in one gulp and he wiped his lips with his sleeve.

"Which bunker you from?" the captain said.

"Orkal C." He returned the canteen. "I must get back to assist in the preparations."

"Preparations?"

"The Egyptians will attempt to cross the canal," the driver said. "Call Southern Command. The radio works." He started the jeep, turned the vehicle around, lowered his goggles, and headed back down the makeshift road.

Captain Shani looked at Zadok but said nothing. The captain seemed to hesitate for a few moments before picking up the radio and taking it into the bunker. Zadok guessed his captain had hesitated in order to review the appropriate questions to ask Southern Command.

Zadok was grateful not to be in the captain's position of having to lead fifty-five men in a battle. But the captain, a rugged, capable, handsome Israeli, about a year younger than Zadok, always exuded confidence. Zadok figured that the attack meant nothing more than the usual artillery duels. Zadok was sure Shani would do just fine.

But Zadok, alone again in his position on the sandbags, began to think about what was to happen. He looked up at the sky, which was totally blue. The sun was rising quickly, the air was fresh and pure and it suddenly seemed life was a privilege.

The news of the impending attack spread through the bunker in minutes. It was relayed to Zadok that the captain had complained to Southern Command that only four days ago he had been asked to relinquish several bazookas and that he would now like them returned. Zadok knew that that kind of request was a waste of time.

Captain Shani gave out a list of orders to fill sandbags, increase fortifications, check equipment, distribute ammunition and supplies, and review procedures. Zadok had no time to think when he was piling sandbags. He was also grateful when he was given the first rotation to sleep for a few hours. Before he went below into the bunker, he looked across the canal.

There was no sign of any movement. Maybe nothing would happen.

He went down the ladder to the familiar dry, dark tobacco smell of the bunker. At least, if nothing else, the bunker was familiar. It had shielded him from the sun, from enemy artillery, from the cold wind at night. He'd spent many boring hours there, but he'd also experienced, through his fellow mates, Europe, Africa, Australia, Russia, and the entire Middle East.

On the bunk below his, he noticed a deck of cards left unpacked after yesterday's gin game. Under his pillow was a letter from his sister. He climbed up to his bunk and lay on his back, his hands supporting the back of his head. He started to think again about what lay ahead. He knew he needed to sleep for as long as he could.

It seemed as if no more than a few minutes had passed, before he awoke. As he stepped out of the bunker, the first person he saw was a Jerusalemite wearing a prayer shawl, and swaying back and forth with exaggerated motions. It was the most earnest, desperate, and physically active form of personal prayer he'd ever seen. Zadok hoped it might help. He went to his position near the canon.

Another soldier, Eli, who loved to hear himself talk, was suddenly quiet. He leaned against the bunker's entrance, and stared across the canal. His behavior, for those who knew him well, brought even more discomfort than his incessant jabbering.

An Iraqi-born soldier recalled his old experiences living in an Arab country.

A recent immigrant from Russia was convinced that the Russians were behind the enemy initiative. He reminisced over his difficulties leaving that country.

One soldier, a native born from Kurdish-Jewish parentage, had a routine describing the kind of woman he was looking to settle down with. He had her description to ridiculous detail. She would be tall, blonde, thin, big busted, with good hip curves, long manicured fingernails, and a non-smoker. He didn't like women who swore or smoked.

Zadok noticed that he was talking much faster now. This time his listeners acted as if they were really interested in what he was saying. Someone said, "What if you found a girl who was a good person and had a compatible personality, but was a brunette or a redhead, instead of a blonde?"

"My dream woman's out there, somewhere, and I'll find her," he answered.

"It might be easier to find a good hair coloring at the pharmacy," someone said.

The Kurd continued at his pace to relate his dreams and where and how he planned to settle down. He even talked about how many children he would have and what they'd look like.

Zadok recognized that it was really his view to the future that made everyone listen, look inward, and think.

The time went slowly. Zadok looked at his watch again. Only ten minutes had passed. Damn, when was it going to happen? Did he want it to happen? No, the shelling was enough. He didn't need to be canon fodder against a full-scale invasion.

A sentry called for Captain Shani, who immediately came running up. The captain took the binoculars, but Zadok didn't need his binoculars to see movement at the opposite edge of the waterway. It became readily apparent that there were boats, tanks, transporters, artillery, bridges, assault barges, anti-aircraft guns, and hundreds, maybe thousands of troops.

Captain Shani called for the radio, but continued scanning the enemy. Finally he put down the binoculars. His face flushed as he looked back at his small unit, back at the Egyptian side, then back at his men. His eyes met Zadok's stare.

"Lovely," he said to Zadok in accented English. It was the first time Zadok ever heard Captain Shani speak a non-Hebrew word.

Zadok and the Iraqi loaded the canon, and waited. Zadok was apprehensive, but he wondered if he could be content elsewhere, knowing that someone else had to be on the front line. He worried about his parents should anything happen to him.

At about noon, the first enemy shell whistled over them and fell about a hundred meters behind. Immediately Shani gave the command to return the fire.

Zadok moved quickly. Men were shouting instructions and encouragement to one another, the guns and canon shook the earth, the sand kicked up and floated in the air. The sun was relentless over them. Zadok was running to carry shells to the canon and held his ears after the loading was complete. In the distance, they could hear the other bunkers.

Over the next half hour, the shooting intensified. The earth around Orkal D was opening up, spitting sand and gravel and shrapnel. The enemy shells that fell short into the canal forced the water up like a volcanic eruption. Then a shell fell right on the sandbags and, after the enormous fireball and smoke cleared, a portion of their fortification was gone.

The enemy blasts came so fast they went for cover more often than they could stand. They were off balance. There was a direct hit at the other end of the bunker. That was the first casualty. Then there was a minor cave-in at the bunker but Zadok didn't think anyone was hurt.

Zadok and the Iraqi had to jump into a hole, wrap their hands over their heads, and hide. The world was blowing up.

As the sun started to descend, the bombardment eased. Now the Egyptians came at them in boats, two rows aimed at each end of Orkal D, with about twenty men in each boat. They were progressing quickly.

Captain Shani tried to use the radio but it was busy. Apparently the commander of Orkal C was hit in the chest and needed a blood transfusion. Because their medic was unqualified for that procedure, the instructions for the transfusion were being given over the radio.

The medic at Orkal D was also now busy and he warned that they were already low in blood plasma.

A fragmentary bomb killed one of the Argentineans and wounded the sergeant. Captain Shani told the signal man to put down the unusable radio and pick up the bazooka. Zadok heard someone praying out loud as the enemy came closer.

When the Egyptians were about halfway across, Orkal D could be more accurate. A near miss was good enough to sink the lead boat. Then a bazooka shell sank another boat. Everyone cheered. They sank a third, so Zadok began to think they might have a chance of holding them back. He believed that all they had to do was hold them off until the reserves came. They just had to make it through the night.

Zadok wondered about the Egyptians' tenacity in this type of combat. He had heard stories of how they had run in 1967. But none of them were running now. It was frightening.

One boat managed to come very close to the eastern shore. When the bazooka shell sank it, they could hear the cries of the enemy. Some were trying to swim, but Shani shot at them with his pistol.

Then Zadok saw one of the enemy boats reach shore about a half kilometer north, in the swamp.

A large Egyptian ferry came down the canal carrying tanks and artillery. The radio was available now, and they told Southern Command what was happening. Southern Command said they already knew about it.

Soon an Israeli Skyhawk passed over Orkal D. Just the sight of it was enough to raise Zadok's hopes. Within seconds it sank a small boat and scored a direct hit on the ferry, which dropped like a dead weight in its own wake.

Before Zadok could realize all that was happening, two enemy surface-to-air missiles flew at the Israeli jet. The second hit and the plane was in the canal. Two more Israeli Mirages thundered overhead, one behind the other. The first turned to avoid a missile, but it didn't work. The pilot catapulted out before the explosion and parachuted into Israeli territory. The second Mirage fired a missile, but soon took one. It spun out of control, into a dizzying nosedive, and crashed in the marsh. The oil fire reached fifty meters high.

In the evening there was a momentary pause and the defenders tried to figure out, as best they could with the night vision equipment, what was happening. With the moonlight alone, they were able to distinguish the macabre sight of hundreds of bodies floating in the canal.

Not even one day had passed, and Zadok was already feeling exhausted, sleepy, and hungry. How long could his adrenaline flow? With an imagination that came easily in the night, he could believe the floating corpses were really frogmen or commandos sneaking in on them.

"Here they come again," someone shouted.

They were using a larger, slightly different type of Russian landing craft now. This time, their artillery rained on Orkal D while their own men advanced in an attempt to give themselves maximum cover. The night turned red from the flash, then instantly turned black again until the next blast.

Zadok was again too busy to think, which was good. When he couldn't think, he wasn't afraid.

It seemed that a comfortable, pleasant day would never come again, that the earth would never stop shaking and that the chill would never leave. Zadok's palms were sore from pressing against his ears. A few shells came too close. They fought with desperation through the night. Each of their shells were precious, but they didn't hesitate to use them, since it was their only protection and they sincerely believed they'd soon be saved. Just before dawn they ran out of flares and had to wait until the enemy was close before beginning to shoot.

The dawn did eventually come and Zadok rejoiced with the first light, as if it meant rescue. The wounded sergeant came out of the bunkers on his own. He was wearing bandages around his forehead, neck, and back. There was a bazooka available for him and on his first shot, he sank a boat.

He looked up at Zadok.

"Not bad for a hungry cripple, yes?"

"Good appetite," Zadok said.

The sergeant's shooting was hot and he soon sank another. Just as he sank a third, he was hit. Zadok didn't realize where the fire came from, but within seconds he saw the Falasha sergeant fall dead from a bullet in the back of his neck.

Zadok turned around. There were snipers on their own ramparts. Shani came rushing down to meet the new danger and was shot in the chest. He fell right before Zadok who instantly jumped down flat behind empty artillery shell crates.

Zadok peeked out and saw Shani dying. Only Shani's lips moved, "Hear, Oh Israel, the Lord is our God, the Lord is one." He kept repeating the *Shema* prayer until the end.

Who was in command, Zadok wondered. The boats were coming straight on them and they were forced to keep their heads down. Some of the men started shooting at the snipers with uzis.

Zadok also began shooting at the snipers. It was a reckless move considering he exposed his very vulnerable position, but he didn't care. He was not going to lie shivering behind boxes until they came to kill him.

The Egyptians answered his fire, but they had many targets to choose from and didn't concentrate on him. He jumped up and ran away from the hole to protection behind sandbags located closer to the captured wall. From there he had a better vantage point to fire, but he also knew time was running out. The enemy snipers were succeeding in allowing their boats to safely approach, and if that continued they'd have established their foothold on the Israeli side of the east bank.

"There's nothing between us and Beersheva," Captain Shani had said yesterday. "If the Arabs capture you, they cut your balls off and shove them down your throat."

You've got to do something, you've got to do something, Zadok kept saying to himself.

Egyptians were using water canon to collapse the heights of sand on the Israeli side of the canal. It seemed to be working.

Zadok saw that the Iraqi had managed to break out and was crawling behind the bunker, in order to get on the other side of the rampart.

There was machine gun fire, and then there was quiet from the rampart. Then Zadok heard in that Iraqi accented Hebrew, "All clear."

The Iraqi stood up, and everyone except him could see that one of the Egyptian commandos was coming up with a knife on his back. Just as the commando reached around the Iraqi's throat, the Russian, who had apparently followed him, took the Egyptian's knife arm in his grip and pushed him down to the ground. The Iraqi fell forward gasping, but free and unharmed. He held his throat.

The Russian forced the knife out of the Egyptian's hand. Free of that danger, he released the Egyptian's arm, and finished him with his own knife.

The Iraqi seemed to want to thank the Russian, but appeared to remember that they didn't like one another. They just looked at each other.

One of the boats had reached them. The Israelis opened fire with small arms, and the Egyptians managed to return the fire. Another boat reached the shore's edge, and the enemy marines were jumping out and storming in the shallow water.

The Orkal D machine guns were successful against the marines, who were not yet to where they could be protected by the slope of the beach. That's where the Egyptians managed to set up their machine gun and a rocket launcher. The Egyptians had used water to easily destroy the sand ledge, which once had seemed so formidable. Then they advanced on Orkal D in stages. The Egyptians' main target was Orkal D's cannon, which was still able to pick off their boats and hold them back.

Then on the left, another boat landed. They must have realized their sudden advantage, and moved on Orkal D quickly, one behind the other, as if they were marching. Lieutenant Uri, who now had assumed command, yelled out, "Look to your left. Forget the front, we'll take them, look to your left."

There were only immigrants there. The South African yelled back, "What?" He hadn't understood Uri's rapid-fire panicked Hebrew.

Then slower, Uri started to repeat. It was too late, the South African was hit. He fell forward, twisting like a crab in the sand.

In about an hour of hand-to-hand combat, the Orkal D defenders managed to kill all of the marines and to hold off the direct advance of the boats on their line. That gave Uri the chance to get on the radio and report what was happening. Southern Command told him to hold at all costs. Zadok had overheard Uri repeat the orders. It seemed to Zadok that it was very easy for them to say that, but was there any other buffer?

It also became apparent that the Egyptians had successfully crossed in many locations and were advancing in all directions. It was a reality whose consequences Zadok was afraid to consider. Uri tried to get through to Orkal A, B, and C, but Orkal C didn't answer. At Orkal A, the officers were dead. Their machine gunner was untrained and during the fighting he'd apparently called in for instructions on how to use the machine gun.

Zadok knew they were surrounded, low in ammunition, and physically exhausted, not to mention the many wounded they couldn't care for.

The Iraqi approached Zadok.

"By the way, thank you. You did a good job," Zadok told him. "And you know you were very lucky, don't you? You had a close one."

"I've had much closer. If you call that close, I should've been killed ten times over. The Arabs can't kill me," he said, with confidence and arrogance. "I didn't make it this far to be killed here by Arabs. That's sure." He smiled and looked straight at Zadok. "There's too many women expecting me."

A young soldier fell to the ground. The Russian carefully examined him.

"Never mind," the Russian said. Zadok and his friends turned away.

"No, no, he's not dead. He's asleep," the Russian added.

"Give him ten minutes," Lieutenant Uri said, "then wake him."

The shock of their own cannon was loud enough to set their eardrums spinning, still it was very understandable that a man could drop from lack of sleep. Noise and discomfort didn't matter anymore. Zadok also longed to sleep, in a way that one might long for an unthinkable, impossible luxury. He considered that giving Ilan ten minutes may have been unfair.

It seemed death at least offered the consolation of sleep.

They were beyond that level of consciousness where rationale presided. The sand had been shot so persistently and powerfully out of the ledge, that it would inevitably hang for days. It was hard to see and feel in the smoke and sand, but they continued.

Here men didn't eat, sleep, or think, they never let up, even for a moment, on their rhythm of shooting. Lieutenant Uri was going around with a fresh canteen to encourage each one of them.

The Iraqi called over to Zadok.

"Yes?"

"The radio. They said Orkal A and C have fallen."

Zadok knew how little ammunition they had left. He realized Lieutenant Uri may have to make a decision and soon. Zadok spoke with some of the wounded. Many were in pain but the medics could do little to help. Zadok began to realize the meaning of courage. One of the eighteen-year-olds, who he knew would bleed to death if he didn't get to a hospital, pledged to Uri that he was prepared to continue fighting. It was becoming apparent that the Egyptians had clearly encircled them, but for the moment, chose to bypass them.

Lieutenant Uri received a call from the commander at Orkal B. Apparently Orkal B had been thoroughly bombed. When the command had come for Orkal B to withdraw, one of their men, who might have been in a state of shock, drove off alone with one of the trucks.

Zadok was picked to drive the jeep behind the truck that was to be delivered to Orkal B. When Uri pointed to him, he felt his heart drop, as if the angel of death had pronounced his fate. He couldn't understand anything that was happening. His legs were moving toward the jeep, but it was as if his body was left behind. He felt that he was marching toward his end. It was an impossible assignment.

The road to Orkal B came down from a hill which afforded a total view of their comrades' attempt to break out of Orkal B and retreat. Zadok got out of the jeep and walked to the truck. Ilan, the driver of the truck, also stepped out of his vehicle. They watched through binoculars.

The commander of Orkal B laid out all the men that could fit on the floor of their one available half truck. They had one tank and they tried to charge their way out. The Egyptians had them totally surrounded and raised the intensity of their fire. The Orkal B defenders managed to make some progress until their tank and half truck were hit.

"Should we try to move the truck closer to them?" Zadok said.

He didn't expect an answer. He knew what he was suggesting was impossible. He wanted Ilan to reinforce his opinion that there was nothing they could do.

The commander of Orkal B must have seen them. Though he appeared to have been wounded, he threw grenades and kept firing, charging in their direction. But he stopped when he realized that his men weren't following anymore. Most of the Orkal B survivors were scattered in a ditch by the side of the track. He went back to his men, and quickly hit several with the butt of his gun to see who was still alive. The commander was counting hands to see if he had any kind of force left to fight with, when the Egyptians moved in on them. They were all captured.

"Forget the truck," Ilan said. "Oh, no, they see us. Let's get the hell back."

An explosion knocked them to the ground. Ilan and Zadok got up and ran back to the jeep, turned around, and drove back at full speed to Orkal D.

By the time they returned to Orkal D, authorization had already been given for them to withdraw. Zadok was grateful. He knew that holding out further meant death or capture. But not everyone reacted the same.

"Why are we retreating?" the Iraqi said.

"Just momentarily. Keep moving," Uri yelled.

"Let's stay and fight them," the Iraqi protested.

"Fight with what? Do you want to throw rocks at them?"

"You want to be captured again?" someone said.

Zadok guessed the reluctance of a few to withdraw was not so surprising after the human strength and effort put into saving this pile of sand. They hated the place but it somehow took on a significant value.

They carefully loaded the wounded in two of the half trucks. They wanted to take all of the dead too, but there wasn't enough time. Zadok climbed in the back of the largest truck and sat next to the Russian.

Zadok realized they were the only force on that point of the Bar-Lev line to be able to withdraw. But he knew that the Egyptians still principally controlled the area, and that Orkal D would be moving down an open dirt road with no protection.

Soon Zadok's fears were realized when two Egyptian jets spotted them. They flew over, apparently on their way to another target. Zadok knew that they would soon be back. There was no protection, no trees or hills. They were wide open.

Uri jumped out of the lead truck. "Out of the trucks. Run. Out. Out. Run."

They tried to carry the wounded out to the roadside where they might stand a better chance of surviving the attack. They dropped to the ground when the truck was hit. They heard shouting from within the truck but for those long seconds they could do nothing. The engine was on fire.

"Anybody hit?" the medic said.

"Two are dead," someone said.

"Hurry up," Uri said. "Move it, faster, move it. Quickly." The smoke was filling the truck and suffocating those still inside.

The jets came in for a second pass, but the men from Orkal D didn't stop.

As they took out the last man on the stretcher, Zadok looked up and saw that the jets were gone. He could breathe again.

Then the truck blew up.

The radio man came over to inform Uri that as devastating as this air attack had been, their losses in personnel were actually light. He pointed out that all their vehicles were destroyed. Zadok saw that all the vehicles were on fire. The enemy pilots figured they'd done their job.

"How do we move the wounded now?" the medic said.

"I don't know," Uri said.

What chance did they have now to escape? Zadok thought. "We'll just have to carry them," the Russian said.

"Too many now," the medic said.

"We can do it," the Russian said.

"No alternative," Uri said. "We'll carry somehow."

Zadok wiped the sand from his eyes and followed them so that he might help.

Chapter Seven

Yet I will leave some of you alive. And I will bring you home into the Land of Israel, and you shall know that I am the Lord. And I will put my Spirit within you, and you shall live, and I will place you in your own land, then you shall know that I, the Lord, have spoken, and I have done it, says the Lord. Though I removed them far off among the nations, and though I scattered them among the countries, yet I have been a sanctuary to them for a while in the countries where they have gone. Thus says the Lord God: "I will gather you from the peoples, and assemble you out of the countries where you have been scattered, and I will give you the Land of Israel."

With the protection of darkness they continued in the open. Orkal D moved like a worm over the desert hills. While some of them were able to keep marching, there were always others in the unit who had to slow down or even stop. They marched not so much with trepidation but with the gambler's anticipation of how the luck would go. They moved quietly, eastward through the black and unnerving night. It had become cold with the wind picking up, blowing the sand, aggravating their burns and malaise, blowing them backward, making it more difficult for the wounded, and for those carrying them.

The terrain was all hill, yet sometimes it was possible to walk around and avoid going up. When they had to climb, it took all their strength. As a unit, too, they drew from whatever reserves they had left. Individualism faded and the unit's character was finally taking shape. Whoever could would pull the weaker ones, and Orkal D inched up the hills.

Zadok was holding the back of a stretcher.

"It hurts, it hurts," the boy holding up the front of the stretcher complained. He had to drop his end of the stretcher.

Zadok lowered his end as well. "What's the matter?"

"My legs, everywhere, cramps." He agonized worse than the corporal lying on the stretcher.

"Both legs?"

"Yes."

Even Eli, the likeable boy on the stretcher, tried to sit up out of curiosity.

"I'm sorry. I can't go on. I can't walk."

"Why don't you try?" Zadok said.

"I can't even straighten them. How can I walk?"

"Try."

"Go on without me. I'm sorry. Forget about me. Now, who'll help carry Eli?"

"Don't worry about me," Eli called out.

"Let me take a look," Zadok said, but the boy screamed as soon as Zadok touched the leg. "We're not going to leave you here," Zadok said and he helped the boy up. Two others came over to pick up Eli. Zadok pulled the boy's arm over his shoulder and helped him up the hill.

Zadok was out of breath by the time he made it to the top of the hill. He let the boy down, and quickly dropped down himself. He pulled out his canteen and finished the last drop and debated whether to throw away the canteen. He decided to keep it.

The Iraqi and Jerusalemite now reached the top of the hill. They put down their stretcher and gratefully lay on the sand themselves, but then they looked at the silent soldier on their stretcher. They called for a medic, but there were no medics around. Zadok went over and reached to find a pulse. But he couldn't. They had carried him up the hill and he had been dead. No one said anything. They seemed to solemnly withdraw.

The Iraqi said quietly, "Someone should say a prayer."

When everyone assembled on the top of the hill, the lieutenant authorized a brief rest.

They had begun to think of their retreat in terms of one hill at a time.

At least it would be downhill now for a while. Some fell asleep within seconds. They were given a few minutes' break and already they were snoring.

Two soldiers argued about whether they'd reach Israeli lines or Egyptian lines first. They decided to make a bet. Either way there'd be a consolation.

The Iraqi and the Russian argued over something else, something petty like who was carrying the greater load, and then the Iraqi left the Russian and came over by Zadok.

"Can't you two get along?" Zadok asked.

"He's an ass. Russians…you know," the Iraqi said. He ritualistically offered Zadok a cigarette, which he declined.

"It changes you, doesn't it?" the Iraqi said.

"What?"

"Death. The real possibility of being killed. Changes everyone. No man can face death and be the same afterwards.

"Haven't thought about it."

"You will. When it's over. Everything'll be different to you. You'll be surprised what will be important and what will become unimportant."

"I don't know if people really change. People forget quickly."

"Maybe for some. You'll see," the Iraqi said.

"Let's just worry about now. About getting out of here alive. That's all I care about," Zadok said.

"That's what we all care about," the Iraqi said.

Lieutenant Uri stood up and called out, "Next year we'll have a reunion. Everybody will come."

"That's an order?" someone said.

"Yes, that's an order," Uri said. "Next year to the day, everyone will come to my kibbutz and we'll look back on this day. Think about that."

"Your kibbutz is too far."

"I live in Eilat," another said.

"How about Netzer Sereni, it's more central," Zadok said.

"Where's that?" someone said.

"Near Ramle."

"That's better. Make it there."

"Will it be all right with the kibbutz members?" Uri asked, knowing that Zadok wasn't a member of the kibbutz.

"Who cares," Zadok said.

"All right," Uri said, "next year we'll meet, everyone now, we meet in Netzer Sereni."

Then Zadok decided to quickly write a letter. He used his helmet as a desk, though he could hardly see the ink. Then he brought the letter over to Uri.

"I just wrote a quick letter to my family in America. I want you to hold it. Just in case. Will you see that they get it?"

"Why worry now," Uri said. "We're almost home free."

"It's very important that they get this letter if anything happens to me. You see, they never felt very good about me coming to Israel in the first place, and now that the war broke out, and they haven't heard from me in days...Well, you know what I mean. They worry about little things like tightening soda bottle caps. I can't imagine how they're taking this."

Uri took the letter. "Don't you worry. This won't need to be mailed."

Zadok sat down again, wrapped his arms around his bent knees and tried to rest, but he knew there wasn't enough time left to the night.

With the morning light, Uri yelled, "Everybody up." He seemed to be becoming more confident in his leadership role. "Move out."

Zadok went back to join the Russian hauling Eli's stretcher. They took the lead position in the column.

They were caught totally surprised when the earth exploded around them. They took cover. The Russian and Zadok put down Eli fast. They didn't drop him, but he shrieked. Many of the wounded had been dropped and Zadok heard their screams continue through the bombardment.

Zadok lifted his binoculars and tried to find the location of the attacking artillery. Red fire, smoke, sand and rock was still flying, so he couldn't see anything.

The attack stopped momentarily, then continued with unusual power and accuracy. They tried to pull their wounded to shelter but there was no protection. Some of the men pulled the wounded and unconscious into foxholes that had been dug out by shells, others huddled behind a few of the rocks that were available. It wouldn't do much good because the bombs were exploding above ground and could wipe out anything in their proximity. They had nothing except rifles and machine guns to fight back with, which were almost useless in this kind of assault. All they could try to do was hover into the sand. The trajectory of the exploding missiles was gradually moving up the hill to their exact location and there was nothing they could do about it.

Zadok finally spotted a tank.

"My God," he said. "They're ours."

Zadok ducked down and felt bits of rock fall against the back of his helmet. "Stop," he yelled, as loudly as he could. "We're Israeli. We're Israeli." Zadok kept yelling into the distant hills until he was hoarse. "Stop. Stop. Stop."

Zadok looked on helplessly as he saw the right flank blow up. Bomb after bomb landed. Survivors of the hits scrambled to get away. He saw that the Jerusalemite was wounded in the legs. He tried a few times to stand up and run, but he couldn't. The Iraqi, who had made it to a hole on the other side, called out to the Jerusalemite that there was an unexploded shell behind him. The Jerusalemite panicked and pathetically began to claw at the sand in order to pull himself away. The Iraqi coaxed him on but probably recognized the futility of his effort. The Iraqi got up out of the safety of his hold and ran back toward the Jerusalemite.

The Iraqi was about halfway there when another shell landed behind the Iraqi. It blew him up.

The Russian also saw everything that had happened. He got up from behind his rock and ran to the Iraqi. He made it safely, examined him, saw that he was dead, then moved on to the Jerusalemite. He slid slowly down beside him, quickly picked the Jerusalemite up over his shoulder and managed to carry him to a boulder on the other side.

Zadok realized that the unexploded shell never went off.

"They're going to kill all of us, do something," Zadok said to himself.

His screaming wasn't doing any good. They couldn't hear with all the noise. "Do something, do something. I have to do something."

The next thing he knew, he was thrown up in the air and spun so that he fell flat on his back. The air was knocked out of him and he struggled to breathe. He saw the blood draining down his arm. His whole body felt numb. It was over for them, he thought.

He looked to his left and saw some human remains and a blood-soaked prayer shawl. He managed to crawl over and pull off the prayer shawl. He straightened himself and held the bloody shawl at arm's length up in the air with his good arm and kept walking, like a drunkard, toward the attacking artillery. Zadok ignored the shells flying overhead, before him, beside him. He ignored the residue of the blasts that reached him, he ignored the pain in his right arm and right side. He didn't care. He was dead anyway. He just didn't care. Why don't they see me, he wondered. He waved the shawl around as he walked. He felt each moment that passed to be the destruction of Orkal D.

Please help us, he thought. Stop, please stop. You'll kill all of us. Please make them stop.

Suddenly, the guns fell silent.

They brought in the helicopters which beat the sand and dry air into an offensive concoction. Amidst the noise of the engines, pulsating earth, screaming and running men and women, medics everywhere, Zadok sat down. He had no more energy. He had done all he could. Two medics came over and soon started arguing over how Zadok should be treated. Finally, the shorter medic acquiesced to the other medic's opinion that Zadok should go to the helicopters. He walked to the helicopter like an aimless ninety-year-old. He now had the luxury to become totally dependent. The rest of the wounded were brought in on stretchers. Zadok sat in the cab staring wide-eyed at the sun flashing between the slowly rotating helicopter blades.

Zadok imagined he could smell blood. There was blood everywhere. Death, too, had a smell to it. He could dispassionately smell the death. He felt the jerk and swift lift of the chopper as it pulled up over the dust. Zadok fell asleep.

In the hospital Zadok didn't have to wait long. Everyone was moving quickly. Zadok was walking to the side to make room for the stretchers with the seriously wounded. He felt lost for only seconds when a nurse came over.

"Where are you hurt?"

"My arm was bleeding."

"Come here, let's take a look."

She ushered him into a small crowded room. He sat down and she started to cut away at his torn sleeve in order to expose the wound.

"My name's Shoshana. What is yours?"

"Robert."

"Ah, an American. Well, you'll be okay. It's just a dirty little wound. We'll fix you up."

Zadok turned to look at Shoshana. He hadn't really noticed her face until now. She had strong, prominent cheek bones, and light blue eyes which contrasted beautifully with her black hair pulled back tight into a long ponytail.

"Thirsty?"

"Very," Zadok said.

She left and came back with orange juice. It was the best he had ever tasted.

"I'll get the doctor. He's very busy, but I'll clean you up while we're waiting."

"Thank you," Zadok said.

Zadok watched the dust rising and roaming and falling in the sunlight to the side of his chair. The hospital was very old but kept as clean as possible. The white plaster walls and ceiling were all cracked like spider webs and the floor was chipped. There were small drops of blood on the floor beside the chair. He realized it was his blood. He looked into the hallway floor just beyond the opening of the room and noticed more blood, most of it dried. That wasn't his.

They were bringing more stretchers past the room. A few of the boys on the stretchers were crying out in pain. The majority were quiet. Zadok was feeling a little better after drinking the juice, though he was still slightly dizzy and his nose was filled with dried blood. He fell asleep.

About an hour later, a Dr. Rosen came into the little room and stopped next to Zadok. "How are you feeling?"

"Better," Zadok said.

"Let me see the arm." He touched the wound.

"Do you speak English?"

"A little," Zadok said.

"Can you make a fist?"

Zadok made a fist.

"Can you turn it? Good. That's the way. You'll be fine. We'll stitch it, wrap you up and you'll be fine." The doctor quickly examined his eyes and throat. "I'll give you a note so that you can go right back to the front, if you like."

"Thanks for the offer, but I think I need to sleep for a few days," Zadok said.

Shoshana stitched the arm and bandaged it, then she went to the next patient. The hospital was busy and suddenly Zadok felt superfluous. There were no beds available for sleeping. He decided to hitch a ride to the kib-butz and sleep there.

Hitching a ride was easy. He didn't even have to put out a finger. The bandage over his obvious wound helped. Suddenly for the first time since coming to Israel, he felt like an authentic Israeli.

"How'd you get hurt?" the elderly man driving the Peugeot said.

"Shrapnel."

"Egyptian artillery?"

"Yes."

"At the front?"

"Yes."

"Ah, how's it going?"

"Things'll improve now that the reserves have arrived."

"There's no doubt," said the old man, who politely offered to take Zadok to the Netzer Sereni gate.

In Kibbutz Netzer Sereni, the women and old men had taken over all the chores. Zadok passed women trying to milk the cows and an old man driving a tractor. No one said anything to him.

He watched his boots make contact with the dusty road. As he stepped he realized he'd see another sunset, another day, another blue sky.

"I'm alive, I'm alive, I'm alive," he said.

As he opened the door to his room, a telegram which had been pushed into the crack between the door and casing fell to the floor. The telegram apparently had arrived only that morning.

He read it out loud, "Great news. Your sister engaged to a wonderful doctor. Wedding next June. Love, Mom."

Zadok shook his head and tore up the telegram. He went to his bed and lay down. Then he kicked off his boots. It felt wonderful. God, he was so tired, so damn, aching tired. In a moment he was asleep, but in about an hour or so he woke up in fright. Suddenly, he thought of his friends who had died. Up to now he hadn't had time to think about them or mourn. He was sick over it and started to sweat.

Most of all he felt anger. He was angry about the failure of the Israeli intelligence services. They had failed and Zadok and his friends had paid the price.

How could they have been so stupid. Some intelligence service. God-damn them.

He counted how many of the defenders of Orkal D had fallen. But not for long; soon he succumbed to the sleep which gripped him in a near coma for fourteen hours.

The next two days he worked with the women in the kitchen. That was enough. On the third day he reported to the Ramle army base for assignment to another unit.

Chapter Eight

And when they come there, they will remove from it all its detestable things and all its abominations. And I will give them one heart, and put a new spirit within them; I will take the stony heart out of their flesh and give them a heart of flesh, that they may walk in my statutes and keep my ordinances and obey them; and they shall be my people, and I will be their God. But as for those whose heart goes after their detestable things and their abominations, I will require their deeds upon their own heads, says the Lord God.

Zadok stayed in the army after completing his mandatory service. The army provided a feeling of belonging, and extended his immigrant benefits, which included tax and housing privileges. He bought a new Fiat free from the sales tax, which was almost as much as the cost of the vehicle.

He liked the army, and figured he would just get frustrated as a civilian engineer. In college he'd chosen the field of industrial engineering because he'd recognized that Israel needed to make cost-effective, quality products in order to become self-sufficient and improve its citizens' standard of living.

Now Zadok felt it was a hopeless crusade. The country wasn't yet ready to become competitive. Zadok became convinced that the existing politics, influence through personal connections, as well as the need to enable reservists and immigrants to earn a living, would for the short term take priority.

He liked to repeat the joke that in Israel there were twenty-nine different words to express the concept of inefficient. The twenty-nine words were necessary to fully convey the subtle nuances and variances of inefficiency in the land. For the concept of efficient, on the other hand, there wasn't even one word.

Zadok volunteered to become a munitions officer. He was particularly interested in the emerging technology of weapons systems. He studied munitions, state-of-the-art armament and the storage and control of military hardware, a field for which there was a clear and current need.

Zadok began to read his grandfather's book. With the help of the dictionary and a few friends, he was able to progress at a reasonable pace through the Hebrew.

The publisher's foreword introduced Reuven Zadok as a kabbalist from Safed and a recognized authority on Ezekiel's prophecies. His grandfather's book in Hebrew was written in a simple, less dramatic style than the Yiddish portion he had received from his Aunt Bella. Zadok guessed that his grandfather was more comfortable writing in Yiddish than he was in Hebrew. His grandfather assumed that the reader was knowledgeable in the Bible and the Talmudic commentaries. There were also references to kabbalistic books, especially the Zohar.

According to his grandfather, Ezekiel was noteworthy amongst the prophets because he personally recorded a detailed description of his encounter with God. That description would eventually serve as a model of sorts to help mystics of later generations differentiate between the genuine divine, and their own eagerness, agendas, and egos that might falsely lead them to believe they had experienced revelations of the genuine will of God.

Ezekiel had been subject to substantial abuse from his contemporaries when he prophesized the destruction of Jerusalem and the Temple by the Babylonians. He was eventually proven to be correct.

Zadok's grandfather defended Ezekiel from critics who claimed that Ezekiel was not a legitimate prophet because he had incorrectly prophesized both the fall of Tyre, and the return of the Jews in Babylonia to the land of Israel. According to Reuven Zadok, the critics had made incorrect assumptions regarding the events described by Ezekiel in assuming those events would unfold in the Babylonian exile period. And they had incorrectly assumed to know the timeline and sequence of events as if the Almighty followed a mortal's calendar.

* * *

After work at his army base, Zadok adopted an evening routine of running several miles and lifting weights. Once a week, on Thursday nights, he went to folk dancing at the recreation center in the nearby town. He seldom danced. He tried to learn the dancing, but his feet didn't seem to have a very good memory. He enjoyed listening to the music, though, watching the dancing, and watching and meeting the women.

At such a Thursday dance session, while leaning against a wall, Zadok noticed a familiar face leading the dance line. How did he know her?

Later, after the music had stopped for a break, he felt someone tap him on the shoulder.

"Do I know you from someplace?" the dance leader said, tilting her head and smiling. "I know it sounds like a line, but you really look familiar."

Suddenly he remembered. It was her ponytail and contrasting blue eyes that were the giveaway. "You bandaged my arm during the war. You're a nurse?"

"Yes, yes. There were so many. But I remember your face," she said.

She smiled again and her face seemed to glow. The music started and she headed back to the dance floor. "See you," she said.

"See you." His eyes followed her as she stepped, glided, and turned to the music.

As the evening wore down, Shoshana came back. "A few of us are going out to a cafe. Like to come?"

At the outdoor cafe, Zadok felt the difficulty of breaking into the conversations of a clique of native Israeli dancers. Zadok frequently found his attention drifting and his eyes followed the parade of passersby. It was a lazy summer night, perfect for an outdoor cafe rendezvous after a sweaty workout.

Zadok did realize that Shoshana had made at least a few efforts to draw him into the group conversation, and in the end it was he whom she asked for a ride home. As he drove, they made plans to get together in two days. He walked her to the elevator door in the parking level.

On their first date, Shoshana expressed her love and appreciation for Israel and the meaning of Israel to the Jewish people. She was a refreshing find for Zadok. He'd begun to wonder at times why his Zionist perspective seemed unique, even in Israel.

In fact, Shoshana was probably more of a zealot than he. She was inflexible in her conviction that every Jew should live in Israel and that every Israeli should be self-sacrificing for the good of the country.

"I don't care about expatriates. Who has use for those emigrants? I have no use for them. Me? No matter what happens, I'll be staying. Even if I'm the last one left, the last one still fighting from the last hill."

Zadok smiled and nodded, but said nothing about his own convictions.

Zadok called Shoshana the next day. "I had a good time last night."

"Me, too."

"How 'bout a movie Friday? There's one I've been wanting to see in Rehovot. Is Friday night good for you?"

"Sure."

Shoshana called Zadok on Thursday night. "Hate to call like this. I'm afraid I'm sick."

"What's the matter?"

"Just sick. I don't know. Maybe the flu. I feel terrible."

"That's too bad."

"Afraid I won't be able to go out tomorrow."

"I understand."

"I'm really sorry."

"Hey, what can you do when you're sick."

Zadok hung up. Something didn't feel right. Shoshana didn't sound sick. It had to be an excuse. She just wasn't interested. Too bad, she was the first woman since Vicki who had interested him. In the next few weeks, Zadok had several forgettable dates with other women.

One day at work, an assistant handed him four messages, of which two were from Shoshana. Later in the day, he traveled to an artillery warehouse. As soon as he entered someone handed him a note, which read, "Call Shoshana."

Lately, he'd been feeling lonely, and was pleased to see her messages, although he was curious about three messages in one day. Maybe she just broke up with someone, he thought.

He called her and they agreed to meet that evening at a park that he had frequently used for running.

"You didn't believe I was sick, did you?" Shoshana said.

"It sounded like an excuse."

"I really was. You never get sick?"

"Of course I do."

"Look, I just wanted to let you know I don't play games. I was sick. If I didn't want to go out, I would've told you. I didn't want you to think the wrong thing."

Zadok knew now that she was very interested. And so was he. As they walked through the park, he felt a strong temptation to pull her body against his, squeeze her, and kiss her.

"I believe you now," he said.

"Good." She could flirt with just a smile.

"I'm glad you called."

"Just wanted to set things right."

"Why'd you wait over a month?" he said.

"I was sure you'd call me back. I thought you liked me. It took a month before I realized you weren't going to call."

"I did like you. Still do."

Shoshana laughed.

Zadok realized that not only did she have a terrific figure, she had a natural beauty. She wore no makeup, not even lipstick. Not like Vicky, he thought.

"How about dinner, tomorrow?" Zadok said.

"Tomorrow?"

"You're not sick, now?"

She turned her head to the side, and seemed to pretend anger.

Zadok laughed. "What's your favorite food?"

"Falafel."

"I think I can arrange that."

"The Arabs make the best."

"Okay. I'll find a falafel stand with an Arab chef."

"But I also like schnitzel."

"Okay, schnitzel it is."

"Do you like it?"

"Love it."

He picked her up the next night, and drove to a recommended Viennese restaurant in Tel Aviv.

"Fancy. I like it a lot," Shoshana said.

"I'm glad. I'm told the food here is good, different from kibbutz food or army food."

"Or hospital food." She sat down and rubbed her hand across the white tablecloth.

The waitress brought them menus. Zadok ordered a bottle of wine.

"So what do you like to do when you're not nursing or dancing?" Zadok asked.

"I read. History, biographies, sometimes romance novels if I'm in the right mood. I'm active in the Freedom party, and the Committee for Soviet Jewry. What do you like to do when you're not soldiering or watching dancing?"

"I run and work out. It relaxes me."

"Folk dancing relaxes me, gives me a workout."

"How long have you been doing it?"

"Since I was little." She eagerly picked up the menu and seemed to enjoy reading it.

"See anything you like?" he said.

"Everything. The veal looks good."

"I'll get the chicken. Want to share?"

"Okay."

The waitress came with the wine, and Zadok gave her their order.

"You're not religious, are you?" Shoshana said.

"No."

"Most of the American immigrants who stay are religious. Why did you come?"

"I came for the oil."

"Oil? In Israel? There's no oil."

"No oil? You don't say."

"Is this a joke?"

"Not a very good one, I guess."

Shoshana raised her eyebrows and tilted her head. "Can you pour me some wine, please."

"Sure." He filled both glasses.

"I was out of step in America," Zadok said. "Most American Jews seemed to have different values, different things they wanted out of life."

"Meaning what?"

"I wanted to be part of Jewish destiny, make a difference."

"You're an idealist."

"I don't think of it that way. It's more an emotional thing that drives me."

"Idealist or not, you're still thinking outside of yourself. The majority don't think that way."

Zadok shrugged.

"Have you thought of taking a Hebrew name?"

"No. Everyone calls me Bob."

"Bob is nice. American names have appeal here."

"I already have a Hebrew name, Reuven."

"Reuven is an old name. If you decide to take a Hebrew name, you should try a name that's more modern."

"Like?"

"How about Uzi? What do you think? I think Uzi is a good modern name."

"Well, I'd be a son of a gun."

"Let me change the subject," Shoshana said. "What're you looking for in a relationship?"

"To have someone in my corner. Life's like being in a prize fight. When the bell rings between rounds, it's nice to have someone meet you and care for you in your corner."

"Too many people go to their corner only to fight there, too."

"Yes, I know."

"Haven't seen you at folk dancing."

Zadok shrugged.

"Will you come next week?" she asked.

"Sure. Maybe I'll even dance."

"Oh, I'm counting on it."

"I'll warn you, I've got two left feet."

"We'll see," she said. Her eyes lit up as if she had a secret.

After a filling and tasty dinner, they went for a walk down Dizengoff Street. It was a pleasant evening, and there were many people. He reached for her hand, and felt a wonderful sensation at the moment of her touch.

They walked for three blocks, until they came to a bench. They sat down.

"Happy?" she said.

He nodded. "You?"

"I'm very happy."

He was hoping she was trying to tell him something. He reached to kiss her, and she responded enthusiastically.

Later that evening, when they went to her condominium, she invited him in. They sat on the couch. Her father was asleep.

"Want a drink? Anything?" she said.

"Yes. I want you to sit here." He patted the couch immediately next to him.

She slid over and he kissed her. They kissed for a long time. Then he rolled his upper body on top, forcing her to lie down.

After he lifted his head, she said, "It was very nice, but you're going a little fast for me."

"Want me to stop?"

"Yes and no. We should stop. Just give me a little more time."

"Don't worry, I won't pressure you." He looked up. "Well, maybe just a little."

She laughed.

Zadok knew he could fall in love with her.

As time passed, he began to dream, night and day, about their future.

Two months later, Zadok again sat on the couch after they returned from folk dancing.

"Your father's sleeping?"

"No. He went to visit his cousins in Jerusalem."

"You mean we're alone?"

"All alone."

"Really?"

"All alone."

He kissed her. Within a minute he was lying on top of her.

She kissed him back, leading him to consider that tonight they might become lovers.

"Shall we go to the bed?" he said.

"I don't know."

"Want me to leave?"

"No."

"What do you want?"

She shrugged.

"What's the matter?"

"I don't want you to leave, but I don't think I'm ready to be sexual."

Zadok thought for a moment. "You want me to stay overnight without sex?"

She shrugged.

"That might be too frustrating," he said. "Well, let me think a second."

"I'm a pain, I know."

"No, you're wonderful."

"I'm not like American girls."

He nodded, but didn't agree.

"Okay, I'll stay," he said.

She smiled and kissed him.

She called him two days later. "Why didn't you call?" she said.

"I just saw you Monday, remember?"

"It was an intense evening."

"A wonderful evening."

"I was afraid I wouldn't hear from you again."

"Why?"

"I don't know," she said.

"Don't worry about that."

"Really?"

"Really."

He began to see her a few evenings every week, and every weekend that he didn't work.

He telephoned to make plans for the weekend. "I have to work Friday, but I'm off on Saturday. You working Saturday?"

"No."

"Great. Want to go out for dinner?"

"Sure. Where?"

"No preference. Anything you want's okay with me."

"What's the matter with you?" She raised her voice.

"Huh?"

"You don't care?"

"I'm just being flexible. I've got no particular preference. So I'm leaving it up to you. That's all."

"Are you a dishrag? No backbone? I want a man with passion," she said.

"Are you serious?" He couldn't believe that she was really getting angry.

"Yes, I'm serious. Don't you care about anything?"

"Would I be in Israel if I didn't have values?"

"You know what I mean."

"Are you premenstrual or something?"

"Yes, but you still annoy me when you act like a limp noodle."

"Okay, I won't be limp. As for noodles, there'll be no Chinese food. How about Greek?"

"Not funny," she said.

"Well, I can't believe we're having our first fight because I acquiesced to your dining preferences."

"You're missing the point. It's not interesting to be with a man who blows with the wind."

"I've got more conviction than ninety percent of the men you know, at least for important matters. Today, I don't care where I eat. What the hell's the matter with you?"

"You don't get it," she said.

They went to a jazz club instead of dinner. They managed to put aside their differences, although Zadok never understood her point of view.

* * *

In a few months, Zadok proposed. They were lying together, and he rolled over and tapped her on the shoulder. He whispered, "I love you."

"I love you, too," she said. "But you're not saying that just because we're lovers, are you?"

"No, I think about you all the time. I want to be with you all the time. No, I think it's more than that. I don't want to be separated from you."

"That's sweet. I don't want to be without you, either. Sure that it's love and not passion?"

"I'm sure. What about you? You sure?"

"I've been sure for some time. I was waiting for you to come around."

"And how could you be so sure that I'd come around?"

"I just knew. I knew you'd appreciate me sooner or later."

He laughed. "I appreciated you the first time I saw you in the hospital when you fixed up my arm."

"Really?"

"Sure, I would've bled to death."

"You're silly."

"Want kids?"

"Of course."

"How many?"

"I don't know, three sounds good. What about you?"

"Six, or as many as my wife wants."

She laughed. "You're definitely silly."

"Silly in love. Been in love before?"

"I've had serious boyfriends. I was engaged once. Want to know about it?"

"No, I want to think I'm the only one you ever knew."

"That's right. You're the only man I've ever known. You been serious with anyone before?"

"Just one. A Moroccan woman who lives in California."

"Did you really love her?"

"I thought so."

"What happened?"

"I guess it just wasn't meant to be. We didn't agree about Israel."

"Not like us, right?"

"Right."

He embraced her until he felt her warmth. "I know I do love you. It's wonderful. Will you marry me?"

Shoshana seemed startled. "Is this a proposal?" She hesitated, lifted her head, and said, "Wait a minute." Then she whispered, "I was worried whether you'd call again."

She sat up in the bed, pushed back her hair so that it looked like it was pulled back by an elastic, and pantomimed putting on makeup. "Okay, now I'm ready. What was it you wanted to ask me?"

Zadok laughed. "Will you marry me?"

"Yes…yes…yes. Oh, my God, yes. Yes. Yes." They kissed. "Yes, I will."

Zadok felt a rare thrill like a lottery winner. She was a beautiful,

athletic, energetic woman, and she was agreeing to be his wife. He was attracted to Shoshana differently from the way he'd been attracted to Vicki,
but Shoshana was a like-minded – emotionally different perhaps, but like-
minded – woman with whom he could share his life. Vicki and he couldn't
agree on where to live, but Vicki was someone he'd never forget. But then
again, perhaps now he could. Marrying Shoshana, a native-born Israeli
with family, could finally integrate him into the society. He looked over to
Shoshana, who seemed to be studying him. Suddenly he thought he might
be getting too sentimental.

The next day they went to a rally in Tel Aviv on behalf of Soviet Jews.
What Shoshana didn't tell him in advance was that she was the primary
speaker at the rally. Zadok stood in the crowd and watched Shoshana step
up to the platform to the microphone. First she spoke about the need for
solidarity with their brothers and sisters in Russia. Then she introduced
a series of speakers, who, in turn, appealed to the sympathetic crowd to
write protests to the Soviet authorities, appeals to the international agen-
cies, and encouragement to the Soviet Jews who weren't permitted to emigrate from the Soviet Union.

"How'd I do?" she said, when the ceremonies were over.

"Great. Didn't know you were going to speak."

"Wasn't important. I just wish I felt like I'd accomplished something."

"You did."

"No. I just may have helped some people feel better about themselves
by creating the illusion that our protests were doing something."

"Maybe you're being a little too hard on yourself. It's better than not
caring or not doing anything. What else can you do, anyway?"

"You mean short of invading Russia?" She laughed.

"Never mind," he said.

After a while Zadok realized that much of Shoshana's political convictions were identical to her father's. It was obvious too that she had considerable respect for her father, a curious concept for Zadok in contrast to the
prevalent generation gap in America. For a brief moment Zadok admitted
to himself that he found Shoshana's respect for her father enviable.

Shoshana's dad, Yankel, was short and stocky, gruff, but amiable.
Zadok guessed he was about sixty-eight years old. He had big wide arms,
biceps, and shoulders, and his hands were enormous. Each finger was the
diameter of Zadok's thumb. It was apparent that the old man's vitality and

passion, his spit and anger, had diminished with age. Yet every once in a while, in the spirit of a dynamic conversation, Yankel's emotions gained the upper hand, and that showed Zadok that Yankel had been a vibrant youth, perhaps a pillar of strength to his family, and a natural leader. There was plainly no muzzle over his emotional response to any issue. He lived for the politics of the day, for the experience he went through in World War II, or for his children. Everything else was less important, even money and his job as a mechanic. It explained his choice of cheap, unmatched clothes that often went unbuttoned, untucked or unzipped. Often he didn't shave for three days.

Most often Yankel spoke quietly, slowly, and gently, rarely revealing the traces of his diminished but still explosive temper. He talked about whatever flowed into his head without attempting to edit or reflect, with no attention paid to the sequence of the stories, or feedback from his listeners.

Every so often he winced from the pain of his digestive ailments or his angina. But his big right hand, which moved up and down automatically as he spoke, told the story of another age, when he might have been physically capable of doing any task, of dealing with any opponent on equal terms. His nose was flat like it had been broken a few times, and his ears had the puffiness of a boxer's ears.

Once Zadok was sitting with Shoshana and Yankel in Yankel's Rehovot flat when a phantom jet thundered low over the apartment building. The window glass nearly shattered. That was the catalyst this day that got Yankel talking about the past. Yankel was a survivor who didn't avoid talking about his personal history in Europe, unlike many other survivors. On the contrary, he sometimes started talking too much about the past, as if all that had transpired since 1945 was of no consequence.

"I love those jets, nice, huh? Good boys we have in these jets. The best. Very good boys. If we'd have had Jewish boys in Phantoms in the war, things would've been different. My town was so small and we were so helpless. Just homes and stores and mud. I remember when the Germans came, and when the Polish militia came. I remember when the Germans came and played marching songs, they drank beer and sang bar songs, the bastards, the killers, they raped the prettiest girls in the town center, while they played their music and drank. I hid inside the fireplace. I'd prepared a hiding place behind the brick. I was hiding there when they marched my parents out and shot them. At night, I came out and buried my parents."

Yankel spoke gruffly but his eyes were teary.

"Then for six months I lived underground in the woods like a mole. How can a man live like a mole? I nearly starved. I nearly froze. No one would help me. I had some money and some gold. It was useless. Most of the time I couldn't even buy food. They stole my house. They were glad we were dead. You should've seen their expression after the war when they found out I survived. I thought they were going to kill me again. I didn't want the damn house. Let them keep the house and the land, who needed their soil? I did hide gold rubles in the walls. May they never find it, the bastards.

"Yes, I was in a camp. They put me in the camp. You know how I was caught? I tried to buy a bread instead of stealing it. They took my money and turned me in to the Germans. I didn't even get the bread. Ha, I should've kept stealing. But I was strong. The Germans knew I was strong and could do the work of two men. I had many jobs in the camp. I measured out the food, if you can call it food. It was a ladle of water with maybe a tiny piece of potato or a piece of fat. I shaved heads. I sorted dead people's clothes and possessions and teeth and eyeglasses. I pulled bodies out of the gas chambers. I stacked the bodies in piles. Big piles of skin and bones, dried out bones. I loaded the bodies into the ovens and I stoked and fired the ovens and I pulled out ashes. I did all these terrible jobs to stay alive. But I was never one of the Jewish police, never a kapo.

"Yes, I saw terrible things. You wouldn't believe. People who walked with no hope, like the walking dead. They were put to the gas when they got to that point. I saw people reduced to cannibalism. Yes, it's true. You wouldn't believe."

"Everything you described was in the Book of Ezekiel," Zadok whispered, looking down.

"Excuse me?" Yankel squinted.

Zadok raised his head. "You just reminded me of something, sorry to interrupt."

*   *   *

Robert Zadok and Shoshana Offer were married in a simple ceremony in Rehovot. The musicians played Hasidic dance music and most of their friends from their folk dancing club attended. Zadok also invited friends from the army and the kibbutz. It was an open house affair and many of the guests invited their own friends to come along. Yankel Offer and Shoshana's brother, Micha, were the only immediate family who attended.

Four uniformed soldiers held up the *hupa*, the traditional bridal canopy. A bearded Orthodox rabbi instructed Shoshana to circle the groom seven times.

At the conclusion of the ceremony, Zadok enthusiastically crushed the ceremonial glass under his right foot. And as he did so he recalled the symbolism behind the ritual – the remembrance of the Temple – and, like an unexpected bonus, it brought even more joy.

Chapter Nine

Therefore thus says the Lord God: Now I will restore the fortune of Jacob, and have mercy upon the whole house of Israel; and I will be jealous for my holy name. They shall forget their shame, and all the treachery they have practiced against me, when they dwell securely in their land with none to make them afraid, when I have brought them back from the peoples and gathered them from their enemies' lands, and through them have vindicated my holiness in the sight of many nations. Then they shall know that I am the Lord their God because I sent them into exile among the nations, and then gathered them into their own land. I will leave none of them remaining among the nations any more; and I will not hide my face any more from them, when I pour out my Spirit upon the house of Israel, says the Lord God.

They moved to a new settlement, on a large hill in the northern Galilee. Their settlement was named Moshav Misgav. The government of Israel was encouraging Jewish settlement in the Galilee because the Arabs had a substantial demographic advantage. It was one more way, they felt, that they could further contribute to the development of the State. It was also one of the few places that they could afford to live.

On top of their mountain they had an open panorama to the Golan and Hermon to the north and to the Judean Hills in the west, which seemed to stand watch over the many communal farms. To the south, the olive trees, greenish rocks and blue hills of the Galilee seemed to project off a canvas. All of it was presented against the backdrop of bright sky, and an eerie transparent mist in the higher elevations. They might on occasion have missed their former proximity to Tel Aviv and its conveniences, and they might have dreaded the long commute to work or to visit friends, but each morning, especially when the sun was shining, was like a new beginning. They would recharge themselves.

In addition to the remoteness, there were other costs. For the first eight months they lived in a trailer home while their house was being built. The trailer was cramped and leaked in heavy rains. Like a lot of Israeli construction, it had no insulation, so they got in the habit of wiping down dew on the interior walls with a towel. After a while they began to run their portable heaters as long as possible to keep the dampness to a minimum. The kerosene stunk and the electric was expensive, so when they couldn't take the kerosene anymore, they sparingly used the electric.

In their first winter weekend, Zadok got sick from the dampness. Somehow it seemed to get into his bones. A glass of brandy helped a little, but he didn't get better until he thawed himself out by holding a limb for a few minutes up against the electric heater. First he put his right hand, then his left forearm, then his shoulder, until he totally thawed himself out. After that experience they were more liberal in letting the heater run.

The plumbing failed often. Usually, just as Zadok began his shower. The hilltop hadn't been fully cleared of snakes or scorpions, a serious issue to the parents of young children.

Each night the men took turns on watch. It was an exhausting ordeal to commute for three hours a day, work a full day, and then walk around the settlement all night. Staying up was enough of an effort, and the men had difficulty reaching a consensus as to what level of watch was required. They finally agreed to provide a cot so that the two men on watch could alternate lying down.

On one such long night, after a hail in the early evening which left behind a field of scattered foxholes and puddles in the deep mud, Zadok stood frozen and in thought. It was the kind of long night that seemed to go on forever. As Zadok stood alone, an old rifle slung over his shoulder, the rain blowing, his face and ears soaked and dripping, he wondered how he could have wound up in such a cold, miserable, impoverished place, surrounded by Arabs. He sloshed in the mud in the middle of the night, exhausted, watching to avoid snakes. What he would give for a decent toilet that worked. Boston University seemed like a hundred years ago.

When the rains ended and the birds of spring came, Zadok's perspective changed. The flowers bloomed quickly and he suddenly couldn't imagine living anywhere else. The cold was forgotten and he relished the breeze that was denied to Israelis living in the coastal plain.

In a few months, they moved into their cottages, a real luxury after the trailers. Everyone was busy improving their new homes at once. Zadok was happy. Now at least he had a shower and toilet that worked. When they moved into the permanent homes, the atmosphere improved immediately. Now they could entertain one another in each others' homes, and the concern that the settlement might fail was no longer routine conversation. The Zadoks welcomed the return of the old camaraderie and sociability between the settlers. They believed that it was a supportive lifestyle, superior to the individual structure of city living. They all said it would be paradise for children, and they all knew that they had no idea if their children would one day agree.

Sunday was a hot day, and the drive home from work was longer than usual. Zadok parked in the designated area away from the cluster of homes and walked to his cottage carrying a bottle of beer.

He remembered that Shoshana had gone to the clinic for her pregnancy test. He was anxious for news.

He entered his kitchen, and put ice cubes in a glass for the warm beer. Shoshana came in.

"Oh, you're home," she said.

He kissed her hello.

"It's warm in here," he said, and he closed the window shutters.

"I was just next door knitting with Hannah. You like these colors?" It was an off-yellow and white.

"Wonderful," Zadok said and sat down.

"I hate it when you're not sincere."

"I'm sincere, damn it."

"Really?"

"I'm sorry, I can't get too excited over knitting. Let's not fight about it. Get the results back on the pregnancy test?"

"Yes," she said.

"Well, are you pregnant?"

She shook her head.

Zadok was disappointed. "Oh, well. We'll just have to keep trying next month. Practice makes perfect."

Shoshana sat next to him on the couch. Then she screamed and burst out laughing. "I'm kidding. Yes, I am. I'm pregnant. I'm pregnant. I really am. I don't believe it. I'm pregnant."

Zadok embraced her. "I can't believe you. You're too much." Again he embraced her.

*   *   *

Driving home one day with Shoshana, Zadok saw a car accident ahead. He pulled over. A child was lying on the side of the road, surrounded by several adults. The child had probably been carried from one of the cars in the collision. A woman was in the shoulder to the side of the road, crying and swinging her fists in the air.

Shoshana took her medical bag and went toward the child. "I'm a nurse," she told the father.

He allowed her to examine the child, a boy around nine or ten. She went to her knees and opened her bag.

It didn't matter to Zadok that everyone involved in the accident was Arab. He was just as concerned as Shoshana appeared to be.

Shoshana stood up. "Have you called an ambulance yet?"

The father shook his head. "It just happened," he said, weakly.

The family's in shock, Zadok thought.

Shoshana came to Zadok and whispered, "It's serious. He's unconscious. We need to get him to a hospital fast. Call an ambulance." Shoshana returned to the boy.

Zadok went to his car phone. He came back to tell Shoshana that help would be coming soon.

Then he went over to the father. "My wife's a very good nurse. She says your boy needs to be looked at in a hospital, and needs to get there quickly. I've been able to get a helicopter. It was lucky. A friend was in the area. He'll take him wherever you want."

The father slightly nodded. "Maimon in Haifa," the father said.

"That's an excellent hospital. We'll take him there."

In a few minutes the helicopter landed on the only visible level clearing near the accident. The pilot was Dov Kesselbrenner, a young pilot in the process of transferring into Zadok's army unit. Dov seemed eager to assist his new boss.

"Someone hurt?" Dov said.

"A boy. Unconscious. They want him to go to Maimon."

"Okay."

Zadok, the father, and two other men carried a stretcher out of the helicopter and brought it alongside the boy.

"Carefully, now," Shoshana said, "I'll tell you how to do it." She instructed while they transferred the boy to the stretcher. Then they carried him to the helicopter.

"You can go with the boy to the hospital," Zadok told the father.

"Thank you very much."

"He'll be okay." Zadok forced a smile.

"What's your name?" the father asked.

"Bob. We're from Moshav Misgav."

"My name's Abdul." They shook hands. Then the father and mother boarded the helicopter.

* * *

Abdul came to visit on the next Sabbath. Zadok invited him in and offered tea. They sat on the sofa.

"How's your son?" Zadok said.

"He's okay, now. Still in the hospital, but making progress. Very nice progress."

"Good."

"That's wonderful," Shoshana said as she put the tea on the table before the sofa.

"I wanted to thank both of you."

"We're happy your son's doing well," Shoshana said.

"It was nothing," Zadok said.

"It was much more than nothing to me. I want to tell you that the emergency room doctor credited your emergency treatment and the helicopter ride with saving my son's life."

"Well, we'll look forward to your son's homecoming."

"May I ask you another question? I'm curious about something."

"Of course."

"Your name's Zadok. Do you know a Reuven Zadok? The writer?"

"My grandfather."

Abdul nodded and smiled. "So interesting." Abdul continued nodding.

"How do you know him? He died some time ago."

"I know," Abdul said. "My grandfather rescued one of his manuscripts. He kept it safe for many years. My grandfather showed the manuscript to me when I was a boy."

"Do you still have it?" Shoshana asked.

"My father donated them to a…what do you call a Jewish seminary?"

"Yeshiva?"

"Yes, that's it, a yeshiva. I don't know which one. Sorry."

"Small world," Zadok said. "Wonder if our grandfathers ever knew each other."

*   *   *

A few weeks later they vacationed in Tiberias. They stayed at a high-rise hotel on the Sea of Galilee. Zadok was pleased to find Shoshana more amorous than she had been in months.

"What do I have to do to keep you this horny?"

"Just take me on vacation," she said.

"Didn't think you could be horny and pregnant."

"See what a vacation can do."

"You mean I have to wait until our next vacation to get you in the mood?" Zadok asked while looking through the window at the lake.

"Stop talking and come back to bed."

The next day they drove into the town center for lunch to find a restaurant that had been recommended.

"I'm not showing yet, at all," Shoshana said. "Am I?"

"No."

"When are you supposed to show?"

"I don't know. I guess everyone's different. And this is your first."

"I'd like to be showing, yes, I think I'd like to."

"And after the baby is born, you'll be impatient to get rid of the belly."

"Of course," she said.

As they entered the city and started to drive up the hill, Zadok suddenly stepped on the brake and pulled his car over.

"What is it?" Shoshana asked.

"I thought I saw something." He put the car in reverse and drove back to the intersection they had just passed.

"I was right," he said.

"What?"

"The street name, look." The street sign read "Reuven Zadok Street."

"It may be my grandfather. Even Abdul had heard of him. He was a biblical scholar of sorts, and, well, this is, after all, Tiberias."

"Let's find out," Shoshana said.

"Forget it."

And then Zadok noticed a street sign for the name of the cross street. It said "RMCL Street." Zadok recalled those same letters from the portion of his grandfather's diary that his Aunt Bella had sent him.

"Are you sure you're not curious?" Shoshana asked.

"Well, maybe a little."

After lunch Shoshana went by herself into the town hall while Zadok waited outside and leaned against his car.

It took her a good half hour.

"Find out anything?"

"Yes, they said both streets were named after religious scholars. And there's a yeshiva in Safed that knows all about Reuven Zadok, they know all about him and can tell us more about his work. They gave me directions."

"Sure you want to bother? I mean, today would be a great day on the beach."

"Come on. I'm curious, and you are too. Let's check it out."

They drove to Safed. The yeshiva was set back from the sidewalk in a narrow ally bordered by high stone walls. The entrance had old script over the archway, and Zadok felt the spiritual presence of the structure even before he entered. He had trouble shifting his mood. This was his vacation, the weather was beautiful and hot, his hotel was plush. The lake was calm, blue, and refreshing, and his wife was horny.

The school was unexpectedly quiet. No lively Talmudic debate or scholarship could be heard. A short, blind, Orthodox man stood alone and greeted them. He ushered them in and directed them to a room in the back. There, a thin, elderly religious man in a black suit and black hat greeted them.

"I'm told you can help us." Shoshana opened with her usual uninhibited style.

"God willing," the old man responded automatically.

"There's a street in Tiberias, named for Reuven Zadok? Reuven Zadok was my husband's grandfather and we don't know much about him. We're told that you may know something about him."

The old scholar rubbed his white beard and looked up. Suddenly he seemed to receive his visitors very seriously.

"You are Reuven Zadok's grandson?"

Zadok nodded. "I'm named for him."

The old man smiled. "I've been expecting you."

"What?"

"Your grandfather told me that he had family who would come after him."

"That couldn't be me. He must have been referring to someone else."

"Where are you from?"

"Boston."

"Father's name?"

"Adam." The old man seemed to be interrogating him, but appeared satisfied by the answers. He smiled and stood up.

"You're Reuven, son of Adam?"

"Yes."

"Would you like to see your grandfather's work?" The old man went into a closet filled with keys, and after retrieving one set of keys, led his visitors to another room filled with file cabinets and boxes of manuscripts. Zadok was surprised at how sloppy everything was. Nothing was indexed or shelved with any organization. He was shown volumes of writing, mostly in Yiddish, in notebooks, loose-leafs, and in hardbound covers. Suddenly he felt as if he'd found a bond. Someone else in his family had left America to live in the Land and had produced the yellowed, dusty, water-stained parchments that he now held in his hands.

"Do you by chance have a manuscript by my grandfather that was rescued and donated to your yeshiva by an Arab family?"

The old man looked elated. He stroked his beard enthusiastically. "Yes. Yes. One moment. One moment."

He returned in about one minute and proudly presented the aged manuscript, tied together by string, to an astonished Zadok and his wife.

"It's his work on Ezekiel that you're now looking at. Much of your grandfather's work was on Ezekiel. He brought back a lot from his travels to Ezekiel's tomb and the library in Iraq. You're welcome to stay and study it if you like."

"Thank you," Zadok said. "Perhaps another time." He put down the papers. He looked over to Shoshana who had picked up a few chapters and was able to read and understand the Yiddish. The old man left them alone.

"What does my grandfather say?"

"It's actually a little interesting," Shoshana said, thumbing carefully through the yellowed and dusty papers. "Something about various interpretations, many of which were incorrect according to your grandfather, of Ezekiel's purpose and prophecy, something about what he was able to learn from the second original text in Iraq. The text was never incorporated into the Bible, but it was an integral part of the original." She picked up another batch and read silently for a while. "He's explaining in this chapter how he was able to discover the real time line for the prophecies that God had communicated to Ezekiel. He talks about how that confusion over the time line had confused students of Ezekiel for centuries. He writes that his insights are similar to kabbalistic secrets in Safed and to the works of RMCL." She carefully returned the papers to the rest of the manuscript.

"RMCL. Those letters again. Is it a name?"

The old man who had brought them the manuscript returned to the room and introduced himself. "You can come back any time," he said. "I'm Haim. I was your grandfather's student. I can help you to understand the importance of what he was trying to do. His work was very important. Feel free to come any time."

"Haim, does 'RMCL' mean anything to you?" Zadok asked.

"Of course. It stands for Rabbi Moses Chaim Luzzato. The letters are pronounced 'Ramchal.'"

"We saw a street sign for him also in Tiberias."

"He's buried in Tiberias. Died of some disease, perhaps the plague. He was famous for his smarts, knowledge of the sacred books, his writings. But he wrote at a time when kabbalism was looked down on by our Jewish hierarchy. They had had enough of false prophets and false messiahs, and it was a while before they realized that Ramchal was unlike any of those pretenders. So much of his work was lost, either banned or destroyed. But we know he was a poet, a scholar, and that he claimed to have received divine messages."

"Divine messages? You mean from God?"

Haim shrugged. "*Baruch Hashem*, bless the name, He has many ways for us to receive His will."

The Zadoks thanked the old man.

Shoshana's eyes turned back to Reuven Zadok's manuscript. "This is very interesting," she insisted. She continued to read.

Zadok sat down. "What does he say that's so interesting?" Zadok asked impatiently.

"Shh. I'm reading. Wait."

Zadok looked to the ceiling and waited. He noticed Haim standing to the side and a little behind him, amused by Shoshana's compulsion to read.

After a while she looked up. "Okay, okay, listen," she said.

"I'm listening."

"Ezekiel was not just a prophet, although being recognized as a legitimate prophet positioned him to lead and to provide explanations for events. His writings were very influential and inspired. In fact, the Jews of Babylon did take steps to preserve their identity even without access to the Temple. And they began to record the oral traditions. Grandpa Reuven says that Jews today – does he mean the thirties? – anyway, Grandpa says that Jews today need to respond as they did to Ezekiel. They need to retain their identity as a people, return to the values of their Mosaic roots, and they should treat others as they themselves would wish to be treated."

"Oh, that's all."

"Don't get sarcastic."

"My grandfather wrote that in the 1930s?"

"There's more. Jews must retain their identity and come together as a people irrespective of differences."

"What differences?"

"He doesn't say. Maybe religious, ethnic, racial, political, whatever."

"Pretty progressive for the time, especially for someone my aunt described as something of a religious extremist."

Shoshana nodded enthusiastically. "We could use more of his thinking in Israel today. You should be proud of your grandfather."

"I'm proud. Can we go now?" Zadok stood up.

"But there's one more thing you should see," Haim interrupted.

He led them out of the back of the building to a courtyard. There was a small cemetery, about nine graves to the right side of the courtyard. "This is your grandfather's place."

Shoshana took Zadok's hand and they stood there quietly, still holding hands, for a long while. Haim had left. Then they slowly walked around the building, past the flower beds, on their way toward the street.

"Wait," Haim called back to them. "Come back, come back," he gestured with his fingers. "I'd like to give you something. Yes, I have something for you." He returned to his shelves of books, scanned the titles with his index finger running up and down against the cracked and torn bindings, and, after five minutes, proudly selected the right volume. "Yes, this is it. Please, take it. My gift. Please." He smiled widely for the first time.

Zadok accepted the old book. He wiped the dust on the cover, looked up to Haim, and expressed appreciation, which was more genuine toward Haim's gesture than the gift itself.

Later, back at the waterfront resort, Zadok's thoughts returned to the yeshiva and its cemetery. He couldn't deny it. He had trouble getting the experience out of his mind. He felt like shouting about his ancestral ties to the land, about his grandfather's contributions. His works must have been significant to someone. What could the old man have meant when he said he'd been expecting him? Could it actually have been foreseen by his grandfather? Nonsense. Yet Zadok had the feeling that something was unfinished, that the old man wanted him to finish his grandfather's work.

Shoshana was smiling at him and looking very proud of herself. He figured she knew he was grateful. He'd never have taken the initiative that she did in order to solve the question of the mysterious street sign.

*   *   *

Another family on Moshav Misgav, an American couple from Philadelphia, gave up and moved back to America. They'd finally run out of money and no longer had the energy or idealism to struggle to maintain a basic standard of living. The ever-present option to return to America made it more difficult for someone to succeed in Israel. America became better than it had ever been. America became unblemished, a perfect society in a perfect land, a place where people enjoyed wealth, opportunity, better recreation, and could accomplish more with less effort. It was always easy to give up the struggle and go back. It was easy to think you were sacrificing something by staying in Israel. Somehow from afar, America seemed so perfect that no other society on earth, in the history of the earth, could compete.

Zadok was discouraged, almost depressed, over his Philadelphia friends' departure. They had struggled together in the trailers, spent many evenings solving the Middle East crises over tea, and then there were the long nights on guard duty. Zadok really got to know someone when they walked together all night. But Zadok hadn't foreseen their giving up. They had talked about building Moshav Misgav together.

Zadok became more entrenched and determined not to let himself run out of money. He started to use candles, rather than electricity, and yelled at Shoshana for serving meat at dinner. He stopped driving for recreation or going into the city. Now that Shoshana had left her nursing job, Zadok's army salary wasn't enough to beat the inflation.

"Forget trying to make ends meet like an American. You're in Israel, you live like an Israeli," Shoshana said.

"What's that mean?"

"Borrow. If you can't make it through the month, borrow enough to get you to the next month. Don't worry so much about money. That's an American priority. And the next month you borrow to get you to the next month. Who lives within their means?"

"Some Americans."

"Rubbish. That's luxury. Life's too short. There are more important things than worrying about money. You're driving me crazy. So what if I bought meat on Sunday and chicken on the Sabbath. It's not the greatest luxury on earth. Okay, I'll cut down to just Friday night, but don't make me crazy. I don't believe this conversation. Look at all the rich American Jews. I marry one who won't turn on a light switch. I'm going."

"Where are you going?"

She didn't answer. He heard the front door slam.

Zadok poured himself a Scotch which, this one time, he didn't really enjoy. Upset and disgusted, he went to bed. On the nightstand was the small book from the Safed yeshiva, the second book written by his grandfather that he had been given. The book was in Hebrew and titled "The Merkabbah Mystics." On the front page was the depiction of a blue chariot and crown, identical to the picture in the other book. So Zadok picked it up and began to read, figuring it'd take his mind off recent arguments with Shoshana.

After a while he heard the door open. She was back, and now he was anxious and apprehensive, a very new response to the presence of the woman he had loved and, he supposed, still loved. He put down the book. While he couldn't read any more this evening, his curiosity had been piqued. He completed it in two days.

The story of the merkabbah (Zadok translated the term to mean "chariot") mystics began centuries ago, during the age of the recognized prophets, when there were many more Jews who aspired – and professed – to be legitimate prophets of God. To be recognized and accepted as a legitimate prophet, however, a prophet had to demonstrate to his contemporaries that he had received knowledge of future events. It was widely accepted that the Creator would reveal future events to a few worthy individuals to build credibility for that individual. The Creator might then, through that individual, reveal his message.

Although not all of Ezekiel's contemporaries accepted his visions as prophecy, there was a group who were inspired by Ezekiel's written description of his encounter with the Lord and his compulsion to deliver God's message to benefit the Babylonian exiles. These students of Ezekiel's became known as the merkabbah mystics after Ezekiel's death, and left a body of literature exploring the meaning of his visions of the chariot-throne that would not only influence future Jewish mystics and kabbalists, but would one day also affect Christian and Islamic mystical practices.

According to Reuven Zadok, Ezekiel's message has to this day not yet been adequately understood because he didn't establish a time line for his prophecies. God had revealed enough to Ezekiel to establish his legitimacy amongst his Jewish contemporaries as a prophet (he foretold the destruction of Jerusalem and the Temple by the Babylonians), but Ezekiel's vision included projections for the benefit of future generations. For example, Ezekiel prophesized the total destruction of Tyre, an ancient city on the coast north of Israel. Nebuchadnezzar did attack Tyre, and, after a thirteen-year siege, broke down the city's walls. The survivors of Tyre, however, managed to relocate to a nearby island fortress. For this reason, Ezekiel's prophecy of Tyre's destruction was evidence for critics that his prophecy was not correct, and that Ezekiel was therefore not a legitimate prophet. Two hundred fifty years later, Alexander the Great did destroy most of Tyre, and the remnants of the city were eventually destroyed by Muslim armies. Ezekiel's unlikely prediction that Tyre would become "like the top of a rock; Tyre will be a place for the spreading of fishing nets" did centuries later come true.

Reuven Zadok was emphatic that while God's dimension was timeless, the esoterica and divine experience that he, Reuven Zadok, had personally received did in fact reveal ways to approximate Ezekiel's prophecies according to humanity's system of time reference. And the author insisted there were more prophecies that have not yet been realized, but will soon unfold exactly as described by Ezekiel. And these events will provide evidence to everyone of God's intent and message.

*   *   *

Zadok came home late on Friday night. "Honey, I'm home," he shouted as soon as he stepped past the threshold.

Shoshana was in the kitchen chopping vegetables.

"For you," Zadok offered while extending to her a dozen red roses.

Shoshana's eyes lit up and her hand stopped chopping. "They're beautiful! You got them for me? Thank you, dear." She lifted the roses up in the air to admire them and then searched for the appropriate vase.

"I love you," Zadok said.

"I love you, too," Shoshana returned. "I hate it when we hurt each other."

"Me, too."

"My dad says we should never go to bed angry."

"Yankel is a wise man."

"Let's try, okay?"

"Okay, I will. I'm sorry if I've hurt you."

"Me, too." Shoshana kissed him again and again.

Chapter Ten

And they shall dwell in their own land which I gave to my servant Jacob. They shall dwell securely, when I execute judgments upon all their neighbors who have treated them with contempt. Then they will know that I am the Lord their God. Egypt shall be a lowly kingdom. It shall never again exalt itself above the nations.

Zadok was promoted and began to travel to Europe in his capacity as a defense systems officer. In dealing with Europeans his English was an asset, and he relished the advantage. Eventually he was assigned to accompany private Israeli defense contractors on a buying trip to Texas.

After Zadok's team finished their negotiations, one of the Americans suggested to Zadok that the two of them get a drink to celebrate the deal.

"Why not," Zadok said.

Colonel James was a little older than Zadok. He had considerably more gray hair, was six feet three inches tall, thin, wore a perfectly creased uniform, and shoes so black and shiny that they reflected the ceiling lights. He inspired Zadok to improve his military bearing and standard of dress. James spoke with a slow Texas drawl that camouflaged his considerable intelligence. Zadok had grown to respect him, a tribute he cautiously and selectively conceded.

In his Cadillac, James offered Zadok a cigar.

"No, thanks."

"Mind if I do?"

"Go ahead," Zadok said.

"Well, where would you like to go?"

"This is your town, Tex, you tell me."

"Ever been to Cow-Town?"

"Where?"

"Never been? Great. You'll love it. I'll take you to Bobby-Bill's place."

"Okay."

"Can you do the two-step?"

"The two-step? I can walk, that's about it."

"Well, you'll love Bobby-Bill's. Big drinks, too."

"Let's go."

James leaned back and adjusted the radio to find a different country channel. He turned toward the window when he exhaled a big puff of cigar smoke.

"You know, I really respect you Israelis."

"I'm glad."

"Better than your American cousins."

"Careful. I'm still an American Jew, too."

"I know, I know, but look what you Israelis have accomplished. And you sure ain't the typical American Jew."

"Look at what American Jews have accomplished in every field."

"True. But I still have more respect for you as an Israeli."

"But I'm sure not unique."

"Sorry. Sorry I brought it up."

"Forget it."

"I was just trying to pay a compliment."

"I know. Forget it."

They pulled into Bobby-Bill's parking lot, and walked past a half dozen bulls.

"They for breeding?"

"For the rodeo."

"Rodeo?"

"Yes, inside the bar."

It was Zadok's first visit to a honky-tonk. He felt almost as if he were visiting a new country. Cowboy hats and shirts, boots, jeans, and big belt buckles were the norm. Everyone was in western wear, and the two soldiers were feeling overdressed.

James took him on a quick tour to the dance floor, the bars, the billiard and game rooms, and the rodeo area. Then they headed back to the bar.

"Hi, honey," James said to a beautiful blonde leaning against the bar. She wore a mini-skirt that seemed to end almost two feet above her knees.

"Hi, soldier," she answered seductively.

"Hey, sweetheart," James called to the bartender, "can you bring a couple of weary soldiers a few beers?"

Zadok stood behind James. There were no stools at this bar. "Thanks," Zadok said when he picked up his Budweiser.

"Don't thank me," James said, "you're buying."

"I am? Okay, then you thank me."

"Thanks."

"No problem. Enjoy."

"Yeah, I really respect you guys."

"So I heard," Zadok said.

"Don't laugh. You never know who your friends are."

"Meaning what?"

"Meaning that we're your friends. By we, I mean the Bible-believing religious community."

"You're religious? Never would've guessed."

"I wasn't always. Some habits and language are hard to break. But I am. I even teach Bible studies to kids on Tuesday and Thursday nights."

"You? Really?"

"Well, you're in the Bible belt now."

"Maybe I should've pushed for a bigger discount for our purchases."

"You guys did all right. Who're you kidding? Besides, I don't represent the manufacturers."

"I know. Just kidding."

"But the evangelical community is really your natural ally."

"You're trying to convert us."

"No, we just believe in the Bible."

"Nice to have friends. I'll take friends wherever I can find them. Another beer?"

Tex nodded.

"But let me ask you something. Many American Jews are apathetic about their Jewishness. They've got no problem with assimilating. But you respect me more?"

"Sure. You find that interesting?"

Zadok nodded. "More than you know."

*   *   *

After they finished the Texas assignment, Zadok split off from the rest of the Israeli group to fly to Boston. It had been a long time since he'd been there. As the jet lowered over the harbor just south of Logan airport, Zadok scarcely recognized the city skyline.

Inside, there was a small crowd just beyond the gate. In the front, his sister Beverly was waiting for him.

"Oh my God, is that you?" he said.

She smiled.

"You grew up. You look so…" Zadok couldn't think of the right word.

He just stepped forward and gave her a hug. He was very glad to see her. Damn, he hadn't realized how much. He stepped back to look at her again. She was wearing a fur, and her hair was neck-length, but set with strategically planned, high-fashion waves. Everything about her was perfect – her accessories, her nails, her scent. She looked very elegant, very much the successful doctor's wife. Was this elegant woman, who clearly stood out from the crowd, his little hippie sister?

Beverly laughed as he silently looked her over. Then she took his arm and led him down the corridor toward baggage claim. Zadok was impressed by how comfortably cozy a big terminal could be heated while it was so frigid outside.

"Mom and Dad are real excited that you're here. They're doing fine, a little slower than they used to be, but all considered, they're doing really well. Dad seems to be enjoying his retirement. Every day, well, almost every day, he's at the dog track. And you know Mom, she's happy as long as there's something to complain about. She loves to visit us, especially Jennifer, my four-year-old. And my hubbie, Kevin, is looking forward to meeting you."

"And I'm looking forward to meeting your husband and daughter."

"Why don't you get the bags while I go bring the car around?"

"Fine."

He waited outside with his luggage and duffle bag only five minutes before Beverly drove up in a big, recently made, silver Mercedes. Zadok put the bags on the back seat and then sat in the front.

"Like the car? It's a special edition, actually. Very hard to get," she said, proudly.

Did she really think he could be impressed by a German car? Yes, very nice, he thought; Hitler liked them too.

"It's great," he said. "Very comfortable. Real leather?" He decided he didn't want to fight with her.

Beverly drove to Weston, one of the western suburbs. Her home wasn't visible from the road. Only after they entered the gravel access road, past the low-hanging maple branches, did the circular driveway and the home come into view. The driveway was draped on both sides by great oaks, and a light snow still covered all the landscaping. Her home was a white southern colonial with two dramatic pillars in the front. Smoke from the fireplace was funneling into the atmosphere, adding to the postcard sense of well-to-do New England. Beyond the pillars were two more columns on both sides of the front door. In the vestibule there was a spiral marble stairway. Zadok chose to step to the left of the stairway as one of the routes to enter the living room. "Your living room's bigger than my house," Zadok said.

Zadok was surprised to see a Christmas tree in the living room, but he said nothing about it. Beverly then led him into the walnut-paneled dining room and then into the kitchen where the nanny was feeding Jennifer.

"And this is my little – I mean, my big four-year-old," Beverly said.

"Hi," Zadok said, trying to be friendly, almost clown-like.

Little Jennifer reminded him how much he was looking forward to having his own children. He couldn't wait for the end of Shoshana's pregnancy.

"Oh, I have something for you, I almost forgot." He reached into his coat pocket, and handed the small, gift-wrapped package to his niece.

She enthusiastically acknowledged Zadok as she reached for the present. She quickly tore off the bow and gift wrapping, and revealed an Israeli doll, a female soldier in khaki uniform.

Jennifer looked at it curiously. "I wanted a Barbie rocker."

"Never mind," Beverly said, "don't be rude. Thank your uncle."

"No."

"Jennifer!"

"No."

"It's okay," Zadok said. "Hey, I'd like to see the rest of the house."

Beverly looked disappointedly at her daughter, then turned. "Sure," she smiled.

"It's a beautiful house."

"Thank you. We enjoy it very much. We're planning to add a few more rooms and a – "

"You're kidding. It's not big enough?"

"Oh, it's big enough for three people and a nanny, but we'd like something a little more. Come on, I'll show you."

She led Zadok through the house, explained their need and plans for a rear addition, and concluded her tour in the living room.

"Jennifer's a cute kid. I can see you in her very clearly."

"Really? I don't see it, but other people have told me that."

"Planning to have another?"

"No. Jennifer's all I can handle. Don't get me wrong. I love her very much, I'm very grateful to have her, but I don't think I can handle another baby, and all that work. How about you, is a baby in the plans for you?"

"Shoshana's pregnant."

"Oh, I didn't know. Congratulations."

"Thank you."

"How far along?"

"Due in three months."

"Wonderful."

Zadok smiled, then got up to study the art which was lined up, museum style, along the living room walls.

"You know what I keep thinking about?"

"What?"

"I remember when, in your hippie days, you called me a capitalist goon. You were an idealist and I was a materialist, remember?"

"Yes, yes, I do."

Zadok laughed. "In that light it's rather amazing to compare our current lifestyles."

Beverly laughed. "We all grow up and it's okay to change as you grow. You know, you can still change your mind about your life. It's okay to change. It's okay to realize that you grow and develop and change."

"You're absolutely right."

"Hey, look, we're starting to agree with one another for a change. Isn't that great?"

"Yeah. A great way to renew a relationship. Maybe to start a new relationship."

The front door opened and Beverly's husband entered, followed by Zadok's father and mother. Zadok followed Beverly on her way to greet them at the rear of the vestibule.

Zadok shuddered when he saw his parents, and for a flash he was their little boy and feared he was about to cry. He was surprised, though he knew he shouldn't have been, to see how they'd aged. They were really old and vulnerable. Suddenly he regretted terribly the circumstances that had alienated them and kept them apart. He wished he could have shared more of their lives. Why did they have to fight? He went over and embraced them.

"My long lost son," his mother said, as she hugged him.

He guessed that she was experiencing the same kind of regret that he was feeling.

Zadok shook hands with his father and Beverly's husband, whom he found to be very accommodating, likeable, and confident. Zadok could see how well Kevin handled and enchanted Zadok's parents. Kevin joked with them and made them laugh, even teased them.

At dinner Beverly announced that Shoshana was pregnant. Kevin smiled and congratulated him. Zadok's mother asked why Shoshana hadn't joined him on the trip.

"It was a business trip," Zadok explained. "Besides, it would be difficult for her to travel now."

"So you should have taken her. I know why you didn't take her. You couldn't afford to take her. That's it, isn't it? You see how your sister lives? And you couldn't afford to take your wife to visit your family?"

Zadok asked his sister to pass the bread. As she reached, Beverly quickly changed the subject to the color patterns in the planned addition to her house.

But later Zadok's mother expressed concern for his being skinny. "Don't you eat enough? Is there food enough where you live?"

"Actually my doctor says I'm a little overweight. I should lose about ten pounds," he said.

"Nonsense. You need to eat. You're too skinny. What's your doctor know? They don't have very good doctors there. I know this. You should hear the stories my cousin Sylvia tells me about those doctors. Why'd you need a doctor?"

As Zadok sipped his soup, it occurred to him that his father had avoided his eye contact, and had made an effort to engage Jennifer and Kevin in conversation, but not him. It seemed to him that his father's contempt for his ideology extended beyond the ideology, to him personally. The realization surprised and hurt Zadok. Suddenly he felt a strange pity for his father. What were the unlikely odds for Adam Zadok that his son would follow the idealism and faith of the old generation from the old country. Each generation was supposed to become more and more modern and move away from the old traditions. Zadok had the disconcerting feeling of knowing pity for his father because he had the misfortune of having him for a son. Zadok studied his father who was joking with his granddaughter. He felt not like a son looking up to his father, but a man looking at another adult male with all his pettiness and humanity.

*　*　*

Zadok was glad to be home in the Galilee, home to the narrow, winding roads that ran through the rock, shrubs and nature reserves. The hills were turning green and the flowers were opening, after a long season of rain. The olive trees and prickly pear, too, were budding. Shoshana was visibly showing. In fact, she was huge. She anxiously described the birthing classes that Zadok had missed, as well as the drum-like sound of the baby's heart beating within her.

His neighbors, most of whom he considered his friends, also seemed glad to see him back, and reported to him that terrorist activity had increased while he was gone. As a result, the underground shelters were cleaned out and prepared.

Shoshana's due date came and passed. Not even a false contraction. Another week passed, and then another. Shoshana feared that she'd be pregnant forever.

In the night a series of enemy Katyusha rockets hit close and everyone was called to the shelters. Zadok and Shoshana were among the last to arrive and as they sat on a mat, they heard another close explosion. Someone offered a chair to Shoshana, who started to decline, but then changed her mind. "Thank you," she said.

It was dark and quiet in the shelter. It was late and everyone was tired. It smelled like mildew.

"Oh, no," Shoshana said, breaking the quiet.

"Forget something?" Zadok said.

"My water just broke."

"What?" Zadok's eyes looked to the floor in search of a puddle.

"Oooh," she put her hands to her belly and looked up.

"Are you sure?"

"Of course."

"What? What?"

Shoshana looked back. Her mouth dropped wide open. There was more than pain in her eyes. Zadok saw terror, denial, disbelief, and then pain, real pain. Shoshana started to pant.

"Is it a contraction? So soon?" Zadok said.

Shoshana continued to pant. Zadok tried to support her upper back. Shoshana's eyes seemed to bulge. When the contraction passed she told Zadok to help her return to the mat. By now everyone was in their corner offering help.

"I don't believe it," Shoshana said, "please, not now."

"Get the nurse," someone yelled.

"She's our nurse."

"Who can help?"

Another explosion, not far away, and then another.

"We can't take her to the hospital," someone said.

"You're right. Too dangerous," a woman said.

Shoshana selected her neighbor, Hannah, to help. Zadok asked the crowd to stay back, which they did momentarily.

"Oh, God," he thought, "don't let there be complications, please don't let anything go wrong."

Shoshana moaned.

The contraction passed. "I want an anesthesia. I want anesthesia, take me to the hospital."

"We can't, dear, it's too dangerous," Zadok said.

"It's too dangerous for me here. I want anesthesia now. Now. Oh, no, not another one." She screamed again. "Do something. Please, do something, make it stop. I can't take it. I need pain relief."

"Let's do the breathing," Zadok said. "Breathe with me."

He started the breathing and Shoshana joined with him.

When the contraction passed, Shoshana yelled, "Get me out of this filthy hole in the ground in this horrible, no-nothing place."

Shoshana continued to curse the settlement, the Arabs, the Russians. She was still cursing when the next contraction started.

It went on for four more hours before the head started to crown.

Zadok was excited, confused, and afraid at the same time. Shoshana seemed totally exhausted. Her face was white, swollen, and soaked with sweat, but between contractions she found the strength to call out instructions to her weary husband, and to Hannah, her neighbor.

"More counterpressure against the head, yes, I don't want to tear. More counterpressure."

When the baby was born and started to cry on its own without aspiration, the neighbors let out a cheer and applauded. "Girl or a boy?"

"It's a girl," Zadok answered proudly.

His hands were shaking. He wrapped the baby and handed her to Shoshana.

"My God," Shoshana said softly, cradling her fresh, new daughter.

"What are you going to name her?" Hannah said.

"Katyusha Zadok," Zadok joked.

"Her name's Tsiporah. It's Tsiporah Zadok," Shoshana said with the quiet but substantial authority of a new mother.

*   *   *

Two years later their son Jonathan was born.

The doctor applied the clamps and instructed Zadok where to cut the cord. "No, between the clamps," the doctor said.

A nurse cleaned and wrapped the baby in a blue and white blanket, and presented him to Shoshana.

"He's beautiful," Shoshana said. Tears rolled down her cheeks.

At that moment Zadok noticed the doctor's expression had turned serious. "The afterbirth isn't coming," the doctor said. "I have to ask you to step out." He began to assemble surgical instruments. The nurse escorted Zadok, while rolling the baby in his basinet out of the delivery room.

Zadok sat down and looked at his son sucking his fingers. He worried about Shoshana and couldn't celebrate yet.

An hour later, the doctor came out of the delivery room. "I think I got most of it," he said, pulling down his mask. "Definitely not all. May have to go back again. We'll see what her body does in the next few days."

"I understand."

"Lucky this one was born in the hospital."

A day after Shoshana and Jonathan came home, she began to hemorrhage. Zadok rushed her back to the hospital. Once again he waited and worried.

This time the doctor was smiling when he came out. "Good news," he said. "We got it all. Come on, what are you waiting for? Go in and see your wife."

Zadok went to Shoshana's side. "How you doin', Mom?"

She was pale and exhausted. For the first time, he noticed circles under her eyes.

"Not a good day," she said, between coughing.

"I know, dear." He took her cold hand.

"The doctor said they got it all."

"It's great news. And they saved your uterus. A very capable doctor."

"So tired. Can you get me a drink of water?"

"Of course." He brought the water. "I'm so proud of you." He helped her sit up while she drank.

At home, neighbors and friends came and went all day long. The kitchen was full of food. Their neighbors did most of the food preparation. Hannah, especially, spent a lot of time helping the Zadoks care for their two young children. Zadok was exhausted by the entertaining, childcare, and wife care.

At the end of a long day, Zadok turned off the light and went to lie beside his wife. He kissed her on the cheek.

"Everyone on the moshav has been so wonderful," Shoshana said.

"They have."

"And you've been a big help. I want you to know I appreciate it. Especially when you do the night changings and let me sleep."

"I'd feed the baby, too, if I could."

"The neighbors brought so much food."

"It's getting eaten. Don't worry."

"Hannah has been wonderful."

"A good friend."

"So wonderful."

"It was nice of your father and brother to offer to help."

"Yes. But I prefer Hannah."

"I understand."

"She brought over so much food. Can you return her dishes?"

"I'll do it tomorrow."

"Don't forget."

"Said I'd do it tomorrow."

"The baby's crying."

"Didn't hear anything."

"Listen."

In a few seconds there was a loud cry.

"Okay," Zadok said, "I'll see if he's hungry or wet."

But he stayed in bed.

"Are you going?" Shoshana said.

"Going, going." He groaned.

The next morning he returned the three dishes to Hannah.

"You're welcome," Hannah said. "Why don't you come in. Just put the dishes on the kitchen counter. Want juice? Tea?"

"Tea'll be fine." Zadok sat on the sofa.

"Just a minute." Hannah was a tall New Yorker with short blonde hair.

In a few minutes she served the tea, and offered lemon, sugar, and milk.

"No, thanks."

"How's Shoshana feeling today?"

"Better. Still weak, but definitely better."

"That's good. You have beautiful children." Hannah sat on the couch next to Zadok.

"I appreciate your help with them."

"I think they take after their father."

"Think so?"

"Good-looking children," she said.

"Thank you."

She took a sip of her tea, while looking directly into Zadok's eyes. She had inviting big blue eyes, and long dark lashes. She seemed to blink a lot.

"It's nice that you can help Shoshana so much. My husband works such long hours. Probably won't be back till midnight."

"I'm taking a vacation so I can be home to help."

"You're working so hard on your vacation. You deserve a real rest," she said. She bent over briefly, exposing her cleavage, and picked up a spoon she had dropped.

She's flirting with me, Zadok realized.

She stroked her hair, smiled, blinked a lot, and leaned towards him. There was a long silence.

"Nice day," Zadok said, pretending to be oblivious.

"Every day's nice this time of year," she said, continuing her stare, pushing her hair back again and again, and squirming in the sofa.

"True," Zadok said.

"Same wonderful boring weather every day. That's what I love about living here."

"Me, too. Except the winter."

"The winter's too wet."

"Yeah, well, better get going. Thanks for the tea."

"Sure you have to go?"

"Shoshana or the kids must be screaming by now."

Hannah nodded.

Zadok felt awkward as he waved good-bye.

*   *   *

The next four years passed quickly. The Zadoks had two more daughters, Rivka and Yael.

Zadok worked hard and became recognized for his knowledge of offensive missile systems. He won the appreciation of an intelligence officer, General Nahum Ben Zion, who brought Zadok into intelligence and rewarded him with progressively more responsibility.

"You Americans are workaholics," Ben Zion said.

"Don't know any better," Zadok said.

"Whatever. I have another assignment for you."

"Thank you."

"Monitoring enemy strength and strategy. Your experience in munitions and offensive systems will be useful."

"Makes sense," Zadok said, smiling wide.

Zadok couldn't wait to tell Shoshana. When he got home, he found two children crying, and two children fighting. Shoshana was yelling at the combatants.

"What's going on?" Zadok said, dropping his briefcase.

"Your children are impossible."

"Everyone to your rooms. I want to talk to your mother."

There were multiple protests.

"Now," Zadok said, raising his voice and pointing. The older children went to their rooms. Zadok carried Rivka to her room, while Shoshana put Yael to bed in a basinet in their master bedroom.

"What's up?" Shoshana said.

"Great news. I got promoted. You're looking at one of Israel's senior intelligence officers on enemy offensive systems."

Shoshana gave him a hug. Her smile seemed to energize her body.

"Not bad for a poor American immigrant," she said.

Zadok kissed her.

"Oh, I've got news, too," she said.

"Good news, I hope."

"Gossip. Sit down, you won't believe it."

Zadok sat on a kitchen chair.

"Want something to drink?" Shoshana said.

"Tell me the news."

"Hannah had an affair."

"What?"

"With a border patrol reservist."

"How do you know?"

"Her husband walked in on them screwing in his bed. Poor man. Isn't that awful?"

"Can't imagine how he felt."

"Hannah's staying on the moshav with her kids. The husband's moving."

"Doesn't seem fair, does it. I'll visit him."

Shoshana pulled back, probably to study his reaction. "Are you shocked?" she said.

"Unbelievable," Zadok said, nodding.

* * *

Fifteen months later Zadok was promoted to full colonel. He was now responsible for the intelligence produced by his unit. He loved the job.

One of his staff meetings was running late. He stood up and impatiently said, "Anything else?"

There was no answer. "Okay. We're done. Thank you." He walked quickly and purposefully out of the conference room, and Dov Kesselbrenner, the former helicopter pilot, followed close behind. Zadok turned and immediately realized that Dov seemed upset.

"Something wrong?"

"Don't know if I should say anything."

"You might feel better."

"Some of your staff, actually one in particular, Mordi, he's not part of your team. He's talking."

"Talking?"

"He thinks you shouldn't be officer in charge. Most of the staff went to the military academy, some have graduate degrees from the Institute of Technology. You're an immigrant with just one engineering degree."

Zadok swallowed and massaged his throat. He had expected Dov wanted to talk about himself.

"Thanks. I'll talk to him."

"You didn't hear anything from me," Dov said.

"Don't worry. You're out of it."

Zadok spoke with Mordi and managed to extract a commitment to work together, but he didn't trust the ambitious native. Zadok decided to transfer him. He knew Ben Zion would support him.

He got home late and poured himself a scotch. He wanted to celebrate, at least to talk, but everyone had gone to sleep. He watched television for a while, and then went to the bedroom.

"That you?" Shoshana was awake.

"Yes, dear." Zadok quietly pulled back the sheets. "Go back to sleep."

"Have to tell you something." Shoshana was very sleepy. "I waited, but got too tired."

"Yes?" He lay beside her on his back.

"I can't believe it. I'm pregnant. Didn't want to be. Too soon."

"I think it's fantastic," Zadok said, clapping his hands.

"So tired. The children are all finally out of diapers, but they're still so much work. How're we going to manage?"

Zadok kissed her. "I'm happy. It's great."

"I'm too tired to be upset."

"Go to sleep."

"Good night."

"Good night," he said, kissing her. He folded his hands under his head and looked up to the ceiling. "What a week," he thought. He had risen to lead his department, had survived a political threat, and had learned of a fifth child in the oven. He couldn't ask for more.

He smiled and fell easily into a nourishing sleep.

Chapter Eleven

I will cause the cities of Israel to be inhabited, and the waste places shall be rebuilt: And the land that was desolate shall be tilled, instead of being the desolation that it was in the sight of all who passed by. And they will say, "This land that was desolate has become like the garden of Eden; and the waste and desolate and ruined cities are now inhabited and fortified." This also I will let the house of Israel ask me to do for them: to increase their men like a flock.

Zadok was relaxing on the sofa, skimming the weekly magazine supplement of the newspaper, and caught the title of a featured article, "A New Understanding of the Chariot-Throne." He recalled the pictures of a blue chariot and crown in his grandfather's books. Was there a connection? The article talked about long overlooked discoveries and new scholarship pertaining to those discoveries. The first discovery of the Dead Sea Scrolls in a cave by an Arab boy in 1947 was not the only discovery of ancient scrolls. Cave 3 was discovered in 1952 and Cave 4 in 1954. The contents originally went to Jordan, but only recently had qualified international experts, led by two American professors, gained access to the scrolls. The results of these studies had just been published. One of the insights from the scrolls concerned the symbolism of the chariot-throne, originally described by the prophet Ezekiel and then by the merkabbah mystics.

Several of the scrolls reference the vision of a God-like figure on a throne which is positioned on a chariot. It had been widely accepted that the description of the vision by Jewish sects during the Roman period was nothing more than another rendering of the Book of Ezekiel. But a new interpretation suggested that at least one of the authors of the scrolls had a vision similar to the vision described and recorded by the prophet Ezekiel. The author of the scroll, certainly a zealot, was describing the same vision, "like the vision that Ezekiel saw," according to one of the fragments. According to this zealot, God "would not allow his people to be oppressed for all time." The zealot interpreted his vision as a mission to prophesy to his people "so that they should stand up against Rome as a great people." There is speculation that such prophecies may in fact have played a role in rebellion against Rome. In any case, Zadok read, experts concluded that it was very likely that the vision that Ezekiel saw, particularly the image of the chariot-throne, had been a part of mystical secrets passed on for generations. It's easy to understand why mystical sects, generations later, would reference the image and compare their plight under Rome to the plight of the exiles under the Babylonians.

Zadok put down the paper. The chariot-throne was depicted graphically in his grandfather's books, and his grandfather had described his own personal encounter with it in the letter Aunt Bella had sent. It appeared that others, over the long span of history – the prophet Ezekiel, the Ramchal, the Roman period zealot and perhaps others – may also have experienced an encounter with the chariot-throne. But what did it mean? How did they tie together? He guessed the questions had fascinated his grandfather, and that the quest to find logical answers had driven the old man for years.

*   *   *

The color portrait of the Zadok family over the television in the family room was usually dusty. It was seldom noticed by anyone, but when Zadok did find himself focusing on it, he usually wanted to take a few moments to study it.

In the picture everyone seemed considerably younger and happier. It was one of the few times he'd put on a civilian suit and tie. He thought he looked the very prosperous American in the picture. Everyone appeared to wear genuine smiles, and matching articles of red and blue; four of the kids were lined up in front and Tsiporah and the parents stood behind them. Zadok felt himself beaming with pride. He realized that he could see himself in his son. Jonathan had his eyes, his cheeks, his coloring. Maybe Jonathan's hair was a shade lighter.

Zadok smiled as he recalled how Shoshana had made an issue over the fact that she'd endured the ordeal of pregnancy and the pain of childbirth, and in the end, all the kids resembled their father. There wasn't a trace of her. They were good-looking kids, Zadok thought. He was damn lucky.

It was time to leave for Jonathan's graduation from basic training. Zadok, Shoshana, and the four girls squeezed into the overcrowded sub-compact. Sarah sat on Tsipy's lap. Zadok was grateful that Tsipy had taken the day off to join the family for Jonathan's ceremony.

They drove to the ceremonial field where the young soldiers would parade. Zadok knew several of the senior officers, who made sure that he and his family had a center row seat in the viewing stands. Zadok had attained real influence.

"Here they come," Rivka said.

The young troops marched smartly into the field to the beat of parade drums. They were all carrying rifles.

"You see Jonathan?" Shoshana said.

"There." Tsipy pointed.

Zadok raised his camera and, though he was an inconsistent photographer, he guessed he'd take a few adequate pictures. To be sure, he snapped a few more.

He had mixed emotions about Jonathan's expressed wish to join the paratroopers. Was Zadok proud of his son? Yes. Was he nervous about knowing his son would be amongst the first into a fight? Absolutely.

Well, it was his son's decision, and the decision had been made. All he could do was provide support. Besides, Jonathan was pretty independent.

When the ceremony was over, everyone went down to the field to meet Jonathan. Zadok gave his son a big hug. Jonathan was much leaner than Zadok, but a few inches taller.

"Dad, you're embarrassing me," Jonathan said.

"Who cares?"

"Me."

"Okay, okay."

*   *   *

A few weeks passed. Zadok poured himself another cup of black coffee and picked up the newspaper. He read:

"A series of thirteen tremors has rocked Israel this past week, with some

minor aftershocks registered last Tuesday. The earthquakes caused no casualties and only minor damage. Last Tuesday, the fourth day of tremors,
the tremors ranged in intensity from under three on the Richter scale up to
five point eight. The epicenter of the tremors was in the Syrian East Africa
rift, which includes the Bekaa valley in Lebanon and parts of Syria."

Zadok thought nothing of it. He drank another cup, kissed everyone
good-bye, and drove to the office.

Zadok greeted the receptionist who also served as his assistant at the
security post in the entrance of the yellow stone ranch-style office building. "Shalom."

"Shalom," she replied from behind her big desk.

Aviva was a middle-aged, trim, well-kept, blonde divorcée, who flirted
with Zadok daily. While Zadok thought she was pretty and fun, he had absolutely no interest in pursuing anything further.

"What's the matter? You don't sound your normal cheerful self," Zadok
said to Aviva.

"Just men trouble, the usual men trouble," Aviva sighed, supporting
her head in her cupped hands.

"Can't believe you have trouble with men."

"Believe it, honey."

"You're always getting flowers and candy."

"Yeah, but always from the wrong type. Why can't I meet a single guy
who's like you?"

"Well, I don't think I'm so rare."

Aviva laughed. "A good man's rarer than a lion in Judea."

"Now I know why I enjoy talking to you. You always make me feel
good."

"Hey, but you don't give me the time of day."

"Now that's not true,"

"You know what I mean."

"What?"

"Don't play naive, dear."

"I'm not."

"Hey, why don't you really let me make you feel good."

"You do, every morning. Now have a good day. I've got to go do some
work."

Aviva let out a deep breath. "That's the story of my life," she said.

Zadok sat at his desk and studied a dated picture of Shoshana and the two oldest, Tsipy and Jonathan. He looked at a beautiful picture on the wall of the oasis of Ein Gedi. He went through his e-mail and papers. It seemed the World Arms Show was to be in France this year. His flight reservations were already made.

Zadok went through his in-box and reviewed his schedule. Today he had a luncheon with a foreign vendor, a meeting with an Israeli aircraft manufacturer, a meeting with Dov, and another meeting with a professor at the Technion. Tomorrow there was a strategy session based on recent field agent feedback.

When it was Dov's turn to enter Zadok's office, Dov was laughing.

"What's so funny?"

"Your secretary's a character, one unique lady."

"What did she say this time?"

"She told me she was in heat, and I better call her by dinner time or it would pass."

"What'd you say?"

"Just laughed," Dov said.

"Maybe I better hose her off," Zadok said.

"What kind of hose will you use?" Dov asked.

"Don't you start."

"Okay, how's the family?"

"Great. Driving me nuts as usual. Going to join me at the French show?"

"Yes, I'm planning to. All I need is tickets and an itinerary."

"Great."

"Fax me your itinerary and schedule when you can?"

"Okay, I'll make sure you get it this time, more than an hour before the flight. So what do you got for me that's hot?"

Dov lifted his briefcase to his lap. "Photographs this time." Dov pulled a file out of his briefcase.

"Of the missiles?"

"Yes. Here."

Zadok took the folder and found six seven-by-nine-inch photos. He put on his glasses, and studied the photos under the light. "So these are the infamous Iranian arrow missiles."

"Yes. Big, aren't they?"

"Who gave you the pictures, the Kurd?"

"Yes. We call him 'Libi.'"

"Libi did a great job. Keep him happy."

"We are."

"Anything else?

"They did a test that Libi witnessed."

"Have a summary sheet on it?"

"Yes. Unfortunately, the test was powerful, pretty damn successful from their point of view. Damn accurate, too. They can hit anything they want in the alpha range."

"Alpha? The entire country would be vulnerable. Let me see."

Dov handed over the summary sheet.

"Damn, if this is true, it's as good as anything we got," Zadok said.

"I know. But I don't know how many they've got or where they're deployed."

Zadok expected that he should be able to access that information from other sources. It was starting to look bad. He was already computing the capability of Israeli defensive missiles against the data on the summary sheet.

"Can you be sure they're as accurate and powerful as described in this summary?"

"Libi was in the test. And there are other sources for verification."

"Reliable sources?"

"Very reliable."

"They have any private agenda to create a war?"

"Who knows."

"What else?"

"That's it."

Zadok stood up and stepped back towards the windows. He began to pace.

"Do you need something else?" Dov asked.

"Let me just think for a minute," Zadok said. Dov looked back to his files.

"See if you can find out their rate of production," Zadok said. "Find out about fossil fuel, or chemical storage near the missiles."

"Will do."

"Tell miss lady-in-heat to come in here as you leave."

"Okay, Bob." Dov got up and left.

In a few minutes, Aviva entered the office. Zadok was in no mood to joke with her.

"Call a staff meeting. Right away. Let's make it tomorrow, Wednesday. I don't care what else they're juggling. Tell them to be there."

"Okay," Aviva said. "I was working on the itinerary and schedule for the trip to France, but I'll just put it aside."

"Cancel the trip to France."

"Cancel? Dov, too?"

"Yes, cancel all foreign travel. Get back to me with confirmation ASAP."

"Okay." Aviva turned to leave.

"One more thing," Zadok said.

"Yes?" Aviva turned around.

"Get my American friend on the phone. Colonel James. Set it up first thing tomorrow Texas time if you can. Still have the number?"

"Yes, I do."

She went back to her desk.

Zadok returned to his chair. He looked at an old photograph of his family. He thought about his kids, all five of them, amazingly unique and different from each other, and they had turned out wonderfully. He thought about the summary sheet in front of him. He didn't want to believe that the pinpoint accuracy was true. But that was his job. He planned to do a damn thorough analysis. He had another source that might be able to verify or dismiss the data.

He brought home two briefcases that day. As he walked from his car to his cottage, he greeted a neighbor, then waved to the boys playing soccer. He remembered when his own son, Jonathan, and one of his daughters, Rivka, were young enough to be in that soccer group. Now they had other interests.

Only his youngest, Sarah, accompanied him for dinner. Even Shoshana was at a community meeting. He and Sarah shared a salad and pasta. Sarah poured on the cheese, but Zadok, mindful of his high cholesterol, used only a little tomato sauce sparingly.

"Play a game with me tonight?"

"Honey, I'd like to, but I have a lot of work to do tonight."

"You're always working. You never play with me."

"That's not true."

"Yes, it is. You always work or play with the others. You never have time for me."

Zadok looked at his pretty daughter. She had been a difficult baby, but how glad he was to have her. She definitely had his coloring: long, black, straight hair, brown eyes, and skin that tanned easily. She was so damned cute.

"Well, maybe for a little while. What do you want to play?"

She shrugged her little shoulders. "I don't know."

"Well, what did you have in mind when you asked?"

"I don't know," she repeated.

"How about cards?"

She nodded.

"Great. Go find the cards," Zadok said.

*   *   *

The next day Zadok decided not to wait for a prearranged conversation with his friend in Houston. Although Israel had its own satellite surveillance, Zadok wanted to see what the Americans had. He telephoned himself.

"What a surprise. How the hell're you?"

"Fine, Tex. And you?"

"Any finer, I wouldn't be able to stand it. Say, do you know what time it is here?"

"I just wanted to be sure I got you."

"No problem, call me anytime. Middle of the night's best, at my home, any time after midnight."

"Thanks."

"And you can even try the office some time, too, you know, like a normal thing. Just for variety. Hey, are you going to the French show this year?"

"No," Zadok said. "I had to cancel."

"Too bad. It'll be a good time."

"I know."

"Well, then, if you're not calling to set up a meet to buy me a drink, what's up?"

"That's what I wanted to ask you."

"Me? Hell, what do I know?"

"More than you'll probably tell me."

"That's a hoot, I know nothing."

"Satellite photos?"

"Yeah, I knew that's what you wanted. I also know that you know that I can't even talk about it. So what do you really want?"

"Just to hear your sweet voice."

"Well, do you feel better?"

"Absolutely. Now will you ask about loosening up on the photos?"

"What photos?"

"Okay. Guess I get the picture. Even though I don't get the pictures."

"You still owe me a drink, maybe two."

"Maybe a drink and a half."

"Great hearing from you. I'm going back to sleep."

He hung up.

Zadok leaned back at his desk and stared out the window. He picked up a pencil and bit on the eraser. His eyes slowly turned back to the computer, so he scanned his e-mail. There were several routine requests, to which he took the time to respond. Then Zadok got up and went to the conference room. His staff was all there waiting. The seven officers were seated facing him.

Zadok stood by the monitor, said good morning, and began to pass out photos of the arrow missiles.

"I think we've been fooling ourselves in the dark. This is the wake-up call. We need to get a better handle on troop or hardware movements, particularly missile activities. And I mean everywhere. I need the data on a real time basis. We've set up the 'hot' desk. I'll be reviewing it regularly and sending the executive summary to General Ben Zion. Travel is cancelled. This is sole priority. I consider it a preliminary war alert. Any questions?"

"Why not just focus on these missiles?"

"Dov has that assignment. But I have reason to suspect that they won't act alone. That's why we need data. We need to know the whole picture. Understood?"

Zadok knew they'd seldom seen him as serious. That was probably good. The occasion called for it.

*　*　*

"I'm tired," Shoshana complained that night.

"Tough day?" Zadok said.

"Unbelievable. All I'm doing is hauling the kids from one activity to another. I feel like a taxi service for the royal Moshav Misgav children. And I do this on top of my job. I don't know how I have any time to go to work."

"I'm sorry it's such a drain for you," Zadok said. To show his empathy, he offered to help.

"Yes, you can help. I was going to ask you. Tomorrow there's a teacher conference for Rivka and Sarah. I can't make it. Can you?"

"Tomorrow?"

"Yes."

"In the morning?"

"Of course."

"I don't know. I've got to – "

"I don't believe it. You offer to help. I ask you one thing – "

"I've got an important meeting with the general."

"You always have important meetings. They're all important. Meanwhile I'm the one who's working, taking care of the kids, the house, the shopping, planning the activities, running the taxi service, and in my spare time serving as the family social planner. You go to meetings and flirt with the secretaries."

"I'm not like Dov."

"I need you to take them tomorrow. It would be a real disappointment for Rivka and Sarah if no one came. I can't do it."

"Okay. Okay. I'll call the general. I'll reschedule."

"You have a responsibility to your family, too," Shoshana said.

"I know. I agree with that. I just…okay, I'll do it."

*   *   *

"Hey," Zadok said to Aviva when he finally made it in to the office.

"Shalom, shalom, deary," Aviva said.

"How are the men treating you?"

"Don't ask."

"That bad or that good?"

"That bad," Aviva responded. "I don't know why I attract the kind that I do."

Zadok laughed.

"You have a lot of messages on your voice mail."

"Figures. Everybody calls the one day I'm late."

"General Ben Zion rescheduled for three o'clock this afternoon, as you requested."

"Good."

Zadok entered his office. There were electronic messages already from the "hot" desk, so he read about troop and missile movements. He felt anxious. He'd hoped he'd be wrong. They were planning an all-out surprise assault against Israel. Was it enough evidence? It'd be proof enough for Ben Zion. His job was to pass the data up. Damn it.

*   *   *

General Ben Zion wasn't alone at the three o'clock meeting. He'd invited an aide, a major, as well as two colonels and a subordinate general. Zadok had brought Dov along.

"It's your show," General Ben Zion said.

"I've got a lot to share," Zadok said. He sat down.

Dov went around the room distributing a sealed envelope to each of the attendees.

"Just shoot to the bottom line," Ben Zion said.

"You see the summaries and the photos. These missiles are locally produced, and have been tested to the specifications on the data sheet."

"What else?"

"Clear indications of immediate expansion beyond the prototype level. I'm including chemical warheads as part of that expansion, although to date, we've seen no evidence of nuclear."

"They're not publicizing it, even to their own. Could they simply be doing research?"

"Of course we don't know their intentions, but I believe for the moment we have to assume the worst."

"Maybe they'll hold the expansion if we let them know we're aware and will respond if they don't stop," the major said.

"That's an option," Ben Zion said. "First we need more information. Then we can lay out the options. Zadok, report to me daily. We can't let this go very long."

"All right," Zadok said.

Dov and Zadok left. Zadok knew Ben Zion would continue the meeting without them.

* * *

The picture looked more and more like a buildup before an offensive action. There were no threats in the media. No large-scale propaganda. That made it more ominous, because a preemptive action by Israel would appear to the world as an act of aggression. Still, given the choice, it would clearly be better to strike first. Zadok looked diligently for proof of their intent. At the same time, he hoped he'd find reason to believe he was wrong about the whole thing. The best he could do was to collect quality data, and let Ben Zion and the politicians make the decisions.

The next day he called Ben Zion for his daily update. "The Syrians have put thirty thousand additional troops into a ready alert. There's no reason for them to think we're about to attack. I don't see it as a defensive move. They're trying to keep it a secret. We see activity in the others as well, but troop levels remain approximately as previously reported."

"Okay. Meet me at the Knesset tomorrow at nine. I'm attending a cabinet meeting. I may need you to answer specifics."

"I'll bring all the data."

"We'll keep it at a high level. But they may press for specifics on anything."

* * *

Zadok sat silently through the first half hour of the meeting. The interior minister brought up the risk of upsetting the peace. The chief of staff seemed to pick up on General Ben Zion's argument for an offensive action. The prime minister listened, but didn't say anything. It became clear to Zadok how differently the politicians behaved behind closed doors, at least differently from the combative, sometimes circus atmosphere portrayed in the media. The group behaved like a club; they were clearly very comfortable with one another, even the opposition. After all, they did it regularly.

However, today's agenda required a certain insight and intensity that wasn't routine. There were real brains and experience in this club, but the smartest appeared to be the finance minister, who questioned the quality and extent of the information. That was when Ben Zion turned to Zadok.

"We've had very reliable sources. We have photographs and testimony from a half dozen sources," Zadok said.

"Something doesn't feel right," the minister said. "If they're that obvious about it, they can't expect it to be a surprise. Yet, several countries are keeping it quiet. Why?"

"I don't know," Zadok said. "I believe it's an attempt to get some element of surprise. It may simply be an attempt to make it difficult for us to preempt them."

"We should make it clear in the media what they're doing," the defense minister said. "Publicize it. They'll either back down or give us the justification, the world sympathy or the international support, whatever it is you think we need so that we can properly defend ourselves."

It was now the interior minister's turn to speak. "What're the chances we could be wrong? What if they just deny it? Does anyone think they'd agree to inspectors? Of course not. We need more proof. Let me see the proof."

"Here's what we know," Ben Zion said. "With Chinese and French help, they've developed a new arsenal that's state of the art. We have reports, highly credible reports, that their tests were successful. They have real accuracy, including the ability to circumvent defensive missiles. And there's no doubt that there have been major troop movements in three countries."

"Reports from whom?"

The prime minister held up his hand and spoke quietly. "It doesn't matter. We don't need to prove anything to anyone except ourselves. We need a strategic military option. Two categories of options actually. Preemptive and strategic responses. How quickly can they be ready?"

"They're ready," Ben Zion said. "I'll review them today and deliver them tonight."

"Good."

Zadok enjoyed being part of the interaction with this celebrated club. He tried to show that he wasn't starstruck. He tried to behave as if it wasn't unusual for him to participate in these meetings. But he could feel his own excitement. He knew he was witnessing something extraordinary. He just wished the issues were different.

Outside of the Knesset building, as they walked to their cars, Ben Zion said, "Continue the daily updates. At any moment they may make a decision one way or the other. Whatever way it goes, be ready."

It was after eleven when Zadok got back to the moshav. Shoshana was making sandwiches. The three kids who still lived at home were in bed. Zadok sat at the kitchen table. "I'm tired, real tired," he said.

"You know, you forgot to take out the garbage again," Shoshana said. "What's the matter with you?"

Zadok got up to get the garbage.

"It's too late now," Shoshana said. "You already blew it. Don't do it now."

"No problem. I'll take it out."

"It's too late. You missed it."

"I love to take out the garbage. I'm taking out the garbage. Nothing can give me more pleasure than to take out the sweet, wonderful, beautiful garbage."

He carried the garbage to the dumpster across the field near the parking.

*   *   *

The late summer was uncomfortably hot, as the thick desert air slowly moved north. The weather and the economy dominated everyday conversations, while the media focused on local and foreign politics. Zadok was, for the first time in his life, unaware of many of the contemporary popular political issues. He was totally immersed in the military considerations that few people knew about. Then there were his personal problems. Shoshana seemed to be more and more emotional, more and more high-strung, and more and more she initiated fights. Every weekend there seemed to be some issue coming up – who did more work at home, how he perceived the intrusion of her friends, how to raise the kids, how to spend money.

"All I do all day is laundry," Shoshana said. "Five kids and two adults produce a mountain of laundry. Then I make meals, and administer to everyone else's needs. What about my needs?"

"There's only three at home. But isn't this life? What do you expect? What does every other woman on the moshav, or in town, do?"

"They have fun sometimes. We don't have fun anymore. It's nothing but drudgery out here in the middle of nowhere."

It scared him that Shoshana seemed both so dissatisfied and unwilling to talk about it. It made him think of, and miss, Vicki Amour. He wasn't sure why. Did he still love Vicki after all this time? He didn't think so. But he imagined that Vicki would've always been even-tempered and soft-voiced, even if she got angry with him.

Then there were the politics of the moshav. So many different personalities that had to live so closely together. Well, he guessed every group had to have its share of characters, dissidents, and outright assholes. At least the moshav did have some exceptional and wonderfully giving people. That made it worthwhile.

The moshav was coming along well. They were even offering cultural activities now, like training the kids to play musical instruments, sing in a choir or perform in a play. His kids were doing some impressive painting. The moshav was becoming established, earning a reputation in the area for its level of extracurricular cultural and artistic excellence. Hell, it was stereotypical middle class.

As hard as that new identity was to accept, it was, in fact, what they'd collectively worked so hard to achieve. Who knew, perhaps some day all the area moshavim would blend together into a small town or suburb. He felt good and proud that he'd been one of the original founders. And, thank God, the kids were mentally and physically healthy. Yes, he had problems like everyone else, but all in all, he couldn't complain.

Chapter Twelve

O mountains of Israel, shoot forth your branches, and yield your fruit to my people Israel; for they will soon come home. For, behold, I am for you, and I will turn to you, and you shall be tilled and sown; and I will multiply men upon you, the whole house of Israel, all of it; the cities shall be inhabited and the waste places rebuilt; and I will multiply upon you man and beast; and I will cause you to be inhabited as in your former times, and will do more good to you than ever before.

The car radio was playing contemporary Hebrew Yemenite music. Zadok had grown to really like it; the shrill harmony and punctuated beat made him feel as if he were dancing. He thought of it as Kasbah jazz. It was similar to Arab music, which had sounded so strange and discordant when he'd first come to Israel, but now he could appreciate and like it.

No music had for him the powerful effect that modern Hasidic music had on him. The old melodies and prayers of the Eastern European sects were contemporized with an Israeli beat. That sound seemed to penetrate his soul, reaching out and welcoming him into the mysterious world of the Jewish mystics. It was almost as if the music created nostalgia for a favorite ceremonial tune enjoyed by an ancestor.

He parked his car on the street directly across from his physician's ground-floor, one-story office building. He was long overdue for this checkup. But he'd been feeling out of sorts lately, so reluctantly he had called to make the appointment. Damn, it's too hot, he thought, as he stepped out of his Ford. He wondered if the car's air conditioning made it harder to adjust to the dry heat.

Fortunately there wouldn't be too long a wait, only four people ahead of him. He hated socialized medicine. Always crowds at the clinics, doctors in a hurry, nurses and aides who didn't care. But he was fortunate to have a personal relationship with a competent doctor who did care.

The doctor grunted after probing Zadok's neck. Then he carefully probed the throat and neck again. After the examination the doctor told him to wait in his office.

This surprised and concerned Zadok. His doctor had never ushered him into an office before. Usually his exams resulted in a pat on the back and regards to his family. On the few occasions he had the flu, the routine prescription for an aspirin-penicillin-codeine pill and a vitamin pill was written before Zadok could finish describing his fever.

His doctor had a thin mustache, reminiscent of an American used car salesman. He was a native in his mid-forties who spoke slowly and quietly. The doctor leaned back in his chair. Zadok leaned forward in his and concentrated on his doctor's every word.

"I don't know why you're feeling tired and out of it, as you put it. My guess is simple fatigue."

"Okay."

"We'll test your blood, just to be sure, but I don't think it'll show anything. Have you been under stress?"

"Yes. At home and at work."

"That's probably the problem. I can recommend a good counselor or therapist."

"Not necessary, thank you."

"Okay. But I'm glad it got you to see me. I'm concerned about something else."

"What do you mean?"

"I want you to go into the hospital for more tests. There's something that concerns me."

"What?"

"May be nothing. Let's wait and see." He turned in his swivel chair and shrugged with an expression of arrogance unique to the Middle East.

Zadok had also learned to be assertive in his own right. He looked straight into the doctor's eyes, a man whom he knew, and raised his voice. "I can take it."

The doctor studied the colonel before him, shrugged again and matter-of-factly said, "There's a lump. I need to know more."

"What lump? What're you talking about?"

"Didn't you feel it when I examined you? There's a little irregularity in the lymph glands. It may be nothing. But, to be safe, I'd like to check it out."

"I thought it was...I don't know what I thought."

"Let's find out for sure what it is."

"But you already know what it is, don't you," Zadok said.

"There's no way to be positive at this point, but, yes, I'm concerned it may be a cancer."

Zadok didn't say anything.

The doctor said, "There's a very good clinic and doctor I can refer you to at Rambam Hospital. Name's Seiderman."

"Hope you're wrong." Zadok got up from his chair.

"Yes, I hope I am."

Days later the diagnosis became official: Hodgkin's disease. Dr. Seiderman explained quickly the conventional radiation treatment. Then the well-respected medical specialist, still speaking at the same quick pace, said, "The bottom line is that if the cancer can't be arrested, you have about a year, two or three at best."

Zadok squeezed the sides of his chair. So be tough, he said to himself. Show them that you still have balls. This can't be happening, can it?

"The statistics are very favorable for successful treatment if it isn't too advanced. First, I'd like to check you in for extensive radiation treatment. I think we've got it in time. But in any case the therapy will improve your chances of survival," the doctor said matter-of-factly.

"Of course, there's the side effects from radiation we've already discussed," Dr. Seiderman continued. "You should also know that there are more experimental approaches."

"Like what?"

"Well, for example, there's the approach that takes some of your diseased cells, injects them in rabbit's blood, and then returns it to your body. The idea is to help your own system recognize the cancer as an invader, and then the immune system ideally can destroy the cancer cells. To help the process along we add another prescription which attacks the cancer. There are many documented successes with this therapy. It started in America."

He explained it very clinically, as if it were a new recipe that may or may not inflate the soufflé.

"I'll think about it. When did it start in America?"

"A long time ago. It's based on a reading by Edgar Cayce, who was known as the 'sleeping prophet.' He was a religious Christian who had a mystical experience when he was young. As an adult he learned to put himself into a hypnotic trance, and then give readings with specific cures for his patients' hard-to-diagnose ailments. And there's much documentation to support his very high success rate. Strange, huh? His patients were the hopeless cases, the ones the medical doctors gave up on. So the therapy I'm suggesting for you is based on one of Cayce's readings."

"You will try both therapies?"

"I'm somewhat confident we're early enough for a cure. The first step is the radiation and medication. Then we can better appraise the situation and discuss all the therapies."

Was this the specialist he should entrust with his life? The doctor spent no more than ten minutes with him, and seemed to treat him like just another case number. What should he do?

When Zadok stepped back out to the street, he didn't care about the long-term, summer heat wave. The sky was still bright as ever, the traffic still jammed. He could be dying. But, damn it, he felt pretty good. There had to be something wrong. Those doctors had to be full of it. Maybe he should go back to the States where they had real doctors. He couldn't accept it. It had to be a mistake. He would just have to find a smarter doctor. "Tell me," he said to himself, "that this is a bad dream."

He didn't go back to his office. Instead he drove around and around, got himself lost, then eventually he made his way to the beach. He walked along the beach, carefully observing the other people who were also strolling. What kind of problems were they struggling with, he wondered. Then he looked up to the heavens, as if to question God, but didn't say anything.

He drove back to his office. Aviva greeted him, but Zadok scarcely acknowledged that he noticed. One of the girls in the front open area must have observed that he looked upset since she brought him a cup of hot tea.

But he couldn't bring himself to do any work. He got up to close his office door. He came back to his desk and kicked a drawer shut. He tossed a folder full of loose papers across the desk. He started to write, but then threw his pen across the room at the door. Then he kicked the bottom drawer over and over. He felt his eyes well, but there were no tears. He dropped his head onto his folded arms, resting on the desktop.

"Everything all right?" a girl called out as she knocked on his door.

"Everything's okay, just fine, wonderful, couldn't be better."

As he drove home, his mind wandered. He needed more time. He felt he deserved more time. Life was so damn short. He had accomplished some things, after all. He'd started a new settlement. He had brought five Jewish children into the world. That was his most significant contribution.

Then there was the war. Funny, he'd faced death in the war but he hadn't felt any of these emotions or concerns. That was different. There was no time to think in the war. You just did what you had to do, and if you survived, you didn't have to worry or think about death. Yes, a war was different. Being a father now made it different for him, too.

Should he say anything to Shoshana? Yes, he'd have to tell her, but it'd have to be at the right moment. How would she take it? What about the kids? God, what should he tell the kids?

He put a cassette of Hasidic music into the tape player.

The heat began to subside as it normally did when he finally reached the Galilean hills. It was a combination of the geographic elevation and the time of day that he normally approached the area. As he turned to climb the snake road up the hill, he heard a strange clicking sound, then the car jerked as if he had popped the clutch. His car stalled.

He let the car's momentum guide him toward the soft shoulder. Don't flood it now, he said to himself. He tried the ignition over and over, but it wouldn't start. He was alone in the Arab area, but he knew these Israeli Arabs and he had friends among them.

He went out to raise the hood. Then he returned to reach for his phone. Before he finished dialing, a pickup truck pulled alongside.

The driver was Abdul. Zadok didn't recognize the passenger.

"Have a problem?"

"Yes, it won't start."

"Need a jump start?"

"Maybe." Zadok shrugged.

The Arabs tried to jump start the battery, but it still didn't work. Abdul invited Zadok to ride in the open back section while they drove him to his settlement.

Zadok looked back sadly towards his broken-down Ford, as the pickup sped up the hill to the moshav settlement.

When they reached the moshav, Zadok jumped down from the back of the truck.

He walked around to thank Abdul.

"Happy to help," Abdul said. "We know you've been kind to us. Wish everyone on the mountain were as kind as you." He waved.

Zadok returned the wave.

Suddenly he felt tired and weak. He began to walk, carrying his satchel, from the parking area to the residential area. As he stepped, he imagined he was getting sicker, that with each movement the disease spread into more and more of his body. The satchel got heavier and heavier. He imagined he could feel the cancer cells floating and tingling. Yet, as he went down the path he knew so well, he still managed to notice, despite the impending darkness, the birds who squealed and took flight as he came too close, the flowers flaunting the beauty of their short lives, the mildly scented gardens, and the white painted rocks along the edge of the stone-in-concrete pathway. And, as if to emphasize it all, there was the orange sunset, seeming almost touchable, brilliant, but serving simply as an environmental accent.

The front door of Zadok's cottage was open. Shoshana was busy in the kitchen.

"Good evening, how was your day?" he said. He noticed a flying cockroach zoom through the door opening.

"You're late. You could've called, you know."

"You wouldn't believe the day I've had. Besides, the car broke down," he said.

"What happened to the car?"

"It just died."

"Where is it?"

"Just north of el-Sacnin."

"Couldn't you have called?"

"When? What's this third degree all about, anyway? Leave me alone, will you? Get off my back."

"I'm not on your back. I just need a little courtesy so I know what's going on," she yelled.

Then their daughter Rivka came into the kitchen. "Daddy, I need five shekels for school."

"I'm talking to your mother now. Can't it wait? I'll be with you in a minute."

"No, now," she wined. "I need it now. It's very important. My friend's waiting."

"Wait outside. I'll be with you in a minute," he said.

"No, I can't, I need it now," she said.

"Damn it, get out," he yelled. "Get out. I've had it with your whining. Leave me alone."

Rivka cried and ran out of their cottage home.

"Why'd you do that?" Shoshana yelled. "What's your problem?"

"Oh, go to hell, too."

Zadok went out, slammed the door, and without a plan wandered down the hill beyond the perimeter of the moshav. He came to a dead olive tree and sat nearby on a boulder. What the hell was he doing, he thought. He was yelling at his wife and daughter, actually beating on the people who mattered most to him. That was verbal abuse. He was losing it, he thought. Damn, he'd better get it under control quick, before he ruined what was left in his life. God help me, he said to himself. He looked up and wondered how he could possibly get through what was to come.

* * *

Zadok made plans for Dov to continue the daily updates to Ben Zion while he went through the radiation treatments. Zadok found it difficult to talk for a few weeks, and occasionally Ben Zion called him to provide feedback and keep him up to date on the situation. However, it was mostly a one-way conversation.

Shoshana had become very accommodating for him, resuming her role as a concerned wife and nurse. She'd taken the news very well, or at least appeared to in front of him. She seemed instantly to fall into her health professional mode, as soon as she began to understand what Zadok had. It was wonderful to see how good and kind she could be. After all, that was the real part of her makeup that had compelled him to fall in love with her. He began to forget their recent communication problems and how short-tempered they'd been with each other. Their relationship seemed to be getting stronger.

And now that he was spending a lot of time at home, he was beginning to see things from her perspective. She worked from morning to night at her jobs, taking care of the kids, managing the household, dealing with moshav issues, and juggling day care so that she could work at a demanding nursing position. He recalled how he normally had come home very late. He'd be exhausted, but if he had any energy at all to interact with the kids, he'd only want to play with them. He had become the good time dad and she had become the authority figure and disciplinarian. No wonder she could lose patience with him.

They hadn't told anything to the kids about his health, except that Daddy was sick and had to go to the hospital. The oldest, Tsipy, wasn't buying the explanation, though. She insisted on more facts. Zadok guessed Shoshana must've told her privately. In the last few days, Tsipy had stopped asking questions and she cancelled her long planned trip to America. Zadok was grateful she would still be nearby for a number of reasons. He felt that Tsipy had the personality and temperament of his father, Adam Zadok. She might easily assimilate into American culture if she were to live in America. No wonder she aspired to visit the country she had heard so much about and to meet new relatives. She seemed to have very similar attitudes to his father's. He considered that he might be similar in some ways to his grandfather even though he had never met him. Funny how personalities, interests, and priorities could skip generations.

* * *

Zadok was lying in the hospital bed considering the unusual rabbit blood therapy that his doctor was prescribing to cure his cancer. He was going with Dr. Seiderman's recommendation, but the idea of a therapy based on a so-called prophet's reading seemed irrational when his life was on the line.

The phone rang.

"How are you feeling?" Dov asked him.

"Never worse, if you really want to know."

"Well, at least you can talk now."

"Yes, it's a little uncomfortable. I feel sick to my stomach all the time. Maybe I'm pregnant."

"Maybe."

"What's going on?"

"The cabinet decided to put a hold on the preemptive option. At least for now."

"That's a mistake."

"I thought you'd want to know."

"Of course, but it's still a mistake. It's just a way of putting off the inevitable."

"I haven't heard from Libi in two days."

"Is he all right?"

"We'll find out."

"Let me know."

"That's all I've got."

"Thanks for the update."

Losing Libi was a significant intelligence loss at a critical time. Still, reports kept coming in, all leading to the same scenario. It was becoming more and more clear what was about to happen.

* * *

Zadok was home now. As he lay in bed at night, staring at the ceiling, he slowly looked over to Shoshana who lay fast asleep in an awkward pose, similar to the fetus position. She seemed to Zadok, even in sleep, exhausted by the effort of working a nursing job and raising five children. Mothering was an endless job, interspersed with moments of unequalled joy, something like a poor investment with a spectacular dividend expected some time in the future. As Zadok lay uncomfortably with his eyes wide open, neither asleep nor fully awake, he studied the mysterious forms and shadows projected by the lattice work enclosing a bedroom window, but he was mostly thinking about how important it was to show his appreciation to his wife.

Suddenly he feared for his children's future. Now he was more awake. Would his children and his neighbors' children enjoy the benefits of everything good they'd tried to create? He knew too much about the security threats. At times like this he wished he had a job that granted him the privilege of ignorance. Then he could sleep at night, and let others agonize over the correct strategies to defend Israel.

He rolled slowly and carefully out of bed, not wanting to disturb Shoshana, and wandered over to a window. He stepped down to one knee, pushed away the shutter, and looked into the moonlit clear night. He listened for a moment to the alluring call of the crickets, and then he thought about offering a prayer. He felt a presence in the empty gray and black cool air, something mystical that wouldn't allow him to fail in his responsibility. It was both meaningful and magical. It gave him a confidence, without logic, that all would work out. It seemed to help. But, he wondered, was it nothing more than foxhole religion, or counterproductive wishful thinking?

Then he went to the living room and practiced deep breathing exercises that he'd learned from his martial arts training. The breathing and arm extensions, generally performed from a horse-stance position, seemed to help. He was surprised how well he remembered the movements.

He went to the kitchen and poured himself a brandy over ice. That, too, seemed to help. So he poured another. Then another. Yes, it seemed to help.

He went back to bed convinced he could sleep now. He was nearly numb, but the damn tightness in his gut was still there. The anxiety and restlessness was still there, too. What could he do about the expected attack? Sure as hell it was coming. He was the only one who knew it. He imagined how different the Yom Kippur War might have been if Israeli intelligence had been more responsible before the attack. He knew that wars could be won or lost before one shot rang out. Now he was the one who had the advanced intelligence, and the responsibility to do something with it. What was the solution? He had to do something. God damn it, Jonathan would be in the front line.

Finally, he fell asleep.

*　　*　　*

He fell into a pattern of one day not being able to sleep, and the next day dropping from pure exhaustion.

When he did sleep, his dreams were vivid, often frightening, and he remembered them. Sometimes he was being chased. Sometimes he was the only one naked in a large group. He had an especially disturbing dream about being captured by the enemy. He guessed it must have been one of the carryover dreams from his Yom Kippur War experience. He still had many dreams, usually nightmares, about the war. Lately he was thinking more and more about that war. In particular, he was angry about the poorly advanced intelligence. He'd been angry about it for years and years. Strange how things worked out sometimes.

In the mornings he'd often be up and gone long before anyone else in his family awoke. Sometimes in the early morning, or later in the afternoon, he'd go to the beach, hoping that the walk or run along the seashore would foster a plan, some strategy to do more than stand on the sidelines while everything unfolded. Suddenly, he felt responsible for everyone he saw.

He was worried, too, about his medical problems, optimistic about things getting better at home, and he was absolutely possessed by the impending military threat. For hours at a time, the threat was all he could think about. There seemed to be nothing good in his life. He'd forgotten how to laugh.

He could say nothing to anyone, not to Shoshana, his children, the other moshav families. Yet, he had spoken at length to his military peers and superiors. The bottom line was still the same, and the tragedy was that the people in power, the politicians, the generals, were all paralyzed. No damned leadership. He mourned the lack of men of character.

The beach was crowded this afternoon. Dozens of windsurfers, kayaks, and sailboats zigzagged in the blue-green waters beyond the bathers. Every forty minutes or so a combat helicopter patrolled about thirty feet over the sea foam, part of the national strategy to protect the coast. On shore, thin, attractive teenagers played beach tennis. Their seniors played backgammon. Young soldiers were surrounded by female tourists. The U.N. soldiers in their blue berets were drinking beer at a beach-side cafe. Scandinavian tourists painted their fair-skinned bodies with thick white lotion. The children constructed anthill castles and sketches in the sand by the water's edge. Attractive women in bikinis did not go unnoticed, nor did they stay unaccompanied by men for long. The older folks protected themselves in the shade provided by the permanent mushroom-shaped structures, or they brought their own umbrellas. They wore big hats, and spoke enthusiastically with their hands, about the old country, old friends and wonderful grandchildren. The middle-aged men and women, like himself, lay back on their lounge chairs or blankets to secure a well-earned moment's rest from their workweek and routine.

Zadok felt responsible for them all, though he tried to dismiss that feeling as destructive and emotional. How innocent, how isolated they were from the threats that surrounded them. He knew they didn't worry because of their confidence in their army, especially their military intelligence. That meant they weren't worrying because of their trust in men like him. God, what was he going to do?

That night began as another sleepless night of staring at the ceiling. He began to think about his son and how much he loved him. But he must've fallen asleep, because he experienced an unusually clear and realistic dream. He found himself summoned to the top of a familiar mountain. It was the tallest of the Galilean hills that surrounded his moshav. There, he was greeted by a bronze figure. It turned out to be a man, and he was holding a flax stalk in one hand and a measuring stick in the other. He was naked from the waist up, and wore a strange, flat headdress. The bronze man was ushering him into a building. It was the school in Safed where his grandfather had taught and studied.

Zadok went into the school and was greeted by the blind man, who quickly disappeared. He was startled to see his bearded grandfather standing in the hall. When he recovered from the shock, Zadok realized that the old man bore a strong family resemblance to himself. He was dressed in a black suit and 1920s black derby hat. He had the look of kindness and sagacity that seems to come with age. Reuven Zadok, his grandfather, asked him what was troubling him. Zadok answered that he knew the enemies of Israel were gathering together with a frightening new arsenal and would soon attack Israel, and he didn't know what to do. The grandfather figure pointed to the bronze man and told Zadok to watch, that Zadok would soon learn what he must do.

Zadok agreed to watch. The bronze man was now clearly in Jerusalem, and carefully measuring and building something. After a while, Zadok guessed it was a sort of sanctuary. The bronze man suddenly stopped his work and turned to Zadok, as if finally convinced that he had Zadok's full attention. He said, "Son of Adam, look and listen carefully to what I do, for you were brought here so that I could show it to you. Declare all that you see to the house of Israel."

Zadok, seeing himself standing in awe, said that he'd comply. Zadok watched him perform the ancient sacrifice and prayer from the time of the Temple.

The next morning Zadok woke long before the alarm went off. It was easy to get out of bed and start the new day for a change. Zadok decided to visit the old yeshiva in Safed.

By six, he started out on his drive to Safed with renewed strength, passion, and purpose.

He had trouble finding the right street at first, but he managed to find several streets occupied by the best artists in the country. Safed was an artist colony as well as a spiritual and historical center. From there he eventually made his way to the yeshiva. He waited outside for a while. When he saw a few students come, he decided to enter the building. The blind clerk, who had just opened up the office by the entrance, seemed to remember him instantly by his voice.

No, he couldn't possibly remember me – too many years, Zadok thought.

The clerk immediately reached to the telephone and called Haim. Within two minutes Haim had joined them in the front office.

"My name's Robert Zadok."

"I know who you are. I remember," Haim said, extending his arm to shake hands.

"I'm impressed that you remember me. It was so long ago. My wife and I were on vacation in Tiberias and we saw the street sign."

"And you asked about Ramchal. Did you read your grandfather's book?

"Yes."

Haim nodded contentedly. "Have you returned to begin some study, perhaps?" Haim smiled. He seemed satisfied that he knew what the answer would be, and proud of the fact that his own little prophecy was coming true.

"Yes. I'd like that."

Haim smiled wider. "Excellent. Excellent. Let's go back to the library. I knew you'd come. It was just a matter of time. Excellent, excellent."

"Fine."

Zadok followed him down the corridor. He felt grateful that no more explanations were required. He was equally grateful that he could begin right away. He felt it was an astonishing efficiency for a school to waste no time. It was also clear how animated Haim was to receive another Zadok.

"I don't speak Yiddish, you know. Is everything written in Yiddish?"

"We've taken care of that. There were instructions to translate into English and Hebrew."

"Whose instructions?"

"Your grandfather's, of course. I did much of the translation myself," Haim said proudly.

"He actually requested that? Very strange, isn't it," Zadok said, but Haim didn't respond.

Zadok followed him into the office library. He remembered the room, the feeling of disorganization and chaos amongst the files and books and furniture. But he seemed to remember more than just the room. Once again he had a feeling of déjà-vu.

Despite the appearance of utter confusion, Haim managed to pull out the appropriate manuscripts. "This will provide a useful start," he said. "I'll keep pulling up the rest, and you can tell me what else you may need. I'll have one of the boys deliver everything to you. We have an empty office down the hall."

"Thank you."

"No problem. I'm very happy to have you study here, just as your grand-father, of blessed memory, studied here. You're welcome."

"Thank you."

"*Baruch Hashem*, blessed be the Name," Haim said.

Zadok began to go through the manuscripts and books. He preferred English over Hebrew, whenever it was available. He attempted to review a few yellowed pages of his grandfather's original Yiddish manuscript which had been rescued by an Arab family. The words were scrawled decades ago with a fountain pen. Looking at it seemed to connect him to the past.

Zadok leaned back in the flimsy chair and scratched his forehead. "How could Ezekiel possibly have really written that? How the hell could one man have had a vision of the future?" he said, out loud, attempting to critique his grandfather's analysis.

He couldn't deny it either. He, too, was beginning to feel the fascina-tion and excitement of the remarkable discovery, perhaps the same kind of excitement that his grandfather once felt long ago. How could Ezekiel have seen the twentieth century from over two thousand years ago? In fact, his grandfather had died before many of the projected prophecies were actu-alized. His grandfather went on to explain Ezekiel's mission to encourage Jews to retain their national identity and not assimilate into the dominant majority culture. The final component of Ezekiel's prophecy would be facilitated by the people's adherence to the values of their Mosaic roots. They should keep what is important in life in perspective and focus and avoid the temptations of vanity and contemporary idols.

He returned to the school every day for the next week.

Zadok began to see Ezekiel as a man struggling to describe future visions that he couldn't comprehend. For example, Zadok imagined Ezekiel describing a modern jet fighter when he said, "The sound of their wings was like the sound of many waters, like thunder. And out of its midst there was fire, flashing continually, as if it were gleaming bronze."

Zadok thought that Ezekiel was seeing the Holocaust when he said, "A barber's razor shall pass over your head and beard. A third part of you shall burn in fire. As men gather silver and bronze into a furnace, so I will gather you with the fire of my wrath."

The second component, the return to the Land, was apparently seen in great detail. Ezekiel said, "The Lord will cause the cities of Israel to be inhabited, the waste places rebuilt. The Lord will take the people of Israel from the nations among which they've gone and will gather them to their own land."

The third component, a return to God's favor, was now the most significant and relevant part of the scriptures and commentaries.

In this vision, God would show himself to the world by intervening on Israel's behalf. God would act against overwhelming forces, and provide sanctuary for the people of Israel.

Zadok felt there was a deeper message in these texts that he must research in order to fully understand.

Slowly a relevant strategy emerged through the fog. He thought he now knew what he must do. But he needed to know more.

Chapter Thirteen

For thus says the Lord God: Behold, I myself will search for my sheep, and will seek them out. As a shepherd seeks out his flock when some of his sheep have been scattered abroad, so will I seek out my sheep; and I will rescue them from all places where they have been scattered. And I will bring them out from the peoples, and gather them from the countries, and will bring them into their own land; and I will feed them on the mountains of Israel, by the fountains, and in all the inhabited places of the country. I will seek the lost, and I will bring back the strayed, and I will bind up the crippled, and I will strengthen the weak, and the fat and the strong I will watch over; I will feed them in justice.

Zadok didn't know where else to turn. He called Tex.

"What do you have in mind?" Tex said.

"Something a little unusual. There are old texts, scriptures, in Iraq. They're Jewish books, very old and valuable. In particular, I'm interested in one book. I don't need the original. A copy would do. You have access to places in Iraq that I don't. Can you help me? It's more important than you know."

"A whole book?"

"No, that would be impractical. Just a section. I'll fax you the details. I've also suggested the likely location. It is near an old canal by the river Chebar."

"You're not asking for an artifact, just a copy of an artifact? Strange.

Can't see what that has to do with weapon systems. You are Bob Zadok, the weapons guy? Don't tell me you've had a religious awakening? You born again or something?"

"Can you do it?"

"If it's there. Of course," Tex said.

"Will there be expenses?"

"Maybe the usual bribes."

"I want a separate accounting for this. This is personal. I'll pay the expenses myself," Zadok said.

"Fine."

"You understand that I'm asking you to do this as a personal favor for me? Not a request of my government?"

"Not a problem. Strange, but not a problem."

"Thank you."

"Anything else?"

"No."

"You owe me big time."

Zadok laughed. "More than you know."

* * *

Zadok became so absorbed by his readings at the yeshiva that he worked through two nights, stopping only for a few hours' sleep when he couldn't go on. There was a sofa in Haim's office and he went to it a few times when he got sleepy. When he awoke, he got up right away and went back to his reading.

Zadok knew Haim was anxious to help. Zadok involved him by asking him a question, the kind of question he knew a Talmudic scholar would relish. "How do you think we know what God wants us to do?"

"Answering that question is the whole basis of our religion. But let me answer this way. No one knows what God's voice was like when he spoke to Abraham or Moses. But somehow they were moved to understand what it was that they had to do. Even when doing it went counter to their own wishes."

"So you're saying that if it happens, we'll know?"

"But be careful not to assume that you know. An assumption of God's wish is like...well, it's idolatry. Terrible acts have been committed throughout history in the name of presuming God's intent. The terrorists speak of God's will."

In a few weeks Zadok received a document wrapped in newspaper from Tex. Zadok opened it with the enthusiasm and anticipation of a child. Yes, it was all there, and he let out a cheer. He needed help with the translation, but now he had the confidence and information to proceed.

Haim helped with more than the translation. He helped Zadok pull together all the pieces to the puzzle.

Many of Ezekiel's prophecies came true in his lifetime. Many came true centuries later. And some had yet to be realized. Ezekiel consistently demanded adherence to strict Temple ritual, which he saw as a way for the people to acknowledge God's hand in the events of man. He described his encounters with the chariot-throne, which were subsequently also described by the merkabbah mystics, kabbalistic books, the Dead Sea Scrolls, Ramchal, and Reuven Zadok, among others. Insights into the practices of a limited number of learned individuals who were able to comprehend the deepest levels of Torah knowledge were passed down from generation to generation of mystics. These secrets needed to be taught privately for fear they would be abused, ridiculed, misinterpreted, or misapplied by the masses, and so the knowledge came to be known as secret.

"These visions all seemed to come during times of turmoil, the Babylonian exile, destruction of the Temple, the first return from exile, the Roman wars. But what was going on during Ramchal's time that was so apocalyptic?"

Haim smiled. "Before the Ramchal's time, most Jews understood that scientific knowledge and Torah knowledge did not conflict with each other. The Rambam, one of our greatest sages, was a scientist and a doctor himself. But as scientific knowledge spread among the nations, some began to lose their clarity, and many began to assimilate into non-Jewish cultures," Haim said. "The roots of the problem were just beginning during Ramchal's vision."

"So the prophecies could have been warnings, not a view of predetermined events?"

Haim nodded.

"Could my grandfather have experienced the chariot-throne first-hand?"

Haim froze at first, then seemed to prepare his answer. "He never discussed it, but he did write about it. The picture in the book, you remember – that was from his experience, his own vision, nothing else."

"I remember."

Zadok leaned back in his chair and rubbed his chin.

"What are you thinking?" Haim asked.

The questioned prompted Zadok back from his daydream. "I have the answer," Zadok replied confidently, sitting up straight.

"The answer?"

"To facilitate the prophecy we must perform the ancient sacrifices as described by Ezekiel."

Haim shook his head but hesitated before speaking.

"It's everywhere in his writings," Zadok insisted. "It's what he cared about. It must be the way to facilitate the final component of his visions. It must be."

"You are serious about this, aren't you?" Haim said, "But no, it's specifically forbidden to perform those rituals outside of the Temple. It would be a grave sin."

"The Samaritans do the sacrifice for Passover."

"They're not Jews."

"I read about Yemenites who did the sacrifice."

"No. There are Cohanim who study the rituals so they shouldn't be forgotten. But it is forbidden to do the sacrifice. It hasn't been allowed since the Romans destroyed the Temple."

"I've read that it was performed in Egypt after the destruction of the Temple."

Haim waved downward and grimaced to show his disgust. "That was a Temple erected by exiles in Egypt, as if they could replicate the Jerusalem Temple. But they were wrong to do so. There is only one legitimate place in the world for the Temple."

"I'm not convinced," Zadok said.

Still soft-spoken and supportive, Haim retained his patience. "Keep in mind that while Ezekiel insisted on strict adherence to Temple rituals, including the sacrifices, he had survived the destruction of the Temple. So he knew how to worship in exile during the Temple and after the Temple. I can refer you to very learned rabbis, perhaps you'd like to see one?"

"Thanks. Won't be necessary," Zadok said while rising.

Zadok decided to personally research a magazine article about Yemenites who practiced the ancient Temple rituals, including animal sacrifice. It seemed that one name on the list had especially good credentials in the long forgotten dogma and techniques. The man's name was Yitzhak Levi; according to a source at the Hebrew University that was quoted in the article, Levi was truly genuine. He had learned the strange, detailed, and elaborate practices as a secret family rite, not from a theoretical textbook. The article said this man had learned the ancient rituals as a youth in Yemen, and continued to the present day.

Zadok drove to find him in a small village called Kfar Timini, serviced by a circular dirt road. The old man lived alone in a stucco hut. Inside there was a bed, a chair, many books, and a silver goblet and candlesticks. A worn camel hair tapestry was on the hard floor. The old man was sitting on the bed. He wore a Yemenite turban, a short white beard, and white side curls that came down over his ears. The Yemenite's shirt was much too heavy for the day's temperature. Zadok wondered if it was the only shirt he owned. The Yemenite's face was dark and wrinkled, toothless save for only two or three broken back teeth.

Zadok asked the old man if he was Yitzhak Levi, though he was sure of the answer.

The old man nodded.

"They tell me you're knowledgeable in the ancient rituals of the Temple Priests and their descendants, the Cohanim. Are you?"

This time the old man shrugged.

"You a Levi?" Zadok said.

"Yes," the Yemenite said.

"My name's Reuven Zadok. I'm contemplating renting some land in East Jerusalem and hiring a contractor to build a sanctuary to the exact biblical measurements. I want to pray and sacrifice there when it's finished. Will you help me?"

The old man said nothing. Then Zadok decided to repeat what he had said much louder and in slow, deliberate Hebrew.

This time Zadok's offer seemed to interest the old man, but the Yemenite still hesitated.

"I'll pay for all the expenses, for everything you need. What do you say? Will you do it?"

Still he was quiet.

"I'm sincere. I want to pray to God in the old ways. I need someone who's really done it before."

Levi made the "tt" sound while shaking his head. It was a Middle Eastern way of expressing there was a substantial roadblock.

Then the old man stood up. He was little more than five feet tall. "If you are speaking of the sacrifice, I have never done it. I have learned how it should be done, but I've never done it."

"Never?"

"The Temple site is occupied. And even if there were a Temple on the holy ground, the sacrifice must be done by a Cohen."

"I've read that you have done it."

Levi shook his head. "Never."

"But before Yom Kippur, there is a ritual with roosters and chickens…"

Levi laughed. "*Kapparot*, you're thinking of *kapparot*. It's a form of atonement. But the animals aren't sacrificed, they are slaughtered in the normal way and donated to charity."

"Sorry. My source was incorrect?"

"There is no Temple. There's nothing to discuss."

Zadok thanked the old man and turned away. He had not found the answer. Haim was right. Damn it. Why did he feel compelled to find a spiritual answer? It was nuts, really nuts. The medication must be affecting his mind.

* * *

Zadok completed his required radiation treatment, but continued taking his medication. He felt better as soon as the treatments stopped.

Soon he resumed his job and his daily updates to Ben Zion. The enemy intentions were becoming obvious as they moved more missile sites into position. There was talk about attacking the missile production facilities, but again inertia amongst the politicians set in. No decision was made except to wait. Zadok pleaded with Ben Zion to continue to use his influence to force the issue. They had to strike now before it was too late.

Large numbers of enemy troops were observed approaching the borders. Finally, the decision was made to call up several Israel Defense Force reserve battalions.

Zadok ordered the command bunker that they had used during the war cleaned up. Then he spent a day there to ensure that the communication systems were working. Zadok also learned that his son Jonathan was stationed somewhere on the northern frontier.

* * *

Zadok went to the Western Wall in Jerusalem and pressed his hand against the cold stones. This time the wall was more than a historic symbol and connection to the past. He was seeking something from the Wall: truth, answers, comfort, help. He was aware that within his heart a trace of spirituality was emerging.

Something was driving Zadok. He decided to visit the Dome of the Rock. He arranged for an Arab tour guide named Ibraham to bring him to the holy site, which Ibraham explained was a shrine for Muslim pilgrims, not a mosque for prayer.

Zadok removed his shoes and followed Ibraham. Then Ibraham ceased lecturing and stepped ahead of Zadok. Zadok just stood there a while looking around, admiring the arches, the marble and mosaics. There were large Roman-style columns supporting the archways and encircling the rock. The light allowed a golden hue to highlight the holy spot. The shrine was a most impressive example of Roman and Islamic architecture.

Zadok focused on the rock, the one place on earth that could boast being credited for so much. This was the site where Abraham prepared an altar to sacrifice his son Isaac. Two Jewish Temples were erected here, the one and only place where the ritual sacrifice was permitted. The Romans built temples to Jupiter on the site. It was where Jesus debated with the Pharisees. It was where Mohammed was carried at night on a winged steed to the temple that is most remote. And where Abd al-Malik built this architectural wonder.

The light got brighter and Zadok shivered. He suspended his disbelief for a moment and accepted his calling to facilitate the ancient prophecy. And as he thought about it, he realized the answer was there all along and he should have realized it. His grandfather had experienced a vision by a river, maybe not like Ezekiel's vision, but he had nevertheless been inspired to write, just as Ezekiel had been inspired to write and to influence the Jews.

Reuven Zadok, his grandfather, was nothing less than a visionary with a message.

*   *   *

The next day Zadok went back to the yeshiva in Safed to meet with Haim. He asked Haim to bring the Hebrew versions of his grandfather's manuscript to a reputable printer. "Tell them to print ten thousand copies."

"What would you do with so many copies?" Haim asked.

"Distribute them free to synagogues, seminaries, yeshivas, schools, libraries, whoever will take them and make sure they're read," Zadok enthusiastically responded.

"It'll be expensive."

"I'll pay for it. We don't have a lot of time to get it done. Can we do it? Can you get volunteers to help with the distribution?

Haim nodded and began to relax. "Wonderful, just wonderful," he said calmly. "You are sacrificing your time and money, not for yourself, but for the people. This is the highest of blessings. The right kind of sacrifice. You are spreading your grandfather's message as he had wished. *Kol hakavod*, all honor to you," Haim applauded. He stood up and shook Zadok's hand.

Zadok assigned a reservist, a burly native from Tel Aviv named Yossi Blumenthal, to manage the logistics.

"Can you truck books around the country?"

"I can do that."

"What do you do in real life, Yossi?"

"I work for *Mizrach*."

"The newspaper? Are you a reporter?"

"Yes, I work for the newspaper. No, I'm not a reporter. I used to be a photographer, but now I work in personnel. More money, a promotion, you know."

"This isn't an assignment that needs any publicity. Can I trust you?"

"Don't worry about it. My current reserve assignment is in the kitchen. I'd take almost anything over that."

"You'll keep it quiet?"

"Hey, don't worry. Want me to do it or not?"

Two weeks later Haim called. "We have a problem."

"What?"

"We need another thirty thousand shekels."

"What? I paid the printer his price in advance."

"We need more copies."

"I don't understand."

"When word got out we were printing Reuven Zadok's unpublished manuscript and giving it away free, we got calls from all over Israel. Actually, from all over the world."

"Huh?"

"We still can't meet the demand. And we need more trucks to deliver the books."

"Okay, okay. I'll see what I can do about the trucks. The money is another matter."

* * *

It didn't take long before the media covered the story of the distribution of free copies of a long lost manuscript. Zadok came home late Tuesday evening, and, just before going to bed, he turned on the television and then sat on the couch to catch the news.

A young blonde from Channel 12 News was explaining that Reuven Zadok was a kabbalist scholar and writer and that the distribution of his unpublished manuscript was stimulating substantial buzz in kabbalist and Orthodox circles. Then she walked over and stood beside Haim near the front gate of the Safed yeshiva.

Zadok laughed at seeing old Haim on television, standing away from the woman and trying to avoid the camera. "Haim is a celebrity," Zadok joked to himself out loud.

"Why wasn't the manuscript published long ago?" the attractive reporter asked Haim.

"Reuven Zadok was my teacher," Haim said slowly, apparently getting past the issue of being on television. And he showed no signs of stage fright. He was loving the role of expert on his teacher and mentor. "I knew my teacher while he was working on the manuscript, and he was very specific about the manner and circumstances under which it should be distributed."

"And those circumstances, are they right for now?"

Haim nodded.

"Can you explain what you mean by circumstances?"

Haim just shrugged.

"Why not give it to a publisher? Why give it away?"

"The circumstances are right to do it now and in this manner."

"And how is it being received?"

"Unbelievable," Haim said, retaining a calm monotone. "We have requests from all over the world. It is like we've released an unfinished symphony from one of the great classical musicians."

Then Channel 12 showed a series of clips, one quickly after the other, of reactions from average on-the-street Israelis. The reporter asked each of them, "What do you think of the excitement around the discovery of a manuscript by Reuven Zadok?"

"Who?" said a college student.

"What the religious have to say has nothing to do with me. Who cares what they say," said a cab driver.

"When the religious community starts to work better with the secular, then we'll have something to read about," said an office worker.

"He's a kabbalist. I have no interest in that stuff," said a middle-aged man wearing a skullcap.

"If he's appealing for all the Jews to come back to their common roots and overlook their differences, I think it's great. What could be bad about that?" observed a young woman pushing a baby carriage.

A week later Haim called again. Donations were pouring in. There was enough money now to print tens of thousands more copies. And they'd added three more printers to keep up with the demand.

*   *   *

When Zadok came home the next day, he discovered that Shoshana was waiting for him and ready to explode. Any improvement in their relationship that began with the discovery of his cancer was apparently gone. "I went to the bank this week to make a deposit in our joint account, and the account was almost empty. All our money gone. Do you have any idea how that happened?"

"Yes, I was going to tell you this weekend."

"You were going to tell me this weekend. What did you do? You were going to tell me after you spent the money? What did you do with it? Or should I ask who did you spend it on? Where have you been all these nights? Who have you been with?"

"Calm down. It's nothing like that."

"Don't tell me to calm down. You make me squeeze change for years. You get upset when I buy meat, leave on a lightbulb, or some other extravagance. And then you go and blow it all in a few weeks?"

"It was for a good purpose."

"What?"

"Well, I…I…"

"What?"

"It's proprietary. National security."

"Oh, so the national budget for security now includes my personal account?"

"No – "

"It's bull. How can you lie like this?"

"I'm not."

"What am I supposed to believe?"

"You may find this hard to believe. But I'm trying to facilitate an ancient prophecy."

"You're what?"

"It's a long story, but do you remember the yeshiva in Safed?"

Zadok recognized that Shoshana was looking at him as if he had gone mad. "You remember?"

She didn't answer.

"It'll all become obvious soon, but I – "

"Get out of my sight," Shoshana screamed. "Get out. Get out. Get out."

* * *

Zadok drove to the underground army shelter. All the way he blamed himself. How could he find fault with Shoshana for feeling the way she did. He could be dying from the cancer, and the last thing he did was spend all their resources. And he didn't even communicate about it. But how could he tell her? What could he tell her that made rational sense? He knew what he had done wasn't a responsible thing to do, especially with five children. Damn, he did dumb things sometimes. And what was he doing while the enemies of Israel gathered for an attack? He was researching ancient rituals, as if he had to do a doctoral thesis or something. Why did he feel he needed to do these things? What was wrong with him? He thought about calling a shrink. His doctor suggested that he see one, didn't he? Could that be the issue after all?

The next day, from the underground shelter, he reviewed the latest "hot line" information, called his staff, and then put in a call to Ben Zion. He scarcely got out his update, when Ben Zion began to yell at him.

"Is this true? Did you call on an American contact to use their operatives? We heard they risked their lives to research a book for you? What's that all about?"

"Well, I asked him to do me a favor. It wasn't an order. And it wasn't research for a book. It was data from a book."

"What's the matter with you? You know how risky that is? Especially now when everyone's on the edge? An operative's like gold now. We're on the verge of a war, and you decide to do archeology or something? There's a time and a place. You know that, don't you? What's so damn important about a damn book? Are you going to school? Have you lost your priorities? I keep pushing the cabinet to move on your recommendations. What'll they think about you and me if they hear about this?"

"I don't know how to explain."

"You're damn right you don't know. I don't want to hear anything more about this, or anything like it. Understood?"

"Yes."

As if to underscore his lost confidence, Ben Zion said, "You get the shelter cleaned out?"

"That's done. I'm there now."

"I don't want to hear anything more like this."

After Ben Zion hung up, Zadok wondered to himself what the general would think if he knew he had seriously considered performing ritual animal sacrifices. In a short time he had managed to lose his health, his marriage, his money, and his career.

"God help me," he thought.

He wanted a drink. He wanted to go running. He wanted to pray at the Wall.

He managed, after a while and after considerable effort, to shake off the scolding and get back to work. He continued to process the intelligence that came in, give appropriate instructions, and do the analysis on the enemy missile systems. That was his job, and he couldn't let anything interfere.

He attempted to sleep in the shelter, but once again he spent most of the night staring at the ceiling. He worried about his son, his country, his marriage, his job, his finances, his health. Still he knew he had to persevere in whatever way he could to facilitate the realization of the prophecy. It was, he knew, an unlikely possibility that the antique writings of a potential visionary would come true, or that his grandfather's manuscript would in some way facilitate realization of the final component of the prophecies. It was very unlikely that Israel's problems would be solved by anything other than her own resolve and initiatives. And if, by some miracle, the prophecy did have a hand in the impending crisis, why did he feel such a strong need to facilitate it?

He knew he couldn't answer his own question. There was something inside, something that had become a part of him, that compelled him to continue. He would work at his job with every ounce of his energy, and, as a backup strategy, he'd continue his new spiritual calling. It was another long night until the dawn.

The next day he worked as hard as he could to make sense of the increasing amounts of data and intelligence coming across his desk. He was exhausted by seven at night, but he decided to go for a run. It was good to run again, a refreshing run, and he felt reasonably relaxed when it was over. He hoped that meant his health was restored. He showered at a public facility, although he hated them because they were filthy and the shower heads were always missing.

He stopped at a cafe and ordered a glass of Israeli brandy. The brandy was harsh, but Zadok wasn't drinking for the usual pleasure of drinking. He needed the alcohol to deal with the unrelenting anxiety over his multiple failures.

He rubbed his face and temples. It seemed hopeless. To his mind, a terrible war was inevitable. The public wasn't fully aware of the danger. The government was failing to deal with it. His own son was on the line to meet the initial frontal attack. His marriage was in danger. Maybe it had already ended and he didn't know it yet. His career was certainly over. War or no war, he figured he'd have to be looking for a civilian job when the crisis was over.

Who would hire him, he wondered. What did he know how to do except analyze input from agents?

It didn't matter, the cancer could grow and then it'd all be academic. There would be no money left for Shoshana and the kids. He'd seen to that. But the moshav might be able to help out. They'd get by. He allowed himself the melancholy thought that maybe they'd be better off without him.

What was he doing about all his problems? He didn't know what else to do except to facilitate the prophecy through prayer. The need for prayer wasn't so bizarre; most people would find that understandable given the circumstances. But he had to be different. He had to get involved with prophecies and visions. Why? What was it that compelled him to pursue prayer and ritual according to the biblical guidelines? Something bizarre that he didn't really understand. But the compulsion was definitely there. He couldn't deny it and he couldn't let go of it.

"Everything's gone wrong," he said to himself. Everything that he touched turned to garbage. What could possibly go wrong next?

When he returned to his desk at the underground shelter, he found a message from Shoshana to call. He did so immediately.

"Hi, it's me. How are you?" he said.

"Fine. You?"

"Thanks for asking. I'm okay, I think."

"I've calmed down. I just don't deal well lately with surprises."

"I understand."

"I still don't understand what you said."

"I know that I didn't explain myself very well," Zadok said.

"Well, anyway, the reason I called is to tell you that your sister called. She sounded very upset. I thought you'd want to know."

"I'll try calling her as soon as we're done. But you've got to give me a little time. Everything that I've been working on will become obvious soon. I can't talk about it now. All I need is a few weeks. Then I should be able to explain. Will you give me the time?"

Shoshana hesitated. "When are you coming home?"

"Tonight?"

"See you tonight," she said.

"See you," Zadok answered, relieved.

He phoned his sister, but only got the answering machine.

Yossi Blumenthal walked into his office. "I took care of your distribution problem. Just wanted to let you know that your grandfather's book is spreading over the land as we speak."

"I'm so relieved," Zadok responded with sarcasm, though he genuinely appreciated Yossi's help without a lot of questions.

After Yossi left his office, Zadok tried dialing Beverly again. It had been months since Beverly had called. Even longer since he'd called her. He was sure the call had something to do with his ailing parents. He prepared himself for bad news. Good news just didn't seem to be coming.

This time Beverly was home.

"Is that you?" Zadok said.

Beverly didn't say anything. It was evident that she was choked with tears and unable to speak.

Zadok wasn't sure she had recognized his voice. "It's me."

Beverly started to cry. "I know," she managed to say in between soft sobs.

Zadok waited until his sister regained some control.

"Kevin and I are finished," she said. "We're done as a couple."

"What? I'm sorry. Really. I'm sorry. Can you talk about it?"

After a while, she started to talk. And once she started talking, the story poured out as if the dam had broken.

"He moved out. Then I found out he's got another apartment where he's been living with his nurse bimbo. I went over and found the little whore in the apartment. I also found hash and coke and other drugs in the closet, and a whole collection of porno videos. They've been having this affair, I found out, since last year. Can you imagine? And I had the bimbo over to my house for Christmas dinner. I was feeding her and entertaining her, and all the while she was sleeping with my husband. I slapped her skinny face when I saw her in his apartment. Then when the word got out about our separation, I started getting phone calls from other nurses and receptionists who had worked for him. Some of them told me that they'd had an affair with him, and that telling me helped them deal with their guilt. Some told me that he'd harassed them, and some said they knew he had had sex with his staff in the office. What did I do to deserve this? I can't believe it. The lawyer told me to hire a detective. It turns out he was using our joint account for trips and gifts for the bimbo and his other playmates. Can you believe it? I paid half the cost for them to party in Key West and Jamaica and who knows where."

"I'm sorry. I'm very sorry to hear all this. I can only imagine how you must feel."

"It hurts, it hurts so much. It feels like I've been beat up. I feel like I've been kicked in the belly." She started to cry again.

"I don't know if it'll help now. But I'm sure as time goes by, the hurt will go away. Time will heal."

"Can you come visit soon? I know you're busy, and it's a lot to ask."

"Of course, I'll come. Just as soon as I can. There's a lot going on right now, but when it all clears, I think I'll be able to arrange a visit to the States."

"Good. Thank you. It makes me feel better just to hear that someone cares," Beverly said.

"Of course I care. Hey, what's a brother for, anyway? You'll be okay in time. I know you will. You'll get past this. Kevin's the one who's lost something of value. Not you. Call me any time that you need to talk. I know you have a great support group with your girlfriends, but I think I can be a good listener, too."

"I know. You're a very good listener," she said.

"Just hang in there. He's the one who did wrong. Don't blame yourself. If what you found out gives you an honest picture of Kevin, you're much better off to finally find out and get rid of him."

"I suddenly realized I didn't know my husband at all."

"I know it's an awful lot to accept all at once."

"It's like I was living an illusion with a stranger. I was married to an image that didn't exist. It was a great image that I created, a perfect little family. I wanted it to be perfect so badly that I created it, my own reality."

"Don't get down on yourself." Zadok realized it was much easier to say.

"I'm not. I'm just realizing what a lying sociopath I was living with. I'm realizing what a fool they all took me for. It's kind of hard to accept."

"I know."

"You'll come when you can?"

"Yes. It may be a while. But I'll make every effort to make it happen soon. In the meanwhile, you call me, okay? And I'll call you, too."

"Okay. I'm feeling a little better."

"Good."

"Have you spoken to Mom and Dad?" Beverly added. "You should, you know. They're getting on."

"No, I haven't."

"I'm suggesting you should for your sake. I think you'll regret it someday if you don't."

"Okay, I'll call them."

"Really? You will?"

"Yes," Zadok said, but he knew he didn't mean it.

"How's Shoshana and your wonderful family? I'm sorry, I'm so caught up in my own issues, I neglected to ask."

"Oh, that's okay. They're fine, thank you. Everything here's just fine. No problems."

"You know," she said, "you really do have a wonderful, simple life there in the moshav."

"Thank you. Yes, nothing much happens out here."

* * *

Zadok was glad to be home. Sarah greeted him at the door with a big hug. She genuinely missed him. Shoshana offered to make him dinner, but he wasn't hungry. After a short jog, he drank two beers, but it wasn't enough to deal with the anxiety.

"Want to talk?" Shoshana said.

"Yes, but I can't tonight. I just need a little more time."

Shoshana didn't say anything, but Zadok knew how unhappy she was with his answers. He didn't know what else to say or do. His attention quickly moved on to one problem after the other, and he was mentally withdrawn from his wife and daughter. He had no answers for any of the problems. Just issues beyond his control. He forgot about the issue with Shoshana, and the other issues in his home and on the moshav. He was far way, floating from one impossible conflict to another, resolving nothing.

Later, in the middle of the night, Shoshana sat up in bed and turned on the light. "I can't let this go. It's bothering me. We have to talk," she insisted.

"It's okay, I'm up. Not sleeping well. Too many problems."

"But I'm your partner, aren't I? I'm your wife, remember. Talk to me. It could help."

"It won't help. Just a mess."

"Tell me anyway."

"There's the cancer. Problems at work. I think I've lost my relationship with Ben Zion. I may have to consider civilian life."

"Why? What happened with the general?"

"He's lost confidence in me. I'm delivering quality intelligence. But he flipped out because I asked my American friend to help me do some research on Reuven Zadok's manuscript."

"You did what?"

"I know. I know. Don't you start. Maybe the medication fried my brain."

"Tell him that. He knows you've been on heavy therapies. Talk to him. You can work through it."

"Think so?"

"It's not so bad considering all the good things you've done over the years. People are sympathetic to heavily medicated cancer patients. I've seen that. Anyone should understand what you've been up against."

Zadok pulled her closer against his chest. "You know, I think I do feel a little better. You were right."

"Always listen to your wife."

"I know, I know."

"Is that why you couldn't sleep?"

"One of the reasons. There's more. Can we talk about the rest another time?

"Men, they hate to talk. There's never a good time."

"How can you live with us? Why do you?"

"God knows," Shoshana sighed. "You can't solve problems without talking them out and attacking them."

"Attacking?"

She nodded. "Do you have time for another slower approach? Rip off the bandage and get the pain over with. Do it quick, don't pull it off hair by hair."

"I'm not as tough as you."

She moved closer and hugged him. "It'll be all right…as long as you do what I tell you."

They both laughed. For Zadok, laughter was especially welcome.

He was grateful she didn't bring up the missing money again. He knew that issue had to be eating away at her, but she put it aside for the moment and was trying to help. She was wonderful. He loved her and felt unworthy.

Chapter Fourteen

The hand of the Lord was upon me, and brought me in the visions of God into the Land of Israel, and set me down upon a very high mountain, on which was a structure like a city opposite me. When he brought me there, behold, there was a man, whose appearance was like bronze, with a line of flax and a measuring reed in his hand; and he was standing in the gateway. And the man said to me, "Son of man, look with your eyes, and hear with your ears, and set your mind upon all that I shall show you, for you were brought here in order that I might show it to you; declare all that you see to the house of Israel."

Zadok joined Yossi Blumenthal in a truck on a mission to deliver more books to Jerusalem. The air was too cool and blowing as they rode through the Judean hills, so they closed the windows. Zadok remembered the red and yellow lilies that had sprouted not long ago at the end of the rainy season in that valley. "Where have all the flowers gone," he said to himself. He feared they were approaching a difficult season with no flowers.

Yossi sang along to the radio as he drove. Zadok had had some misgivings over enlisting Yossi in this mission. His career and reputation, already in jeopardy, would certainly be destroyed if Yossi leaked the story. Zadok was relying on his judgment of Yossi, whom he liked and trusted. Yossi might have a rough exterior, but he was a good man with a compassionate heart. Zadok was confident that Yossi's promise to keep the enterprise quiet would be kept. Anyway, Zadok was grateful for the company.

They arrived at the school where the students were already waiting in anticipation. Yossi opened the back of the truck and pulled out a four-wheel dolly. He put it on the road and began to stack cases of books. He pushed the four-wheeler into the school, followed by six students each carrying a carton of books.

Zadok, now alone outside, looked up to the heavens, and specifically asked for the prosperity and security of Israel as promised in the scriptures. He went on specifically to ask, for the first time in his life, for God's hand in working out his personal and health problems, and protecting his family. "Amen," he said as he finished the prayer and turned back to grab and lift a carton.

"Well, what did you think?" Zadok said as Yossi returned. They climbed back into the cab.

"Weird stuff. Why are you doing it?"

"That's exactly right. It is weird stuff. No one would believe it. So there's no reason to talk about it. That's why I need you to keep what you see to yourself."

"I promised. Don't worry about me. But there's enough media coverage, so don't be surprised if your name gets into it."

"Glad you came?"

"Sure. I like weird stuff."

"What's that say about you?"

"Don't start," Yossi said. "What the hell do you think it says about you?"

Zadok laughed.

"I'm serious," Yossi said. "I mean why are you doing it?"

"I'm not doing it. They're doing it."

"But you're helping them. They tell me you financed it all. Is that true?"

"The manuscript has a worthy message. Why not share it?"

"Maybe I should read it one of these days."

"Maybe," Zadok agreed.

On the ride back, the music on the radio suddenly ended, and, thankfully, so did Yossi's accompaniment. Then they heard the announcer read military codes. "Bar Kochba's shield. The sword of Maccabbee. David's sling."

"They're calling more reserves," Yossi said.

"Something's going on. This is different."

After a few minutes of codes, the familiar beeps that began the news program were heard. The announcer reported that enemy missiles were being launched against Israel. That was all that was announced on the radio. Then the broadcast returned to calling reserve units.

"Step on it. Let's move. Let's get to the bunker as fast as this thing will go."

This was it, Zadok said to himself. It was finally happening. He hoped that the preparations they'd implemented would be enough.

The traffic was slow, sometimes not moving at all. Valuable hours passed.

They heard sirens as they came into the coastal area. Hitchhikers were everywhere. Teenagers were already out brushing blue paint over automobile headlights.

As they approached the base, there was a small line of traffic that moved too slowly for Zadok. He jumped out of the truck, thanked Yossi, and jogged toward the center of the base.

In fact, many people were running everywhere and in every direction. The nearby air raid sirens were piercing, forcing the officers to shout instructions even louder. Trucks, overloaded with troops, were already moving out, though more reserves were just coming in to join up with their unit. Adrenaline was gushing.

A long caravan of tanks on transports was coming to form, with soldiers swarming like ants above, around, and inside the tanks.

The jets were streaking regularly overhead, cracking the sound barrier with each pass.

In the rear center of the base, a little concrete structure stood alone, at the edge of a fenced-in field. The only other protrusions in the field were the air inlets, shaped like futuristic flying saucers. The were about six of these saucers, and they were reputed by design to increase survival probability, even in a nuclear attack.

Zadok ran to the bleached white entrance, then down the two steep narrow flights. The underground office was full with people standing, walking, or at the work stations. More people were still coming. Dov was already at the main computer terminal.

"What's happening?" Zadok asked.

Dov didn't hear him – there were too many conversations going on. Zadok approached closer and repeated his question.

"Missiles incoming," Dov said while maintaining his focus on the computer screen. "Large numbers of enemy troops ready to come in after the air assault."

"Targets?"

"So far strategic locations, not population centers. The bastards seem to know where our defenses are."

"Do we know where the missiles are coming from?"

"What we know, we've already communicated to Central Command. Many of our defensive missiles have been knocked out, but we do have a substantial air cover. We could've done a lot more, if only those politicians had listened to you."

"Forget that. That's history. Our job's to help win this thing. Now exactly where did the missiles hit?"

"Don't know yet. This thing just started."

Zadok reviewed the reports coming in. The enemy arsenals were enormous. Israel was very badly outnumbered and outgunned. It didn't look very good. This would be a different kind of war. He was afraid for the nation, but he couldn't show it. He knew it would be very costly.

Word came in that Tel Aviv had been hit. They didn't know how or where, but it appeared to be extensive. Then they learned of some successes in intercepting offensive missiles, but there were more failures as well. The air force wasn't doing well in going after the missile batteries. Zadok's team was trying to find accurate coordinates for the enemy missile sites. There were so many sites, and they only had information on an estimated 40 percent. Projections of enemy troop strength kept going up, as did the projections on the size of the enemy arsenal.

Zadok began to pace. He kept feeding the data to Central Command, but there was too much confusion to get a full picture of what was going on. He didn't know if the front lines had been shelled or penetrated. He did know there would certainly be a ground assault, as soon as the missile attack ended.

Then a report came in that two major air fields had been hit, with significant damage to the hangars and a few jets on the ground. It was becoming clearer that Israel's war resources and strategy had been seriously punctured.

Zadok and Dov looked at each other. "It's not going very well," Dov whispered, clearly discouraged.

"It'd be nice to get some good news," Zadok said. "Wars are still won by the quality of the men in the field. That's when we'll win this thing."

There were direct hits against Israel Defense Forces positions on the northern frontier.

Hours passed. It was becoming difficult to evaluate the intelligence coming in. Zadok wanted to be sure that his team's analysis was accurate and complete. At the same time, he knew that a delay in passing critical pieces could be a mistake. Zadok stood behind Dov as he put data into the computer. Sometimes Zadok went to the adjacent work station in order to toggle between several screens.

Then the shelter began to shake. At first it felt like little vibrations which they barely noticed. They ignored it.

Then the shaking increased more and more until bits of ceiling started falling.

"There must've been a close hit," someone said.

The concrete was cracking and dust and stones were falling on them. Phone lines started going dead. The computer went dead. People lost their balance and fell down. Zadok held onto a column. Someone was holding a handkerchief against a bleeding nose. A young girl screamed. A few people ran to the stairs but the exit had become blocked. There was a puddle of blood on the floor. A large crack on the tile floor was getting wider and longer. The floor started to open.

Zadok wanted to ignore the tremors. He wanted to keep his focus on the big picture of the war.

"We've been hit," Dov said.

"Isn't it supposed to be nuke proof down here?" someone yelled.

At first Zadok figured they had sustained a direct hit, but the tremors and shaking kept getting bigger and bigger. It just wasn't ending. Zadok wasn't sure what was happening.

A whole hour passed of shaking and people holding on, some people falling, of dust and stones and concrete chunks dropping on them, and it was still going. There was no choice but to finally shift their focus to the very real problems in the shelter.

It was useless staying there. All the data stopped coming in, and they were unable to do the computer analysis with the data that they did have. Zadok went to help in the effort to open up the exit. It was slow because dust was everywhere and it was becoming difficult to see. It was getting hot as hell in the shelter, and many of the men had taken off their shirts. It appeared that a cave-in had closed off the stairs, and they were digging with file drawers to recreate the opening.

Then the lights went out, and in a few seconds the emergency lights came on.

They heard the sound of concrete crumbling. All eyes looked up to the ceiling.

Zadok was beginning to feel very hot and claustrophobic. He took off his shirt, and took a swallow of water from a canteen that had been offered. He returned to clearing a path. The team worked another half hour before reaching the exit.

When they finally saw sunlight, through the freshly cleared passage leading up to the stairs, they cautiously filed, one step at a time, one after the other, through the gap between the concrete slabs.

At first Zadok was momentarily blinded. The outdoor air was pure and wonderful, but, oddly, Zadok started to cough relentlessly. When he stopped coughing, he gratefully breathed in the dustless air. Then he realized that the tremors were continuing. The ground was still shaking. Well, at least nothing was falling on him any longer.

Then he became aware of loud explosions from far away. He assumed it was missile hits.

"What the hell's going on?" Dov said to him.

"Don't know," Zadok said.

Zadok saw Yossi and called him over.

"You all right?" Yossi asked.

The question reminded Zadok that he was caked in white dust and wearing an undershirt.

"Been out of communication for hours. Is there a phone line working?"

"We've been using the radio phone. I'll show you. Follow me," Yossi said.

Zadok and Dov walked behind Yossi. "Know what could be causing the shaking?" Zadok said. "Was there a nuclear hit? Multiple missiles hit nearby?"

"No, nothing like that. The missile attacks stopped two hours ago."

"Stopped?"

"It's over. You haven't heard? It's over. No more missiles."

Zadok stopped in his tracks and stared at Yossi.

"Heard it confirmed on the radio," Yossi said.

"But the shaking, and the explosions?"

Yossi shrugged.

Central Command confirmed that the missile attack had suddenly stopped at about the time the tremors started. There was no ground assault as yet, but Central Command had no intelligence on enemy troop movements or whatever else was going on.

"What do the pilots say?" Zadok said.

"No feedback."

That was an odd answer, Zadok thought. What did it mean? There certainly had to be resources they could use. Hadn't the air force penetrated enemy air space?

He turned to Dov. "Let's get a ride to the helicopter pad. We're flying to the northern frontier."

Dov nodded. "Okay," he said, but Zadok could sense his reluctance.

Zadok and Dov sat in the back of the helicopter, and the pilot sat alone in the front. Zadok was immediately aware that the tremors underfoot were absent. He'd gotten used to them, but now airborne, he couldn't help notice the different feeling underfoot. It was like the feeling of coming onto land after having been at sea for a while.

The air was gray and warm, almost foggy. There was a strange smell everywhere, something like foul charcoal, but he recognized it as a smell of war. He had smelled it before, long ago. Perhaps, he concluded, it was the forgotten smell of death. The cracking and explosions kept getting louder as they flew north.

As they approached the northern border, Israeli jets streaked by in all directions. The jets appeared to be without focus, going back and forth, always staying in Israeli air space, apparently unable or unwilling to go further north. The noise of the jets added to the eerie percussions coming from the north.

They flew about ten kilometers into enemy air space, when they first realized the air had become much cooler, and a wind hit the chopper, jarring it slightly off course. The pilot instantly corrected for the choppiness. Then they noticed bits of ashes, big as silver dollars, floating everywhere through the sky, like a light snow. They kept the course due north until the great cracking noise was so loud and offensive that they all had to put their hands over their ears.

Momentarily distracted because of the ashes and the explosive noise, they now took in the sight ahead.

Zadok rubbed his eyes. So did the others. The scene was cloudy, and perhaps what they thought they had seen was incorrect. Denial began to fade.

It was like a scene out of a science fiction or horror movie. They knew that they would be unable to advance further north.

Lightening bolts were shooting everywhere with no more than ten seconds between strikes, and no more than a kilometer between every bolt.

They turned the helicopter to the side to improve their view.

Everywhere to the north, as far as they could see, the heavens had filled with ominous black and gray electrically charged clouds, hurling lightning, followed by thunder. It was the tremendous pounding of the thunder that they'd heard so far away. There was so much thunder that the claps overlapped and became almost continuous. In addition, there were hailstorms shelling grenade-sized hailstones. Below, the earth seemed to be moving. Fires were everywhere. Some of the fires were triggering explosions, some were spitting rock like a volcano. Buildings seemed to be falling into the earth – they were consumed and gone. Smoke was shooting out of the ground like geysers in many, apparently random, locations.

"What in hell…" the pilot said.

It was more than an earthquake. The earth was opening up.

"I don't believe what I'm seeing," Dov said.

Zadok didn't say anything. He knew what was happening. More than anyone else he shouldn't have been surprised. But he was. He was as much in awe as the others.

It was a surreal vision, one that made them look four times, and still it wasn't enough. It hooked them hypnotically and made them feel like part of a disturbing dream.

They flew westward along the edge of the lightning storms, and when they came to a possible opening in the lightning and hail, Zadok wanted to fly into it. The pilot refused.

"That's guaranteed suicide," the pilot insisted, yelling as loud as he could in order to be understood.

Dov pointed to an area where the earth could be seen to be moving.

Zadok panned the view with field glasses, and was able to watch several structures in the process of collapse. The earth just seemed to open up, exposing fire and smoke, at just the right locations to destroy enemy positions.

The lightning seemed to get closer and more intense. The thunder made ripple sounds, louder and louder, then reaching a deafening climax, a pounding blow.

The pilot did agree to try to fly higher to get over the clouds. But the wind was too strong and forced them down in a sudden roller-coaster drop that brought their hearts to their throats, their white knuckles to the overhead restraints.

It appeared that the helicopter had been brought under control, then they experienced another rapid drop. This time Zadok and Dov fell to the floor. Zadok could see the earth coming at him faster and faster.

The helicopter was straining, against the background clamor of thunder and flashes and the cacophony of pelting hail.

There was no time. It would be over in a flash.

The earth swelled larger, coming fast at them.

They were within fifty meters of crashing when the pilot managed to level off, and then to swing quickly up to regain altitude.

They flew for only another thirty-five minutes before it started to get dark. They also were getting low in fuel. They decided to fly back to a nearby base.

Zadok was back on the shaking ground, so he called Central Command, but what could he tell them? Like the pilots, he could only describe what he'd seen from the border area, and that they were unable to penetrate enemy air space. There was still confusion over what was going on. Zadok wanted to tell them about the prophecy, and what he had done to facilitate it. He knew this wasn't the time. No one had the patience to listen to the kind of story he had to tell.

The thunder continued unabated.

Zadok realized that no one would believe his story. Only Yossi and Haim had any idea what he had done. He needed proof of what was unfolding.

"I've got to go back at daybreak."

"Why?"

"I've got to take photographs. It's the only way to document what's happening."

"That's fine," Dov said. "But can you tell me what's happening?"

"It's the realization of the ancient prophecy of Ezekiel."

"Come again?"

"Long story."

"If you've got an explanation for what's going on, I'd like to hear it."

"Fine, but first we need to get a chopper and a pilot who'll be willing to volunteer to bring us in. Even if the lightning continues. It's not an assignment I'd like to order someone to do. And we need cameras."

"I can fly the chopper," Dov said.

Zadok had forgotten that Dov had been a helicopter pilot. "Aren't you a little rusty?"

"Very rusty. But what other fool will volunteer for this mission?"

"Okay, let's do it."

Dov went to get the cameras. Zadok went to his briefcase to retrieve an old book.

When everything was set up, Zadok told Dov, "You may find this hard to believe, but the Holocaust was predicted long ago."

"Why are you bringing it up now?"

"It's relevant."

"Don't we have things to do now?"

"Indulge me. Just listen."

"Well, what difference did it make? Obviously no one would've believed this prediction, as you call it. No one was saved because of it. Besides, it's easy to predict major disasters."

"Okay, that's true. But the same prophet predicted the rebirth of Israel in the wake of the Holocaust."

"Well, I don't really – "

"Here's an old manuscript someone wrote that I recently received. I'd like you to read it. I think it'll address some of your skepticism."

"When the hell am I going to read this? Do I have time to go to a library?"

"We're not leaving until daybreak, or slightly before. You're going to see things you won't understand unless you read it."

"I won't understand what I will see? I already don't understand what I saw."

"The same prophet predicted what's happening now. What you'll witness will be the realization of the third and final component of Ezekiel's prophecies."

"And just what's this third component?"

"Well, I'm not very good at explaining these things, but apparently it's a way for God to show his hand by saving and redeeming Israel in this conflict. Why don't you read the manuscript? It has biblical portions and commentary."

"I don't know about this."

"Good. Read."

Dov tossed the folder containing Reuven Zadok's book into his satchel in a manner that showed his opinion of the whole subject, and went to one of the barracks. It would be a good idea for both of them to get as much rest as possible, Zadok thought. Tomorrow would be an incredible day.

*   *   *

Yossi agreed to join them and help with the cameras. Zadok was pleased because he knew his own photographic abilities could very well be inadequate.

They approached the frontier just before dawn. It appeared that the lightning, thunder, and hail were over, but the air temperature still dropped as they came near the target zone. The fires also continued, but some of them were starting to burn out. On the other hand, the earth movements were definitely still active.

"Okay, it's light enough," Dov said. "Here we go."

They crossed into enemy air space.

"Do you see anything that can shoot at us?" Yossi said nervously.

"Don't worry," Zadok said, with straightforward confidence, "they won't be able to shoot."

"How do you know?" Dov said.

Yossi also seemed surprised by Zadok's willingness to accept a new role as a consultant in the whole affair.

"Just be ready with the camera," Zadok said.

They held their breath. Then Yossi started his damn singing again. He must have been nervous, Zadok thought.

Nothing below except fires. Sometimes smoke. Sometimes a half truck or tank that had been burned out.

Then they came to the first of the missile bases that they would photograph that day.

Dov approached cautiously and slowed down the engine. He decided to come in from the right flank and just skirt over the edge of the fortress. He was the first to see anything. "Holy…" his voice trailed off.

"Oh, my God," Zadok said.

Yossi put down the camera because he didn't believe what he was seeing in the viewfinder.

"*Baruch Hashem*," Yossi said, which sounded peculiar coming from him. It was probably an expression recently picked up from being around religious students when he was delivering books.

The enemy missile launchers were destroyed and chewed into scrap metal, and the famous arrow missiles that they'd so feared had all been destroyed and broken into pieces. Buildings were sunken into the earth so that only bits of roof, gables, or chimneys were visible. There were sporadic fires. Blackened human parts and burned up corpses were everywhere. What had been trucks or other vehicles were now either burned out shells or twisted remnants, some barely visible above the ground. There were no more roads leading into or out of the place. It had become an isolated sample of hell.

Dov now shared Zadok's confidence, and he flew quickly over the site, darting from one smoking remnant to another. As he flew to each new location and realized what it was he was looking at, or who the grim remains might have been only yesterday, he kept saying, "Holy…holy…holy…"

Yossi was furiously clicking or zooming away with the cameras.

Zadok reached for the radio. What he'd been expecting was now confirmed. It was clearly safe to communicate.

"This is Central Command. Come in."

"Battery el-Tubal is totally destroyed. Confirmed destroyed. Will proceed as indicated in plan to the next battery in the flight plan."

"Roger. You've been approved to proceed."

"Suggest releasing the other choppers to proceed with the documentation." That was the signal for fifty helicopter crews to fly north.

"Roger."

At the next sight there were a few survivors of the lightning and hail. The survivors saw the helicopter and came out into the open with white flags and tried to surrender. But the ground was still moving and there were missile launchers still intact.

The business of destroying the arsenal was unfinished and there would be no mercy. Fires kept shooting out of the earth. The missile launchers fell into an open gulf; there was a tremendous black cloud of smoke that covered the earth. When it cleared, there were no more missiles, no more launchers, no more troops that could be seen trying to surrender. There were only several deep ragged caverns that seemed to go on and on down to the center of a fiery red earth.

Zadok, Dov, and Yossi spent the rest of the day flying on their predetermined route, collecting photographs and videos. Only after they'd returned to their base, and started to review the photos in a bunker, did the full effect of the sights hit them. They held the photos firmly and stared as if the photos themselves had become as significant as the burning bush. Yossi acquired an empty gaze and didn't say very much. He looked like a man who had touched an angel. Even Dov seemed to be changing his attitude. At least he wasn't sarcastic anymore.

Eventually, their passiveness turned into enthusiasm, and they began to aggressively assemble and catalog their photographs. The next day they had much more data from the other choppers as well as from a few land-based missions. Zadok supervised two teams for the next two days trying to make sense of everything they'd collected.

General Ben Zion called. "How are you?"

"Busy and very tired," Zadok said.

"It's an incredible story. I'm sure you understand why I was so skeptical."

"Of course."

"The Americans are asking questions. They don't understand all this. They think we used some new weapon or bomb or something."

"That's understandable."

"Think you can set them straight? We really don't mind sharing this with their military. Maybe they can help shed some light on it for us. They've got satellite photos that might be different from ours, and they're willing to share now."

"You asking me to go to the States?"

"Just a quick trip. A meeting in New York. A meeting in Washington. Then home. You don't have to go right away. You can finish what you're doing. Just let me know the date you want and I'll set it up."

"Fine. If I'm going to New York, I'd also like to go to Boston while I'm there."

"Of course. I'm going to Washington in two days, so I'll meet you at the meeting there. We'll be just a few hours at the Pentagon. The ambassador will join us."

"That's fine." Zadok was pleased by the apparent opportunity to visit his sister.

"I appreciate this."

"I'm happy to do it," Zadok said. "I want to set the record straight. I don't want all kinds of rumors and falsehoods. I want to deliver the facts as we know them."

"Great. See you in Washington."

Yossi came in. His empty gaze was gone now, replaced by a seemingly anxious passion. "You've got to let me tell about the prophecy. Otherwise, the whole thing will never be properly understood. It'll all be in vain."

"Do you think they'll believe you?"

"I don't know. Some will. And then we have the photographs and you and Haim."

"Will anyone but the religious find Haim credible?"

"I can make sure it's done right. The way you would want. Will you release me from the promise to keep it quiet?"

Zadok hesitated a moment, but then relented. "Declare all that you see to the house of Israel," he said.

"What?"

"Nothing. I appreciate what you did for me. Do what you think's best. Just keep me out of it."

"You got it. Thank you."

*   *   *

It took two more days of work in the underground bunker to complete the analysis. There was no doubt that the enemy threat was over. There was no longer an enormous arsenal and war machine facing them. But how it all happened was not quite so clear.

Zadok drove home to the Galilee that night.

It was late when he arrived. Shoshana was alone reading a newspaper in the living room.

"Hello, how are you?"

"Fine. You must be tired. Want me to make you something?"

Zadok could sense that something had happened. Shoshana seemed exhausted.

"Thanks for offering, but I'm not hungry. Everything okay with the kids?"

"They're fine."

"Jonathan okay?"

"Yes, he's fine."

"Something wrong?"

"I don't know what to think. The TV crews were here today. They came to our house."

"What did you tell them?"

"I didn't know what to tell them. I'm a little shook up by all the attention."

"How did the kids take it?"

"They had a good time, I think. I don't think it bothered them."

"Good. Well, I came home to pack. They want me to go to the States for a few days. It'd be a good chance to see Beverly, so I'm going."

"What's going on?"

"You mean about the prophecy?"

"Yes, I think so. There were newspaper reporters also here today. They were asking everyone in the moshav about you. I had to stop answering the phone. They say you're in the middle of this thing. I don't understand. I know you started to tell me about it, and I know I didn't give you a chance to explain. I don't know, it doesn't make sense."

"I'm not sure I understand myself, but I'll tell you what I know."

He related everything he had done at the yeshiva and with the old manuscript while he packed. Shoshana listened and helped him find the things he wanted to put in his bag. She just listened, neither accepting nor denying. She seemed to be withholding judgment. When the packing was done, Zadok kissed her and went to the door.

"Call me when you land?"

"Okay," Zadok said.

He drove back to the base. He reviewed with Dov the catalog of photographs and slides that Dov had already selected to be appropriate for their presentation.

"Good job," he said. "These should be pretty convincing."

"Thank you."

Zadok turned back to Dov. "Ready to go to the airport?"

Chapter Fifteen

The word of the Lord came to me: Son of man, set your face toward Gog, of the Land of Magog, and prophesy against him and say, Thus says the Lord God: Behold, I am against you, o Gog; and I will turn you about, and put hooks into your jaws, and I will bring you forth, and all your army, all of them clothed in full armor, a great company, all of them with buckler and shield, wielding swords; Persia, Cush, and Put are with them, all of them with shield and helmet; Gomer and all his hordes.

Zadok suddenly realized he had been staring at the obliging stewardess and looked away. He had absolutely no interest in other women, but her face had the compelling delicate beauty that suggested a gentle and sweet inner self. Besides, he noticed that her eyes seemed drawn to Dov, whose confidence and smile could, when he wanted, enamor anyone.

Dov was short, about five feet six inches, but ruggedly good-looking. He had dark, thick brown hair which he combed straight back in wide locks. He had a square jaw, prominent chin, and considerable strength in his arms and legs.

Zadok leaned back in his chair, properly returned to the "upright" position as instructed for landing, and looked out the window into the fog of clouds. He was amused that Dov was oblivious to the casual attraction evident in the pretty stewardess's face. Dov didn't usually miss those signals. Zadok's amusement faded as he realized that this was one more reminder of his middle-aged status. Was it that long ago that he might himself have been the recipient of such flattery? Welcome to the trauma common to middle-aged men, he thought, when all young women become beautiful. The only consolation was that he had finally developed a little ability to read faces. He had never been a very good poker player in his youth.

All in all it hadn't been a bad flight. Other flights back and forth to America or Europe had put him in ninety-degree temperatures because of defective ventilation, or in chairs that didn't lean back, or in the last row adjacent to where the Orthodox conduct their morning prayers, or in the seat next to a baby with colic, or next to the passenger who got into a fight with the chief steward.

Dov reached across him and pointed at a great bridge and two sky-scrapers that seemed to project out of the sea of New York real estate. The glamour of traveling had faded a long time ago for Zadok, but this time was different – the purpose was very different – and he was feeling like an anxious tourist.

Ah, old New York. It wasn't the size and scale of the buildings and bridges, nor was it the diversity of entertainment, or the extremes of wealth and poverty that he had come to appreciate about America. It was more subtle: the bounty of central heating and air conditioning, the telephone system, the distribution of foods and materials, the depth and availability of services and skills, the nursing care, the orderly queues, the massive markets, and to some extent the know-how and follow-through.

"Don't forget the file," Zadok said to Dov as they were getting up to retrieve their coats from the overhead compartments.

"Not a chance," Dov said. He was holding onto the satchel full of pictures even while putting on his waist-length black leather coat.

Tsiyon, their travel companion from security, stepped up behind them. "Wait for everyone else. Then we'll go," Tsiyon said in a soft monotone. Then predictably Tsiyon looked around, always careful, always detailed in his approach to everything. He was a big man, uncomfortable in his tight-fitting suit, with thin black and white hair, and thick exaggerated features, especially his ears and lips. He had a scar which brought curious character to his half-hairless left eyebrow, and it was easy to see the deep lines of experience above, around, and below his eyes. Zadok thought Tsiyon must have been tough as hell as a young man, but then again, Tsiyon was still tough. Tsiyon was born in Iraq and could easily have been taken for an Arab, but socially he had more the characteristics of a proper Viennese, and he was considered very competent.

"Fine," said Zadok with a touch of resentment. He and Dov sat down again and waited impatiently for the crowd to file out. The stewards looked at them curiously at first, then seemed to withdraw as they finally recognized Zadok.

Zadok was pleased that the New York customs inspector allowed him quickly through. The inspector stamped and returned the passport without any questions.

Dov also made it through customs pretty easily.

As Zadok entered the main terminal, the rush of warm air felt good, but soon he became aware of activity at the end of the ramp. There was a crowd waiting for them.

"Thought this was to be a discrete arrival," Zadok observed.

Zadok looked at Dov and felt irritated by his apparent amusement at the attention.

Tsiyon swore in Arabic, startling Zadok because it came from a man who never cursed. Immediately, perhaps reflexively, Tsiyon's eyes began scanning the crowd and terminal.

Two tall young men, apparently Israeli security stationed in New York, stepped forward out of the crowd of reporters to greet them. Tsiyon knew them and, immediately, he angrily challenged them to explain the apparent security leak. They shrugged.

Flash bulbs started going off as the group approached within ten feet of the crowd. Zadok was aware they were being videotaped by several people. They kept walking and their audience followed. The New York state police helped them pass through the reporters who began hurling questions.

For a moment Zadok wanted to hide or run out of the terminal, but he managed to find within his recently developed extroverted skills whatever he needed to deal with the situation. He stopped in his tracks, faced the inquisitors, and promptly received a half dozen questions before he had the opportunity to address even one.

"What's the purpose of your visit to the States?"

"You believe the prophecy?"

Zadok wanted to answer that he absolutely did believe that the third component of Ezekiel's prophecies had fully materialized. But he had been so busy, he hadn't prepared himself to deal with the media. He said nothing while he tried to piece together an appropriate answer.

"Can you confirm the sketchy reports coming out of Syria?" another reporter said.

Zadok held his hand up. When he had comparative quiet, he said, "I've been asked to brief General Baler and his staff on technical aspects. I'm not a politician – we deal only in scientific facts. I'm only here to review technical data and evidence with the appropriate authority. One thing that I can assure you is that we've deployed no secret weapons. And we've initiated absolutely no offensive actions."

"Hurry," Tsiyon whispered. "It's no good to stop."

"Okay, I'll take just one more question," Zadok said. He pointed to a reporter with a white beard.

"How do you respond to assertions that there's no earthly explanation for recent events?"

Zadok smiled. "My function isn't to express opinions, especially theological. My purpose is very much an earthly one, and – "

Zadok felt pressure from behind pulling him down. Then he heard a gunshot. Before he knew it, he was on the ground. He rolled over to see that it was Tsiyon's large hands that had pulled him down. There was screaming.

Zadok looked himself over.

A woman screamed. A policeman blew his whistle. Zadok felt foolish on the floor, but he was unhurt.

He looked over his shoulder to see Tsiyon, who was standing and looking forward, his pistol drawn. "Thanks," he said.

"Never mind," Tsiyon said, reaching down to help him to his feet.

Zadok dusted himself off.

"Never mind that," Tsiyon urged. "Let's go. Come."

Tsiyon led Zadok to the front of the building. People were still hiding. He saw a large group of police in a huddle.

"Don't look at them. Keep moving. Go faster. Go, go," Tsiyon shouted.

Zadok started to trot through the airport building, and as he passed the baggage and car rental booths, he kept imagining hearing the gunshot over and over. He couldn't shake it. The bullet may have missed, but the reverberation penetrated over and over.

It finally occurred to him that he was in debt to Tsiyon. Maybe the man was as good as his reputation.

Zadok was very much aware of the stares from the airport passengers, crews, and visitors. He hated being conspicuous.

He was quickly ushered to a waiting limousine and was asked to lie on the floor. Two security men he'd never seen before were seated on opposite sides and were looking through the one-way tinted glass. Their Uzis were in their hands.

Zadok studied Tsiyon's face. He was hard to read, but still the man projected confidence. Was the confidence justified? No way to know. Surely Tsiyon had been through similar experiences. He could fall back on those situations and lay out his options. Yes, Zadok was safe with Tsiyon's protection, or at least he hoped so.

Zadok rubbed his hands through the plush carpeting. Son of a bitch, what a way to ride in a limo. This was ridiculous. After all, he was a colonel in the army. He sat up. No one objected.

Zadok focused on the television, which wasn't on, and then the bar in the back of the limo.

"What happened? I mean, why would anyone want to kill me?" Zadok found himself talking to the back of the front seat, without expecting an answer.

Tsiyon's deep voice returned a thoughtful response. "The world can't wait for you to tell what you know about the prophecy. But there are many who'd prefer you never say anything. Fulfillment of an ancient prophecy has serious implications. Don't forget that all armies need to have God on their side. To be specific, we know of a German group, an American group, a few Muslim groups…"

"Sorry I asked," Zadok said. "Where's Dov?"

"In the car behind us."

The limo sped to a Manhattan hotel commonly used by Israeli businessmen. Zadok and Tsiyon got out, and the limo sped on to a decoy location that was to be set up at the Plaza Hotel.

"Go straight to the elevator," Tsiyon said. "We're checked in, I've got the room keys."

Two small adjoining rooms had already been reserved for them and registered to a large Israeli conglomerate, Cori Industries, Limited. The rooms were small but freshly painted and carpeted and the furnishings were new. It was about as attractive as a small, antiquated Manhattan hotel room could be.

Tsiyon ordered room service for both of them. Zadok turned on the television and watched his airport arrival, as seen by a Channel Four news crew. Then he thought about his sister in Boston, whom he wanted to see on this trip. Now it might not be possible.

Also in the room were two American newspapers, a French newspaper, an intercontinental English newspaper, two Israeli newspapers, one news magazine, and one book on the struggle for Jewish continuity in America. Apparently, the local consulate wanted to keep him abreast of his media coverage. Zadok recalled that he had at first wanted to keep everything quiet, but that probably would have been impossible. Now apparently even the government had decided to join in on the media game. He thumbed through the papers and magazine. All had an article on the prophecy, and most of those articles had some mention of him. The magazine had his old high school picture. He read a statistic in the continuity book that those who identify as Jews in America now numbered less than three million.

He was feeling hyperactive and at the same time tired from sitting in an airplane for twelve hours. He had wanted to call his family in America and in Israel, but Tsiyon had said that it would be taken care of. His family would be reassured, but he really needed to talk to his sister. It was his private motive for coming to the United States. He wanted to meet with her and comfort her. He knew she was going through a hard time. Maybe there would still be a chance he'd get to Boston.

Was he missing the kids yet? He wasn't sure. It was good to get away once in a while. He hadn't seen a lot of his children lately, yet it was when he was away from them that he most appreciated them. Yes, he missed them already.

He heard Tsiyon knocking on their adjoining door.

"That you?"

"Yes."

"Come in."

Tsiyon entered and carefully closed the door behind him. "They caught today's shooter."

"Who is he?"

"An American. Not one of the expected groups."

"Expected?"

"A loner. One of the local police called him an 'Oswald' type. His name is Smith. No one to worry about."

Zadok was not feeling emotionally in control. His stomach had the jitters and he was nervous without knowing why. He tried not to show it, so when Tsiyon went back to his room, Zadok went to the bathroom and washed his face. He took a few deep breaths, but it wasn't enough. His hands were trembling and he wanted to puke.

Zadok decided to change into his jogging T-shirt, shorts, and a sweat-shirt. He needed to run in order to relax. He slipped a note under the adjoining door to explain to Tsiyon that he had gone running. Then he took the elevator to the first level where he saw Dov sitting on a bar stool in a lounge at the back end of the lobby. Dov was ordering a drink for a woman in a gray business suit. He had his own way of working off stress.

"Hello," Zadok said.

Dov turned around. "Hello, hello, hello."

Then Dov turned back to the trim, black-haired, professional-looking woman. "There's my boss."

"Join us," Dov called, "come on, join us." Dov spoke in accented English, his words slurred.

Zadok hoped Dov wouldn't get too drunk. "No, no. I need air. I'll catch you later."

"Okay. He's an American," Dov told his new acquaintance.

Zadok was always amazed at how easily Dov picked up women. By now, he shouldn't be. Not that Zadok was interested in chasing women, but he did respect – perhaps in his youth would even have envied – men who'd developed the pastime into a skill.

Dov was blunt. He didn't beat around the bush, he'd just ask if they'd go to bed with him. Surprisingly, it often worked.

Dov was always bold. Zadok still felt like he was an introvert, living in a country of extroverts. His children, too, thankfully, had an abundance of self-confidence.

On his way to Central Park, Zadok studied the Americans passing him on the sidewalk. Though he wasn't jealous, he could be impressed by affluence when he found it around him. He imagined he could smell the money in their pockets. He stopped to study the merchandise in the retail windows. So much jewelry, he thought, who could wear it in public? He stared up at the great office buildings. Despite his American upbringing, despite his frequent trips to America, England, and France, he was still somewhat of a provincial poor dolt.

Yet he had chosen a life that promised no wealth. He could have taken a path like the executive in a mohair top coat who passed him. Nevertheless he was really comfortable that he'd made another choice.

There was something else in the faces of these Americans in this most affluent part of Manhattan. He wasn't sure if it was a look that came of material comfort or maybe it was just the lack of sunshine. Prosperity looked good. It was a look that he'd disdained when he was younger. Now it was pretty damn fine. The American look was still the world standard.

Then he heard noise from across the street. He turned and there was the Plaza Hotel. Without intending to, he'd approached his decoy location, the one place he was expected to be and therefore should have totally avoided. He pulled the hood of his sweatshirt over his head and pulled down tight on the drawstrings. There were several groups outside the hotel. One group was marching, holding signs which were too far away to read. Another was praying – in fact several groups seemed to be caught up in different prayer sessions. Off to the side separated by police were protesters. Then there appeared to be a few people performing a public fast.

He had no idea about any of these activities. He never imagined when he left Israel that in America there would be the level of public interest and media involvement that he was experiencing.

Suddenly he was concerned that he'd be recognized. He turned away and picked up his pace. Tsiyon would go nuts if he knew what Zadok was doing, but then Zadok needed to do it and wasn't afraid of taking chances in America. Despite the attack at the airport, he doubted there was any more real danger to him. In Europe he would have felt different.

Still, seeing the crowd outside the Plaza gave him second thoughts. He quickly walked away, not slowing his pace until he reached Central Park. There he ran a few miles. Then he walked back a different route to his hotel.

Dov was no longer in the bar.

Zadok went to his room and, with considerable difficulty, managed to retrieve the note he had left for Tsiyon.

Good, Tsiyon wouldn't know what he had done. He poured himself a glass of scotch and took a shower. When he came out of the bathroom, he looked at his watch, which he had left on the night table. It was exactly twenty-four hours since he had left Israel. His eyes scanned back to the newspapers and magazine. There was a time when it would have meant something to him to be featured in such a cross-section of the world media. That was before he learned what it meant to be on the verge of a nervous breakdown. It was before he prayed in deep desperation for help. It was before he reached the point of doubting his own sanity. It was before a medical opinion forced him to terms with his own mortality. It was before he accepted how very human and ordinary he was.

Not anymore. There was no ego boost for him now. It meant nothing. Less than nothing.

It had been a long day. He felt a little better, more relaxed. Now perhaps he could sleep.

* * *

"No more women," Tsiyon scolded, pointing at Dov.

This constant yelling and fighting was a hell of a way to start the morning, thought Zadok. He had just finished his raisin bran and bananas and coffee, and Tsiyon's words triggered concerns over his own marital issues.

He knew he'd taken his wife for granted. He also knew he'd been non-communicative recently. There were, he had thought, good reasons for his behavior. Now he blamed himself for everything which had led to the current strain in his marriage. He hoped it wasn't too late.

Dov was about to respond to Tsiyon's morning threat, but Tsiyon continued before Dov could get out a syllable. "These women, these pick-ups of yours are security risks. It stops now, or you're on the next flight to Ben Gurion."

"Get off my case," Dov said.

"You're irresponsible and I – "

The phone rang.

"I'll get it," Zadok said.

"No."

Tsiyon held up his hand like a traffic cop.

He picked up the phone himself, listened for a moment, and then handed the receiver to Zadok. It was Moshe Avieser, the New York consul general.

"Shalom, shalom, how are you? You weren't hurt in the shooting at the airport?"

"Thank you, I'm fine," Zadok said.

"A terrible thing. Such a welcome for you."

"I'm okay."

"Good. Wonderful. And your wife and the children?"

"Don't know. I haven't spoken to them. Tsiyon tells me they're fine and that they know I'm fine."

"I see. Well, please, give them my regards when you can talk to them."

"I will."

"Listen, I have some news. I think good news for you. As you know, your Pentagon briefing's scheduled for tomorrow. We've just scheduled a briefing for you at the White House for the day after."

"You mean with the president?"

"I presume he'll participate, at least for a while, in the meeting."

"Thank you. Yes, that's good news. I'll be honored if the president attends."

Zadok smiled as he considered the president's possible reactions to the information he'd reveal. And the best part was that he had pretty convincing proof that the improbable had really happened. Zadok grinned wider as he daydreamed about the world response and the societal impact, when all the details of the prophecy inevitably surfaced.

After hanging up, Zadok challenged once more Tsiyon's restriction against contacting his family in Israel or his sister in Boston. Tsiyon agreed to set up a controlled call with his wife, but only for a few minutes, and he could make no reference to his whereabouts. It would have to wait until they got to their safe house in Washington, D.C.

Zadok agreed.

*   *   *

They decided to drive to Washington. Tsiyon had arranged for a car and driver to wait for them just a few yards beyond the hotel's entrance. Tsiyon sent Dov ahead and accompanied Zadok through the lobby to the front door and sidewalk.

There on the sidewalk, a disheveled old street person with a stubbly beard and white mane was parading back and forth in front of their hotel with a hand-scribbled sign which read, "The end is near, justice is mine sayeth the Lord."

"Why are you here?" Zadok said to the old man. "Isn't everyone else over at the Plaza?"

"God told me to come here," the old man answered, sounding defiant and without interrupting his march.

Zadok looked back to Tsiyon. "Makes you wonder, doesn't it."

He got into the car.

*   *   *

Somewhere in Maryland, Tsiyon got a call on the car phone, the topic of which he quickly relayed to Zadok. Their decoy room at the Plaza had been ransacked. No one was hurt but the hotel room suffered extensive damage.

"Someone's after you," Tsiyon said. "I don't like it. As soon as you're done at the White House, we'll go home."

"Fine with me," Zadok said.

"And me, too," Dov said. "I'll gladly trade in you old watchdogs. I could use some wine, women, and song." He sounded as if he had been deprived for years. He looked at Tsiyon and broke into a nervous-sounding laugh. "Ah, never mind," he said, as he turned to the window.

Zadok looked out his own window as well. He was glad that Tsiyon had approved his call home, though the call would have to wait until they got to the safe house. On the other hand, he had no idea how Shoshana would respond to him.

When they got to their brownstone in Washington, after Zadok took a shower and poured himself a scotch, Tsiyon set up the phone call to the Galilee.

"Is that you?" Shoshana said.

"Yes, it's me. How are you?" Zadok asked carefully, reflecting the recent strain between them.

"Fine, we were so worried," Shoshana said in a manner that communicated she had genuine concern for his safety.

"Quiet, children. Quiet. Yes, yes, it's Daddy. We saw you at the airport when they shot at you. It was on television. What's happening? Where are you?"

"I can't talk about that, but I'm okay. Now I regret coming for this, but I was the one who wanted the story explained accurately. I wanted to do it myself, so I've got no one else to blame."

"Everyone's talking about it here. Have you seen the Israeli press? Nothing but the prophecy on the front page. The children want to talk to you and I've already put the little one to bed. Oh, well, she's up now, she's here. I'm going to put on Sarah, hold on."

"Daddy?"

"Yes, Sarah, how's my little girl?"

"When are you coming home?"

"Soon, dear, as soon as I can."

"Rivka hit me on my arm before and it hurt." One by one, three of Zadok's five children came on the phone. Except for Sarah, the youngest, they each left their instructions as to which present they wanted brought back from America. The oldest, Tsipy, and the second oldest, Jonathan, no longer lived with their parents, so weren't there, but Zadok's wife reported that Tsipy was hoping for a miniature television.

Zadok said good-bye to his children and to Shoshana. He went over to the window. He had a great view of a big, old oak tree and a few people walking below. It already seemed a long time since he'd left the Galilee.

Zadok returned to lie down on the sofa and to read the substantial *New York Herald*. He read dispassionately every detail of the airport attack.

"Colonel Zadok is safe and unharmed, and there is every reason to expect he will continue to fulfill his destiny."

It was a curious concept, to fulfill one's destiny. There had been so many hard choices, and whenever he'd turned off from the mainstream, he never knew if it had been the right choice.

Later, they heard that the Pentagon and White House briefings were to be postponed. They assumed it would only be for a day – two, at the most – so Zadok decided to stick it out a little longer.

But the real problem surfaced with the evening television news: "It's being widely reported," the newscaster said with an artificial earnestness, "that Robert Zadok, who is scheduled to meet with Pentagon officials to review what some are calling the fulfillment of a biblical prophecy, is reported to have been treated in a mental hospital in Brooklyn for over three years and has been committed on at least four occasions. According to these reports, he's been treated for delusions. A few professionals at that institution have stated that Zadok is capable of fabricating evidence to support his delusions. Zadok is currently serving as a munitions officer in the Israeli army."

Zadok stood up in the middle of the broadcast. "The hell's this garbage?" He dropped his glass. "No, can't be." He stared at the television in disbelief.

"Unbelievable," Dov said. "I have the proof on film."

"They haven't seen the pictures yet," Tsiyon said. "We'll get to the bottom of this nonsense." He went to the telephone.

"I don't believe it," Zadok repeated, while falling back into his chair. "I don't believe it."

"Here's another drink," Dov said, handing him a glass.

"What do you make of it?" Zadok managed to ask.

"We know we have opposition. Someone shot at you, right? They went through the room at the Plaza, right? This is more opposition. What else is new?"

Zadok tried to think through what might be happening. The postponement had to be linked to this. The hell with them, he thought, now he wanted to go home anyway. But if he went home suddenly it'd be as if he were admitting he was a fake. Still, it was tempting. In a few days hopefully he'd be able to tell his story and go home.

Tsiyon said, "Our security office in New York wants to talk to you. They want you to help them get to the bottom of this." He handed the phone to Zadok.

"My name's Ari Ben David and I work for Israel security. Could you answer a few questions for me?"

"Be happy to." Zadok was pacing the floor while holding the phone.

"Ever been institutionalized?"

"Now, wait a minute – "

"We need to ask these things so we can properly counter the media's sources. Have you ever been institutionalized?"

"No."

"Treated by a psychiatrist?"

"No, but they told me I was crazy when I said I was moving to Israel." He said this routinely because it was an old joke he'd told many times.

Ben David didn't laugh. "Spent any time in Brooklyn?"

"Drove through a few times – oh, and I think I visited a great aunt when I was a kid."

"Any family that was institutionalized or treated for mental or nervous disorders?"

"Don't know, I don't think so. Look, are you going to get to the bottom of this, or are you just going to ask me stupid questions? What's the matter, you don't believe me, either? Anything else?"

"No, that's all. Thank you."

This is turning into a joke, he thought.

He imagined he could feel his blood pressure rising. He decided that he needed to go running and went to change into gym clothes.

"Where're you going?" Tsiyon said.

"Running."

"You crazy?"

"Seems to be the question, doesn't it?"

"You can't go out that door."

"Fine, I'll go out the back."

Zadok ran three miles, came back, showered, and went to bed. But he couldn't sleep.

He lay in bed reviewing everything that had lead up to the fulfillment of the prophecy. And what he knew he'd seen. And the pictures he had taken, and the pictures others had taken. Hell, he wasn't the only one who'd seen it. There must have been a hundred others who had gone north and experienced and seen what he had. Could he be wrong?

Could their conclusions be wrong? Could they all have imagined it?

More to the point, could his unit's analysis of the evidence be off the mark? What the hell, maybe his critics were right. He was a lunatic who lived in a world of delusions, a sort of never-never land.

Coming on the trip had been exciting at first. He'd desperately wanted to share with the world what seemed to him incontrovertible evidence of an extraordinary event, a possible link between current and historical military-political realities and the spiritual side of man. And he wanted to keep the American military informed about the changes in the strategic balance, about new information on enemy missiles, and to assure them that Israel had not implemented a new weapon. Somehow it had all turned into a joke, a headline for the *National Starlet* or the *National Parody*.

He got up and paced some more, and when it didn't help, he went to the living room window to study the silhouette of the old oak tree. After a while he started to think again about how it all began, about the past and the early years, about how it had been for an idealistic young immigrant to Israel.

Chapter Sixteen

On that day when my people Israel are dwelling securely, the enemies of Israel will bestir and come from their place out of the uttermost parts of the north, a mighty army; you will come up against my people Israel, like a cloud covering the Land. In the latter days I will bring you against my Land, that the nations may know me, when through you, o Gog, I vindicate my holiness before their eyes.

And the mountains shall be thrown down, and the cliffs shall fall, and every wall shall tumble to the ground. I will summon every kind of terror against Gog, says the Lord God; every man's sword will be against his brother. With pestilence and bloodshed I will enter into judgment with him; and I will rain upon him and his hordes and the many peoples that are with him, torrential rains and hailstones, fire and brimstone.

Their choice of apartments in Washington, D.C. seemed wrong to Zadok. They were in an Asian and black neighborhood, at least a few blocks from the federal consular areas. They stood out too much, but Zadok knew he wasn't the expert. Maybe the neighbors were less likely to be spies. He was sure Tsiyon had a good reason.

There was something nostalgic about these once-proud, run-down brownstones that Zadok appreciated. Perhaps it was the hint of grace and craftsmanship under the layers of paint or the detailed woodwork and high ceilings. He appreciated the familiarity of the pull-chain toilets, tiny bath tiles and four-legged bathtubs, the chandeliers and the parquet floors. It was familiar and comfortable and reminded him of a long forgotten piece of his life in Boston.

Intruding through the slightly ajar and cracked wood living room window was the unmistakable smell of greasy Haitian cooking. There were sidewalk kids shouting while rollerblading or shouldering their boom boxes.

Zadok returned to wrapping the presents that his children had requested. He had given the wish list to Tsiyon, who had arranged for the toys to be picked up. Zadok taped a card with each child's name over the gift wrap, and then carefully placed the presents in his suitcase. He sprawled out on the couch, turned on the television, and wished he were home.

"Can we go home now? I'm tired of this. I don't want to play this game anymore," Zadok joked.

"Let's go," Dov added quickly. "It was never supposed to be like this. Whoever heard of foreign diplomats hiding out for their lives. I feel like I did in the war."

Dov was right, Zadok thought. They were supposed to be on a technical mission; if they couldn't be welcomed comfortably, they should go home.

Zadok didn't answer Dov. He just stared at the television. An evangelical minister was being featured, proclaiming his support for accepting the validity of the biblical revelations witnessed, photographed, and documented by dozens of people. Even if Robert Zadok were proven to be suffering from a mental disorder, the minister preached, it was not a valid reason to ignore what scores of intelligent, normal, and even nonreligious people had reported.

Zadok had to agree that the minister's logic made sense. Take Zadok out of the equation – yes, that made sense. The hell with me, but not everyone could be crazy.

"Look at the body on that one," Dov said.

He was staring out the window, describing various female physical attributes as they paraded on the sidewalk.

Tsiyon seemed to be ignoring the conversation. He was working on the six or seven groups that were known to be potentially dangerous and in the States now. He never talked much about what he was doing or what his concerns were, about whom he was following or eavesdropping on or looking for. He just did it.

Zadok wondered what Tsiyon could be thinking. For certain, Tsiyon disliked Dov. Tsiyon seemed to think Dov was obnoxious and useless, but he hadn't seen Dov in action, as Zadok had.

Zadok was putting his trust, his life in Tsiyon's hands. He wondered if Tsiyon thought he was crazy. Perhaps he considered the whole expedition a sham. Perhaps he simply didn't believe the evidence.

Zadok studied Tsiyon, who was quietly going through the files, making calls. He looked into this man's eyes and wished he could get a sense of the intelligence, makeup, and character of the man. His gut was telling him it was okay to relax. But was it really? Was he willing to bet his life on this man's competence? Perhaps it was moot – at the airport, he already had.

Someone knocked on the door and Tsiyon pulled his gun. Dov and Zadok went into the back room and picked up their Uzis.

Zadok felt his heart race. This could be it. He wasn't expecting any visitors.

He felt the cold shaft of the Uzi and he double checked the clip and pushed in the safety. Never had he expected to be a front line soldier again, but here he was once more. It had a familiar feel. He swallowed.

He heard the door open slowly.

He took a quiet breath and held it.

He waited.

He peaked into the living room and listened.

It was a man in white jeans and a T-shirt, delivering a pizza. Tsiyon said nothing, took the pizza box, and closed the door. After the pizza man left, Tsiyon opened the pizza box to find another file. Zadok exhaled. He went back to watching television and Dov went back to looking out the window.

"Don't lean out the window," Tsiyon scolded Dov, "you're exposing yourself."

"Exposing oneself has a different meaning in English," Zadok said with a bit of a smirk.

"You know," Dov said to Tsiyon, "There is cholera in Israel and that's not healthy. You're getting to be like a case of cholera."

Tsiyon yelled, "Fool, you can get yourself killed if you want, but you're exposing all of us along with you."

"Maybe if we had a little better security, we wouldn't be shot at."

"That's not the point."

"Isn't it? You're so worried about me going to the window so I can breathe in this little hole. Meanwhile, your people can't do anything about getting us off a damn plane in one piece."

"You want to get through the airport? I'll get you through the airport and onto a plane so fast – "

"Do it, you useless – "

"You're on report." Tsiyon pointed at him.

"Who cares."

At first Zadok had tried to break up their bickering, but now he gave up. They'd had too much exposure to one another in too small a place, for too long a time.

After the screaming match had run its course, Tsiyon went back to reading the file in the pizza box. He looked up proudly, revealing a compelling little smile. He announced that the Pentagon meeting, only the Pentagon meeting, had been rescheduled for Thursday.

"Why is someone trying to discredit me?" Zadok said.

"My guess, it's a hostile government."

"Why?"

"They can explain almost anything to their own people. It's a different thing to the outside world. It's a serious matter for God to intervene against them. It could easily bring down any government."

"But the evangelist said I didn't matter. And he's right."

"He's an evangelist. He's easy to persuade about miracles and acts of God and prophecies. Most people aren't so easy to persuade. They need to create doubt, and the easiest way to do it is to go after you."

"After me?"

"Yes, make you seem like a lunatic capable of fabricating evidence. Or else they could…"

"Could what?"

"Kill you," Tsiyon said.

Zadok paused to gather his thoughts.

"But I think that wouldn't be as valuable to them as discrediting you," Tsiyon added.

"That supposed to make me feel better?" Zadok said.

"That's why we should leave immediately," Tsiyon said.

"Book us on a flight home the night of the meeting," Zadok said.

"Hallelujah." Dov saluted Tsiyon, who didn't seem to appreciate the sarcasm.

Zadok just remembered he had one more present to pack, the television for Tsipy. He went over to the kitchen area to cut up more wrapping paper.

Zadok decided he agreed with Dov's sentiment, if not with his style or mode of expression. It just wasn't right the way things were going. But the meeting was on for Thursday. He could wait a few more days. Then they could go home.

*   *   *

In a Pentagon boardroom, after the handshaking was completed, Zadok sat with Dov on his left and the Israeli ambassador to his right. Except for Ambassador Mazor, all the Israelis were in uniform. General Ben Zion sat on Ambassador Mazor's right. Across the conference table sat General Baler, U.S. army, and four of his aides. There were also three representatives of the U.S. State Department at the far end of the table.

Zadok ran his fingers along the walnut table. It was cold, like the atmosphere. The furnishings were contemporary and pleasant, with green and gray wallpaper and carpeting, more pleasant and comfortable than he expected from the military. But the first impression of the meeting made Zadok feel awkward.

General Baler was a distinguished-looking executive, with a full head of white hair, combed neatly with a part. He didn't hesitate to stare right in the eye of the people addressing him or listening to him. The brightly colored medals sewed onto the general's dark uniform only added to his presence.

Ambassador Mazor said, "In response to your government's request for clarification of the recent military developments in our part of the world, or at least what we know of them, I've brought General Ben Zion and his assistants, Colonel Zadok and Captain Kesselbrenner. These men are our experts, the men who are most intimate with the situation, and can best answer your questions."

"Welcome," General Baler said. "I understand that you've had some inconveniences getting to this meeting."

"No problem," Ambassador Mazor said.

Sure, no problem for you, Zadok thought, exchanging glances with Dov.

General Ben Zion said, "Not long ago Israel was severely threatened."

"That's an understatement. You're very modest," General Baler interrupted.

"I thought you were dead," another American general added.

"We have a lot of confidence in ourselves," Ben Zion answered. "But as you know, our neighbors were developing long-range tactical missiles with the capability to zero in on Israeli population centers. In fact, the intelligence and satellite photos which you recently provided for us showed we were in more danger than we realized. But we were aware that the Chinese and the French had provided weapons systems, and perhaps more dangerous for the long term, they helped assist them to develop and apply homegrown technology. More than anything else, that probably gave them the confidence that they could launch a successful, coordinated offensive against us.

"The situation was very grave, very serious for us. A preventive strike might have led to the possible retaliatory use of the missiles that we didn't destroy. Unless we could wipe out one hundred percent of these missiles, an early attack was too risky. Not a desirable option.

"And, as you know, we didn't want to be the ones to initiate an offensive. We had worked too hard to establish the relative quiet, and we were afraid to irreparably damage it. It would have undoubtedly undermined the more progressive and peaceful elements across our borders. We elected to prepare our citizens for an attack, and to make it plain, unequivocal, and unmistakable to our enemies that if we were hit, we'd retaliate tenfold. We were afraid they might convince themselves they could win with one, totally preemptive strike. It was very tense and uncomfortable.

"Reserves were called up on a limited basis. Many citizens in the border areas were living in shelters. But we took no offensive action. There was much debate, but we fired no missiles, flew no missions, made no attacks, did no sabotage.

"Then they began their joint campaign against us. And it looked as if we'd made a serious strategic mistake, because in the early hours they were successful, and they appeared to have gained the momentum to prevail. Somehow, mysteriously, the missile bases were destroyed. Totally destroyed. I honestly don't know how, but they were. And we had nothing to do with it. Even military bases and air fields were destroyed. Even missile bases we didn't know about were destroyed. The population centers appear to be relatively unscathed, but the military threat was destroyed. Their ability to wage a modern war was taken away from them."

"How'd all of this happen?" General Baler asked.

"We honestly don't know," General Ben Zion said.

"You're asking us to accept an awful lot," General Baler said. He settled back in his chair and paused. "It seems to be either another party was involved or you're keeping something from us, a new weapon, a secret weapon, perhaps."

"We know it's a lot to accept. We've asked the same questions. A third party involved – who? We don't know who could have done this. But we know that a terrible threat is no more. We have men who have seen the change, or the results of the change, with their own eyes. We photographed the results. We have the pictures with us."

Dov handed out about a dozen five-by-eight-inch photographs. General Baler studied them first, then began passing them around the table. The Americans began to whisper, huddle, and debate, but so quietly that Zadok couldn't make out a word. They held some of the pictures up to the light and pointed out certain features. Some of the pictures were difficult to interpret, but it was clear that all the photos featured damaged military hardware.

Then Zadok took over the presentation. He stood up and turned on a slide projector.

"All of what I'm about to show you, I witnessed personally. I assure you that what you'll see is legitimate."

"We know that it's legitimate. What we don't know is how it happened."

Zadok didn't respond to the comment. This wasn't a suitable forum for him to explain what he knew of the prophecy and the role he'd played. This was not the opportunity to expose his personal conviction. He was at this meeting in his role as a military officer, and he knew he had to confine himself to that role.

The first slide he showed was of a map, with a red line that traced the route his men took by helicopter over hostile territory in order to take pictures. The missile batteries were in blue, and he explained the strategic location of the various batteries and air fields and how the enemy could have easily mounted an effective offensive because of their joint capabilities in range, accuracy, and destructive tonnage. In fact, the enemy had actually commenced an initiative that might have been successful.

The Americans nodded. He knew he was speaking a language now that they should understand. These were men of facts, figures, strategies, and military science. Zadok figured they would be confused by and suspicious of mysterious explanations, or an avoidance of explanations.

"This next slide," Zadok said, "shows what we found when we flew over the first missile site. These were locally produced arrow missiles. Long-range, reasonably accurate, can carry chemical, nuclear, heavy conventional. We believe that all of the missiles exploded at or near their launch site. It's possible that they were armed, and that one accident at one site could have happened. It is not possible for the same accident to happen over and over at different locations at the same time. It is not possible. Perhaps I should say it's not very likely for the same accident to happen to missile sites and to jet hangars at the same time."

He went to the next slide which showed three fighter jets destroyed on the ground. The hangar in the background had totally collapsed. Then he signaled Dov to turn to the next slide.

"This next slide," Zadok explained, "shows what we found when we flew over the mountains. We didn't know about this site beforehand, but we couldn't help notice the top of the mountain missing when we flew over.

"This next site is totally inaccessible. It's high, secret, totally fenced and well secured. As you can see, sabotage would've been difficult, very close to impossible."

General Baler still seemed skeptical. "Maybe you have an army of engineers carrying heavy explosives to deploy behind enemy lines."

Zadok responded, "We don't, but even if we did, they'd never get through these security compounds. Here's one that blew up underground where it was stored. Nobody knew about it because it wasn't even uncrated yet."

General Baler studied the slide, then picked up the photos on the conference table and studied them. "No one could walk or drive through that maze." He had the evidence before his eyes but he still seemed unconvinced. He returned to the photographs and he sorted and studied them again. "Could the Syrians have done it themselves, you know, perhaps to get a newer generation of replacement armaments from their suppliers?"

"Not likely. They already had state of the art. Replacement wasn't automatic. They appear to have no reserves left which makes them vulnerable internally and externally. In fact we took advantage of the opportunity to help ourselves to fuel reserves. Enough to fuel our power plant for six to ten years."

"Gentlemen," General Baler said, "it's my job to get to the bottom of things, to ask questions and not accept statements without studying them, without thinking things through. But you've either gone to great lengths to perpetrate a charade to prove to us that the threat is gone – and I'll be damned if I can figure out what you have to gain from that – or you've got a situation here for which I have no explanations."

Zadok signaled Dov for the next slide. "Here's what used to be a cliff. This picture is what it used to look like. Now on this next slide is the same geography now. The cliff has collapsed. Very substantial earthquakes, or should I say earth movements, somewhere in this vicinity."

"Could that be the explanation? Everything is the result of earthquakes, tornados, and natural disasters?"

"A possible explanation for some. Certainly there were earthquakes and hailstorms, but I think you'll agree after reviewing the evidence that the devastation is too focused to be dismissed simply as a natural disaster. A nation's military might probably cannot be destroyed by random natural disasters. Let's look at this next slide."

"What is it?"

"Fire – gas and oil fires, mostly. Up and down the whole coast."

"Incredible."

"What caused it?"

"Don't know," Zadok said. "Next slide. This ancient town experienced multiple earthquakes, floods, fires. It looks like Dresden. I have three more of the same."

"Unbelievable."

"This next slide was taken in the capital."

"Is that what I think it is?"

"Yes, it's a dog with a human limb in its mouth. The next slide is a pack of wild dogs feeding. The next is a flock of vultures feeding on human dead in the streets."

"Jesus," General Baler said.

"Here's one more of the fires at the port. There may have been an attempt to either import or export munitions. In any case, it's all in flames here. In this next one, the terminal building is in flames at the port. Don't know what the cargo was."

"Where'd those vultures come from? I've never seen so many," General Baler said.

"You're right," Ben Zion said. "It's unusual."

Zadok continued. "As we flew northeast, we took this next series of pictures. Fires, quakes, floods, major wall and building collapses. Here's a highway bridge that collapsed and destroyed the road below. The highway and telecommunication networks have largely been incapacitated. Yet the international media to date has had trouble getting in to document the extent of the damage."

"You needn't worry about that. I think the word's gotten out," General Baler said.

"Perhaps you're right. We continued in a loop westward before heading south. That's when we passed over an air base."

This photo impressed the military men the most as they took in the extent of the damage to all kinds of aircraft.

Dov lingered a moment on this slide, then went to the next one. "More missile batteries," Zadok said. "At this base there were very few personnel casualties as far as we could tell, but all of the arrow missiles were exploded."

"I see more birds," an American said.

"Yes," Zadok agreed. "There were a few corpses and a few birds feeding, but not on the scale of the Magog or capital experiences."

Zadok was pleased with the way the meeting was going. It was almost over. A few more questions, and his country's obligations in the matter would be fulfilled. The meeting would be over. The Americans asked for an inventory of destroyed equipment. Zadok had some of that information, merely a projection, and he gave it to them.

Soon he'd be home. They'd go back to the apartment, pack, and fly to Ben Gurion. He couldn't wait. "Any questions?" Zadok said.

"How do you explain all this in your own mind?" asked a white-haired American diplomat who reminded Zadok of his accountant uncle. "I mean, how do you sort all this out? What conclusion do you come to on a personal level?" The white-haired gentleman was seated in the very center of the end of the table, clearly a power position, but Zadok didn't recognize him.

Zadok looked to Ben Zion. The Israeli general was quiet and looked back without expression. Zadok took that as a signal to answer freely.

"We live in a part of the world which has seen the unusual over the years. It doesn't matter whether you believe in miracles. A miracle is an explanation for the unusual. So I guess what I'm saying is that the unusual isn't so unusual in our neighborhood. And it really would be interesting if it was all predicted long ago, wouldn't it?"

"That's a little too packaged," General Baler said.

"We are aware of anti-Semitic activities to make it appear that we are perpetrating a charade on the world," Ambassador Mazor said. "We're aware of it and we know that you're aware, also. We'd like you to investigate further yourselves. You can do this directly, through the United Nations, Red Cross, or Red Crescent. We, too, want to understand what's happened. We want you to investigate and also to share what you learn with us. I agree that it's all very unusual, as Colonel Zadok has said, perhaps even bizarre. But certainly you and the other Western countries would have more co-operation than we would."

"That's an interesting proposition, but as you know, the world press has, to date, had trouble getting in," the white-haired American diplomat said. "For the time being, anyway, we're pursuing it with other resources. But we do acknowledge your request and will certainly explore it as an option."

At that time, they decided to end the meeting. After its official close, they all spent a few minutes on small talk, and then they left.

Zadok and Dov rode together back to the brownstone. Zadok was pleased, almost happy about the day's events. Still he felt an uneasy need to talk more and share his feelings. What the hell, the mission was over and they'd soon be home.

"I thought it went well," Zadok said.

"Maybe," Dov said. "But we really don't have to be concerned. The truth will come out – it always does – and then they'll have to accept what we've been saying."

"Our enemies can't hide or rebuild everything."

"But we know that's what they're trying to do. They're trying to rebuild everything to discredit you."

"They won't be able. There's the satellite photos, for one thing. If the

Americans get motivated enough to get in there and investigate, they'll find no other explanation. I think they're interested enough to find a way to go in now, don't you?"

"I bet they're already trying to find an explanation besides the prophecy," Dov said. "Maybe you should've let General Baler hold on to a natural disaster explanation. That's what he was really looking for."

"But you know as well as I do that there's no way natural disasters could do what we saw. It has to be the realization of the final component of the prophecy."

"But think about what kind of man General Baler is. Do you think he's going to accept a revelation going back to ancient scriptures, over a natural phenomenon?"

"As you said, the truth will come out."

"A year ago, what would you or I have said to all this?"

"See your point," Zadok said. "Yes, you're probably right."

"Baler's pretty sharp, too."

"I got that impression."

"His mind was going a thousand miles per hour," Dov said. "We have no idea what he was really thinking."

"Hopefully he'll share what he learns, or already knows," Zadok said. "It'd be something if he validated the prophecy."

"He seemed pretty crafty. But if he did share anything with us, that would make this miserable trip worthwhile, wouldn't it?"

"Yep, he'd be the best one to do it."

After he returned to the apartment and packed, Zadok was still on a spiritual high. The meeting had gone as well as he could've expected. He could feel his adrenaline pumping. Waiting in the little apartment had taken its toll, but now he felt liberated and invigorated.

The Americans seemed cordial, receptive, and he thought they'd react. And, hopefully, there should be no more question about his sanity. He felt he had been legitimized. He knew that he had left everyone a little frustrated because there were no explanations, no logical summaries. But he had been as straightforward as possible and he thought that his sincerity had come through. After they thought about it for a while, they'd surely have to consider the prophecy as a possible explanation. That pleased Zadok. At the very least he was convinced that they would cease pressuring the Israeli government to give over information. After all, that too had been his objective.

Zadok went down the back stairs without anyone noticing, and came out of the apartment building wearing his sweat suit, a baseball cap, and sunglasses, ready to begin his last run through the Washington neighborhood. He took a few strides and thought about the day's events. He guessed that everyone would like to accept that providence could have a hand in the affairs of man. It was just that people were skeptical. They wanted to believe, they just didn't want to be seen as foolish. Maybe he'd helped them. It would be nice to think so. Too bad people needed an excuse or proof. Did they need proof about atomic structure? The hell with it, tomorrow he'd be home. Thank goodness.

He turned a corner and dodged an old tree branch decaying in the sidewalk. Then he heard a gunshot, and instantly he felt a sharp pain in his thigh. He fell to the pavement. Damn, it really hurt. He reached to the back of his left thigh and felt a dart. He pulled it out, but it was too late. He knew he was losing consciousness fast.

He felt someone pick him up. Before he knew it, he was riding in the back of a station wagon. But he wanted to go home so badly. Not now, he was so close. He was losing it.

Chapter Seventeen

So I will show my greatness and my holiness and make myself known in the eyes of many nations. Then they will know that I am the Lord. I will strike your bow from your left hand, and will make your arrows drop out of your right hand. You shall fall upon the mountains of Israel, you and all your hordes and the peoples that are with you; I will give you to birds of prey of every sort and to the wild beasts to be devoured. You shall fall in the open field; I will send fire on those who dwell securely in the coastlands.

Zadok was aware of little balls of light everywhere, flickering, flashing, shooting in and out, up and down, back and forth, like an explosion of particles. He couldn't make them stop, nor could he pull his thoughts together. Something had happened. There was nothing he could do about it. Little lights in all directions. He kept trying, out of an animal instinct to regain control of his own thoughts. He was unable to reflect or to develop a strategy.

When he could think again, he realized he had no idea where he was or what had happened.

He felt pain coming from his leg and he remembered. He remembered the dart. It still hurt. He remembered being loaded into a station wagon. How foolish he felt. Why did he have to go running – especially when he knew about the threats and when he knew he was so ready to go home?

God damn it, he did stupid things sometimes.

He was still wearing his sweat clothes, and the discomfort around his wrists made him aware that his arms were bound behind his back. He was in a commercial building, perhaps an old factory or warehouse. The room was small, about thirty square feet. He was lying face down on old wood floors, blackened by years of dirt. The floors were buckled in several spots and he was lying on one of the mounds. He rolled to the side in order to find a more level area.

There were large windows in the room, so Zadok guessed it was late afternoon, judging by the sunlight brightening the large-paned, opaque glass, reinforced by heptagonal blocks of embedded wires. He didn't see any light fixtures, so he guessed it would be pitch black at night.

He soon felt the need to urinate. He stood up and looked around. He saw a door. He slowly walked over to it, turned backwards when he got there, and reached to turn the cold knob. The heavy metal door moved in a few centimeters, but it was locked. He kicked the door.

"Hey, anyone there? Hello? Hello?"

Hell, I've got to go, he thought. He was also aware that he had a headache. A bad one. What the hell did they knock me out with, he wondered.

"Hey, open up, I got to piss," he shouted, while kicking the large, metal door.

"I feel like a dog," he said out loud.

He knew he couldn't hold it in much longer. He tried to pull down his sweat pants and underpants from the back. It didn't go very far. So he urinated in his gray sweat clothes, and went back toward the windows to sit in the corner.

"I've got to be the stupidest guy on the planet," he scolded himself. "How do I keep getting into these jams?"

At least he was alive. Then again, his kidnappers chose to keep him alive. What did that mean? Why did they choose to keep him alive? Perhaps he was fortunate after all. But then again, perhaps he'd have been better off dead. He wondered if they'd leave him alone. Should he start planning his escape? Would he starve before he was found?

He lay down on the black floor and tried for a while not to think about it. He became aware of the headache, the wrist and leg pain, and his wet pants. He thought about Shoshana, the kids, the Galilee sun and hills and olive trees, rocks, shrubs, the little village cottages with orange roofs, the army, the trip to America, Dov, Tsiyon.

Good old Tsiyon. He should've listened to Tsiyon. Well, maybe Tsiyon would get him out of this mess yet. Zadok had to have hope. What else could he do but hope?

At night, Zadok was able to sleep only for a few minutes at a time. When he was awake, he tried to make himself more comfortable, but he couldn't. The floor was too damn hard, and the temperature too damn cold. He was shivering. If he could only get warm, then he'd be able to sleep.

In the morning, he finally fell asleep. But not for long. He was awakened by the intrusion of the creaky metal door opening. Zadok was instantly wide awake, ready for anything, afraid and curious at the same time. Three men came in. Two were olive-skinned with black curly hair. They carried small automatic rifles. Zadok assumed they were Arabs. The third was approximately fifty, with thin, blonde-white hair and glasses. He was wearing a white medical gown and carrying a satchel.

One of the Arabs signaled Zadok to stand. Zadok slowly got to his feet and the Arab put his gun to Zadok's temple and held the back of Zadok's sweatshirt. The older man carefully removed a syringe from his satchel and started walking toward Zadok. When he got close enough, Zadok kicked at the man but missed. The Arab holding the gun to his head shouted in a frightening shrill. It was unintelligible but clearly a threat.

Zadok managed to pull himself totally free of his grip. He quickly moved so that the gun was no longer on him. The two Arabs and the older man came at Zadok again, but he started kicking and managed to force them to keep several feet away. Then the second Arab, the big burly one, said something to the others, who promptly stepped back. The big Arab then charged quickly at Zadok, managing to shoot a swift kick into Zadok's solar plexus. Then he instantly landed a punch to his jaw, and when Zadok bent over, another quick chop to the back of the neck.

Zadok was on the floor. He realized his mouth was bleeding. He looked up and saw that the tough Arab was now holding the syringe.

"Ugly ba – " Zadok started to say, but the big Arab stepped on the back of Zadok's neck, pressing him into the floor, pulled up Zadok's sleeve, and inserted the needle in one quick motion into Zadok's forearm. Zadok squirmed but couldn't free himself.

This ugly Arab was the muscle, the enforcer; Zadok couldn't do anything about it.

He was aware they were talking, but he couldn't understand. He wasn't even sure what language or dialect they were speaking.

"Get away from me," Zadok said, spitting blood and saliva.

The big Arab turned back toward him and kicked him in the face by the left temple. Zadok let out a yell and slid over almost three feet.

Zadok tried to rub his temple. He knew it was swelling already. Zadok wished for an ice pack, a glass of water, or something for the bleeding. He was so damn thirsty.

In a strange way, Zadok was almost glad to be in pain. He was so angry with himself that he accepted the pain as a sort of just punishment.

He heard the door slam. They must have left. Thank God. He hoped they'd never come back. Weren't they going to feed him or let him go to the bathroom? Live with it, Zadok told himself. Rise above this. It won't last forever. You'll come out of it, he told himself. Say a prayer. What prayer? Was there a prayer for kidnap victims? In Judaism there were prayers for every situation. He wished he knew. Tsiyon would come. They'd negotiate for something. There had to be a reason he was still alive. Maybe the injection was a food supplement? "Right, they're just scientists testing a new, high-protein health food," he said sarcastically to himself.

He guessed now that his captors weren't Arabs. Perhaps they could be Iranians. He recalled how he'd made many Iranian friends when he had worked at the Netzer Sereni metalworks, and had ingratiated himself with several teams of Iranian buyers.

God, his head hurt. His mouth hurt. His leg hurt. He was cold, sleepy, wet, hungry, and very thirsty. Time went slowly. Nothing to do but worry. When would they come again? What would they do next time?

Hours passed. It was dark in the room, but still light enough to see the door from across the room. He heard the key go into the door and saw the door slowly open.

It was the same two goons who had come before, this time accompanied by a third. Zadok looked for but didn't see the older one who reminded him of a Nazi scientist. The sadistic burly one was carrying another syringe. The other two were holding pistols.

Zadok stood up. He wanted to resist them. He couldn't stand the thought of allowing them to inject him with poison again. As they approached, he told himself to begin kicking, just as he had done before.

But his legs didn't respond. The big ugly one inserted the needle just where he had before, and Zadok just stared at him. Zadok had enough pain, and he couldn't fight anymore.

He slid down in the corner, disgusted. He was afraid of the injections and what they could be doing to him. Why were they giving him injections? What could it be? Drugs? What good would it do for them to make him an addict? Besides, he wasn't feeling high or up or down, he was okay except for the beating he'd received at the hands of the ugly one.

What did Tsiyon say, they'd either kill him or discredit him. Well, they hadn't killed him yet. They wanted to discredit him, Tsiyon had said. How? If he were proven to be unstable, unreliable, if he were a former mental patient…

Was that it? Did they want to make him an obvious kook? How could they do that? By giving him drugs? That was it, wasn't it? Medicine to make him go nuts. God damn this. He really got himself into it this time, didn't he.

Zadok might have been a little satisfied by his deductive reasoning, but he was shocked by the conclusion, which now seemed obvious. What was he feeling? Did he sense any damage to his mental state? No, he thought he still had his full brain capacity. But then, how could he be sure?

Oh, God, he said to himself. He rolled over on the floor and just stared. Give up, he thought. He felt his nose running and saliva dripping from the corner of his mouth, but he didn't respond to it.

It was not a good situation to be in, but then hell, he might be dying from the cancer anyway. That was almost a consolation.

He was a liability to Israel if he were alive and confirmed mentally ill. He was better off dead. But how could he commit suicide, what could he use? He thought about it some more. He sat for about an hour and wrestled with the decision. It was the only option. Zadok stood up and looked around the room. He went over to the window and kicked the glass. He hurt his foot and he fell backward to the floor. "Damn…damn."

He got up and tried again and this time kept his balance. He kept kicking with his heel until he put a crack in the glass.

He turned backwards and probed carefully with his fingers until he felt the shattered area. Then he felt the primary ridge and managed to pull out the glass corner.

He checked to make sure it was sharp enough. Good. Was he really doing it?

He went back to the corner, and confirmed that he could reach each wrist with the sharp edge. He sat down almost comfortably in the corner.

This was it. He could do it. He might as well. He was dying anyway. Better to do it this way than let his enemies use him to their purpose. It was the only way left for him to fight back.

He thought about Shoshana, and the children. He thought about his sister. He missed them all. He wished he could see them again. He wished he could say something to them.

He thought of funerals he had gone to. He pictured the coffin next to the open grave. How sad he had felt for the young ones. He'd been sad even for the older ones. They'd all been terrible. Now, he thought, he'd be joining them. It occurred to him for the first time in his life that death wouldn't be so bad if the alternative was worse.

What was the happiest time? His wedding? When his children were born? Yes, they'd been the best of times. It seemed he appreciated life and understood what was important now that he was on the verge of losing it all.

He thought about Shoshana. He loved her very much, and felt bad about their fighting and differences. They needed one another. Life would be too tough without her. Just as his grandfather had written about Israel, it is better to overcome differences within the family than to fall victim to forces from the outside.

He took another deep breath. "Okay Zadok, let's do it, time to say good-bye."

He took another deep breath and pulled the sharp edge of the glass over his left wrist. He cut it. It hurt but he didn't pull away. He could feel himself bleeding.

Was it deep enough? He wasn't sure. It was difficult to do with his hands bound behind him.

He tried to pass the glass from his right hand to his left hand so that he could sever the arteries in the right wrist. Damn. He dropped the glass.

He started to probe with his bleeding left hand to find the glass. He felt drops of his own warm blood seeping into the floor behind him.

He found the glass. Then the door opened and the goons and the German-looking doctor came in. The big one approached him first. Zadok instantly looked to see if he was carrying a syringe. He didn't see one.

The little goon asked him something in the unintelligible language, then the ugly one changed expressions when he saw the blood. His face flushed and got even uglier. He ranted as he pulled the glass out of Zadok's hand.

"You don't do this," he said, in awkward English, waving the glass razor in front of Zadok's eyes. The ugly one's effort to speak English surprised Zadok.

The ugly goon left the room for a moment and returned with a black sack and roll of plastic tape. He taped up Zadok's wounded wrist and put the sack over Zadok's head, all the while shrieking hysterically at Zadok in the strange language.

Then Zadok felt his legs being bound together. He couldn't move them. They must have been bound together and secured to something in the room. It was hard to breathe in the heavy bag.

He heard his kidnappers walk toward the door and the door slamming. Now he lay motionless on his side in the corner, unable to see, move his hands, or breathe easily. And he was still alive. He'd have no choice but to serve as a pawn in his enemies' grand plan, whatever that might be. He realized that spending the rest of his life in an insane asylum might be what he had to look forward to. He couldn't imagine it. He feared what was to come.

God, why didn't you let me succeed with the glass, Zadok thought. It would've been easier and better.

Time went by slowly. Zadok had time to think about everything, but most of all he kept visualizing how he'd been captured, over and over and over. He knew he'd lost. Things couldn't be changed. He gave up. There was no hope.

Then he heard gunshots. Automatics and voices. Then it was quiet again.

What now?

Chapter Eighteen

Then those who dwell in the cities of Israel will go forth and make fires of the weapons and burn them, so that they will not need to take wood out of the field or cut down any out of the forests, for they will make their fires of the weapons; they will despoil those who despoiled them, and plunder those who plundered them, says the Lord God.

Ethiopia, and all Arabia, and Libya, and the people of the Land that is in the league, shall fall with them by the sword.

Therefore thus says the Lord God: I swear that the nations that are round about you shall themselves suffer reproach.

I will save my flock, they shall no longer be a prey.

They shall be secure in their Land; and they shall know that I am the Lord, when I break the bars of their yoke, and deliver them from the hand of those who enslaved them. They shall no more be a prey to the nations; they shall dwell securely, and none shall make them afraid. And I will provide for them prosperous plantations so that they shall no more be consumed with hunger in the Land, and no longer suffer the reproach of the nations. And they shall know that I, the Lord their God, am with them, and that they, the house of Israel, are my people, says the Lord God. And you are my sheep.

I will make an everlasting covenant of peace with them; and I will bless them and multiply them, and will set my sanctuary in the midst of them for evermore. My dwelling place shall be with them; and I will be their God, and they shall be my people. Then *the nations will know that I the Lord sanctify Israel, when my sanctuary is in the midst of them for evermore.*

———————————————

They let his legs down first.

Zadok's arms had fallen asleep and his mouth was very dry. He was hurting everywhere. He was exhausted, thirsty, and hungry, and almost too weak to care. Whatever will happen, will happen, he thought.

No one said anything to him. The bag was still over his head. His arms and legs were still bound.

"It's about time," he offered with feigned confidence, hoping to generate a favorable response.

"Now, is that any way to greet us?" a familiar, powerful Texan voice said.

It was the best response he could've hoped for.

Someone removed the dusty black hood, and Zadok could see again. And breathe again.

"Hell, we couldn't let you waste away in here. You still owe me a drink." Colonel James was in khaki uniform, open at the neck, and smoking a big cigar. "Besides I hate to see these kind do anything to Americans – especially in America. Ain't particularly hospitable, don't you think?"

Zadok was wheezing. He tried to speak, but nothing came out. Someone brought him a glass of water.

"I'm very glad to see you. I never thought you could look so beautiful," Zadok whispered, smiling.

"Oh, I bet you say that to all the guys."

An FBI agent freed Zadok's hands and helped him to his feet.

"You going to be able to walk?"

"I think so."

"Well, we've got some of your friends and an ambulance downstairs. Think you can make it?"

"Yeah."

He started to walk out of the little room with the help of one of the federal agents.

"We'll do that drink another time. How about your next trip to Fort Worth? There's a great new honky-tonk you're going to love."

"Sounds great," he managed to respond, weakly.

"You take care now. Don't get yourself tied up again. I'll keep you posted on the cleanup over here."

"Thanks."

They helped Zadok into the ambulance and gave him a hospital gown to put on. He lay down flat on his back and soon realized that there were real doctors in the ambulance, not emergency technicians. They proceeded to examine him.

Then he happily noticed that Tsiyon, too, was in the ambulance.

"Water, please, anything to drink?"

They gave him orange juice.

"Where are we going?"

Tsiyon looked to the medical team. "That depends," Tsiyon said.

"So far so good," one of the doctors said.

After a while they agreed that he was well enough to travel. Zadok was feeling grateful. He wanted to go home.

They gave him a piece of bread, cheese, and yogurt, and it was the most wonderful meal Zadok ever tasted in his life.

"Want to go home?" a doctor asked.

"You kidding, of course, I can't wait."

"You can go home tomorrow."

"Great, that's what I wanted to hear. Right answer. Thank you, thanks a lot."

"You're welcome."

"What day is tomorrow?"

"Saturday."

"Saturday," Zadok repeated slowly while rubbing his bandaged arm. He looked back to the doctor. "Can we leave at night, after the Sabbath?"

"You're sure?"

Zadok nodded. "Don't want to ride on the Sabbath."

"Then that's what we'll do. We'll arrange it that way."

The next day, after the sun went down, Zadok was moved from the hospital to an ambulance. Within the hour the ambulance proceeded onto a remote airfield. A private, unmarked Boeing 727 was waiting for them. The jet was also staffed with a full flight crew, security, and medical teams.

"How'd we rate this?" Zadok said.

"You may not realize it, but you're a celebrity. Your ordeal's pretty well known, too."

Before boarding the plane, Zadok was interviewed by police and federal agents. Then he was carried onto the plane.

Zadok lay down and was beginning to feel a little stronger. "One thing you should know. They were injecting me with medication. I think they used a drug to make me hallucinate, you know, to discredit me."

"Did you hallucinate?" a doctor said.

"No, I don't think so."

"Don't worry about it," Tsiyon said.

"What do you mean? Why shouldn't I worry? Easy for you to say. It's not your brain."

"I'm sorry. I know that sounded insensitive. It's just that I know what you were injected with," Tsiyon said.

"How could you know?" Zadok lifted himself up on his elbows, so he could look right at Tsiyon.

The medics resisted, pulling Zadok back down. "Please. I'm taking your blood pressure. Besides, you need to rest. Please lie down," the doctor said.

Zadok reluctantly complied.

"You were injected with water," Tsiyon said. "We infiltrated the group and were able to substitute water for the hallucinogen."

"Which one was your man?" Zadok figured Tsiyon wouldn't answer. Zadok was sure it was the big ugly one. He certainly had the opportunity to change the syringe. He had seemed hateful and sadistic, but at the same time genuinely upset at the suicide attempt.

"Never mind," Zadok said, "but what took you guys so damn long, especially since you knew what was going on?"

"It really wasn't very long, considering everything we had to do."

"There you go again. Easy for you to say."

"Sorry. Everything's okay now."

Zadok felt angry and betrayed, but he was too tired to argue or fight. He went to sleep.

When they arrived in Israel, Zadok was carried from the jet to an ambulance on a stretcher.

"I'd rather walk," he complained.

"Just enjoy the ride," Tsiyon said. "When have you ever been treated so well?"

The next morning in a private hospital they took more blood, urine, and x-rays. Then they wheeled him to a private room. He fell asleep again.

He was in a half-awake state when he started to think about the problems he'd left behind. He had been so consumed by the military threat, his responsibilities as an intelligence officer, and his spiritual compulsion to facilitate the prophecy, that he'd nearly forgotten his personal problems.

The threat against Israel had passed. The threat against him personally was also over. He was safe now. But suddenly the other issues, the ones he didn't really want to deal with, hit him like another kick to the kidney. He found himself coming awake to worries over his future good health, his marriage, his finances, his career.

He wondered if he'd be forgotten by his friends, and find himself in a permanent mode of trying to establish his credibility, and perhaps his sanity.

He wondered about Shoshana. She had been supportive after all, especially given his somewhat erratic behavior and terrible communication. How would she process it all now? He was missing the good times he'd enjoyed with her.

The anxiety that had kept him from sleeping normally for months was coming back. He felt the need for a stiff drink. Finally, he fell asleep for a few hours.

He woke up in the dark early morning and caught a glimpse of the moon. It was just a tiny sliver, emerging from the near-total darkness of the previous night. He remembered learning from Haim that the new moon is a reflective opportunity, a reverent new beginning. Rabbi Moshe Cordovero, a seventeenth-century kabbalist from Safed, accordingly established the day before each new moon as a "little Yom Kippur," complete with atonement and reflection and prayer. Zadok had had plenty of time recently for reflection and atonement and prayer. And he had reached the stage where he was no longer skeptical about these esoteric rituals. He fell asleep again.

When he was awake in the morning, he picked up a few of the recent and not-so-recent magazines. He found it interesting to see how the press in Israel had chronicled his travels and problems. There were even articles about his personal history, who he was and what he'd done. It seemed that even in Israel, there were forces that wanted to discredit him. They had different motivations than his foreign attackers, but they wanted to undermine any spiritual experience. Zadok read the next paragraph over three times. He was pleasantly surprised to read that his most prominent defender was none other than Nate, his old shipboard roommate, now apparently president of the Association of Americans and Canadians in Israel. Good old Nate, he thought. He had lost touch with Nate a long time ago.

Another article talked about political progress in Israel, as the left and the right moved together, each making concessions to pass major initiatives. And the party leaders seemed to be making an effort to diminish their inflated egos and take personality out of the debate.

The religious parties had formed a coalition with secular representatives to reduce strife and find an acceptable compromise between extreme positions.

Perhaps, after all, Reuven Zadok had really affected and influenced people to overcome their differences. At that moment Zadok decided he would make amends with his parents, no matter what it took. He'd call them when he got home.

He rubbed his cheek. He hadn't shaved in a while. The stubble would be a good start if he chose to grow a beard. Maybe it was time to let it grow. Yes, why not.

He continued catching up on the news. He had just come to the article about his rescue and return to Israel, but had read little more than the bold print when a nurse came in. "Your family's waiting outside. It's visiting time. Do you feel up to seeing them?"

"Absolutely." He sat up in the bed and put down the paper.

Would Shoshana be there?

Little Sarah ran in first. When she saw him, she called out to the others, "Here's Daddy. I found him." Then she ran to Zadok. Her hair was in a French braid, and she was wearing a new denim jumper. She was so cute that Zadok didn't want to let her go from his embrace.

Tsipy, Jonathan, Rivka, Yael, and Shoshana followed. Each of the children gave him a hug when they came into the room. They all seemed to have grown and matured. Then Jonathan, in his paratrooper uniform, looking very handsome in the red beret and gold wings, shook his hand. The girls gave Zadok another hug all at once.

Shoshana smiled at him but didn't say anything, letting the kids take center stage. Zadok thought she seemed glad to see him but couldn't tell where they stood. It would have to wait for later, when they were alone.

"We got your presents," Tsipy told him.

"Thanks for my present, Daddy," Sarah said.

Then Yankel, Shoshana's father, came in and shook hands with Zadok.

"What happened to your wrist?" Yankel asked.

"That's a story for another time. Anyway, the bandages should come off soon."

"Liked your present," Rivka said.

"I'm glad," Zadok said. "How were things on the front for you?" he asked Jonathan.

"Piece of cake," Jonathan answered.

"I bet," Zadok said. "Tell me about it later, when you're not showing off."

Then Dov and Ben Zion entered the room.

"Boy, they let everyone in here, don't they," Zadok said.

"You know, you've got some pretty nurses waiting on you," Dov said. "I'm always turned on by babes in white uniforms."

"Easy. Shoshana will have me moved to another floor."

"Sorry, I just can't help myself sometimes."

General Ben Zion, thankfully, stepped in and changed the subject "Well, a lot more people want to see you. They want you to attend another cabinet meeting."

"Now?"

"When you're feeling better, of course."

"Sure," Zadok said.

"They want to give you a medal or something."

"That's nice, but right now I'd rather have a few days off to rest."

"Whatever you need. I just wanted to prepare you for the circus that's down the road."

"Here's your grandfather's book back," Dov said.

"Read it?"

"Yes. I read it."

"Well, what do you think?"

Dov laughed. "If I didn't see it with my own eyes…"

Tsiyon came in. Zadok introduced him to Shoshana as the man who'd saved his life on at least two occasions.

Then Yossi and Haim came to visit.

Zadok introduced them to everyone. Suddenly Haim had status, and everyone shook his hand as if he were the most holy man in the land. Ben Zion, Dov, even Shoshana, would have received him very differently only a few weeks ago.

Then a small contingent from the yeshiva came, including the blind man. They said a prayer for his health at his bedside.

By the end of the day, he had another dozen visitors, mostly intelligence people and neighbors. Abdul and a few Arab friends came to wish him good health and offer their prayers. But the visitor that surprised him the most was Beverly.

"That you?"

She went to give him a hug. "I know you tried so hard to see me. I thought the least I could do now was come to see you." Tears were rolling down her cheeks.

"Thanks, sis."

"You look pretty good, all considered."

"All considered, I feel pretty good," Zadok said.

"Well, I thought you guys might need some help."

"We can always use help. But maybe we can help each other?"

When it was time to leave, Shoshana approached slowly, leaned over and kissed him on the mouth. She lay her head sideways on his chest. "We were so worried," she whispered.

He responded by placing his hands on her back. He wanted to speak volumes to her, how much he had missed her, how much he had thought of her, how much he loved her, but the words just didn't seem to come. He just patted her back.

"I'm so glad you're home," Shoshana said sweetly as she lifted her head up. She kissed him again.

*   *   *

The next day Dr. Seiderman came to see him. "I think I have some good news for you. Actually, some very good news."

"I could use some."

"There's no evidence of the cancer. I think we've got it."

"I'm cured?"

"It looks like we got it early enough. It's a very curable cancer if it's diagnosed early enough. Very fatal if it isn't. You were lucky that your doctor picked it up when he did."

"That *is* good news! Thank you."

"There's one thing you could do for me?"

"Of course."

"Could you autograph this for my grandchild?"

The doctor handed Zadok a pen and piece of stationery.

Zadok was surprised by the request, but wrote on the note above his signature, "from a grateful patient."

After Seiderman had left, Zadok cheered so loud the nurses came running to investigate. And after the nurses had left, Zadok lay in bed staring at the ceiling, his hands folded, and kept saying out loud, "thank you, thank you, thank you…"

He began to think about everything, including his family. He worried about his oldest daughter, Tsipy, because she seemed to share none of his convictions. She seemed like his father. He and Shoshana had tried hard to expose her to their values and priorities. Nothing had taken.

Zadok felt guilty about how he had raised Tsipy. He must have done something wrong. He used to think that religious practice wasn't so important if you lived in Israel. Perhaps he had been wrong about that.

Why were the generation gaps throughout his family tree so intense and yet so typical? He recalled the ups and downs with all his relationships, especially with his parents and his wife. Now he would have the time to sort it all out and work on those relationships.

His mind shifted to the prophecy. Was there another explanation for the events?

* * *

On late Tuesday morning, Zadok was released from the hospital. Shoshana had come alone to drive him back up to the Galilee.

As they exited the hospital, they made their way through a group of reporters who had been waiting in the parking lot.

When the newspeople recognized them, they seemed to instantly snap to attention. They called out to him as if they really knew him, calling him "Bob" and his wife "Shoshana." Some were taking pictures, others videotaping.

"How'd the kidnappers treat you?"

"Was the kidnapping also part of the revelation?"

"What did you do when you got the news he was coming home?"

"Have you decided which book deal to accept?"

"How do you feel about all of this?"

"What do you say to the Israeli skeptics and critics?"

"What plans do you have?"

Zadok turned to Shoshana and whispered, "The last time I went through something like this, they shot at me."

"Hopefully, that didn't start a new tradition," she said, smiling.

Zadok turned to the reporters. "I'm fine and glad to be back in Israel. I can't wait to go home. I'm also grateful to our security service and the American FBI. They both did a great job." He waved to them.

They took more pictures as he smiled and waved. He took Shoshana's hand and walked with her to their parked car.

A reporter called out, "Is there another prophecy coming to realization?"

"Yes, I prophesy that Shoshana and I will be home for the rest of the week, and that no reporters will be on our lawn."

A husky hospital orderly had volunteered to carry Zadok's belongings to the car. He followed them through the parking lot, and loaded the suitcase and packages into the trunk. The flowers went into the back seat.

A reporter called out.

"Yes?" Zadok said.

"Welcome home." The other reporters joined the greeting.

"Thank you."

Shoshana did the driving. Zadok leaned back and fell asleep. When he awoke they were approaching the Galilee, and the air was getting cooler, a familiar and friendly greeting. He turned on the radio and they were playing one of his favorite Hasidic melodies.

They began the climb up and down the hills. The irrigation sprinklers were active everywhere, creating a mist in the foreground. The sun was turning orange, but still nurturing the fields.

"You know," Shoshana said, "I really want to get back to where we used to be. I know I haven't been the easiest to live with."

"Me, neither."

"I know I doubted you. I didn't support you at a time when you needed it. I've regretted that. Can you let it go?"

"I have."

"Really?"

"I know I was bad. I regret that, too. But I've had a lot of opportunities to think about you and the kids. I began to appreciate what I had. I felt upset and desperate because I thought I'd lost everything. I probably never knew how much I'd miss you until I thought I'd never see you again." Zadok reached over to hold Shoshana's hand. "Can you forgive me?"

At first Shoshana didn't say anything. She just smiled. Then she said, "Yes."

"I want to make it work, too," he said.

"Should we get counseling?"

"Might be a good idea."

"I'm glad to hear you want to make things better again," she said. "I didn't know what to expect. Especially with your celebrity."

"My what?"

"You know, I thought it might go to your head, or something."

"Don't worry about that," he said. "My feet are well anchored to the ground. Hell, I'm the guy who was rejected by his own parents, remember?"

Shoshana offered him a sandwich of pita bread and tehina. He munched on the snack.

"I love you, Shoshana. I've really missed you," he said.

"That's sweet to hear. I haven't heard that from you in a long time. I think that's what I needed. I love you and I've missed you, too."

"And that's what I needed to hear."

He took her hand again and kissed it.

"You know, people are very jealous of you in the moshav," Shoshana said.

"Of me?"

"Yes, you're the recipient of this great attention from the media and politicians. And they think you did nothing to deserve it. You were just lucky, they said. Oh, yes, you'll find many people are jealous and resent that you've been singled out for recognition and success."

Zadok laughed at the irony. He stopped laughing when the pain in his lower back, where he had been kicked, returned.

"What's so funny?" Shoshana said.

"I don't know. I guess things can seem different than they are. People can be petty."

Zadok knew he'd been served a large portion of humility. Should he share with Shoshana the extent of his self-doubt?

Zadok resumed looking out the window.

He thought about his recent experience in the Diaspora. He still felt bad because of the continuing disintegration of the Diaspora Jewish communities. There was a little consolation that what was happening had also been part of the prophecy. Still, it bothered him.

They approached the summit of one of the hills which provided a generous view over the immediate valleys and ponds. There were varieties of fields with green crops in every direction, between precision dirt paths. Rocks and shrubs filled the inclines of the neighboring hills. In the distance, the terrain provided shades of browns and beiges and greens that touched each other, the colors blending together in some places and contrasting in others. The rolling landscape seemed spread out like kneaded dough, until it stopped abruptly in the horizon before the steep, pale blue mountains.

The sun was getting lower now. Still no clouds. The land seemed finally at peace. A solitary bird flew overhead and disappeared behind the rise of the next hill.

Zadok already felt at home.

He reached for Reuven Zadok's manuscript, the book of secrets that Dov had just returned to him, and started to read it again.